the pink and the grey

anthony camber

First published in 2012 by David A Smith
Print revision 3 — 14 March 2013

Copyright © Anthony Camber 2012

Anthony Camber has asserted the right to be identified as the author of this work in accordance with the Copyright, Designs and Patents Act 1988. All rights reserved.

St Paul's College and the characters and events of this book are fictitious. Any similarity to real colleges, or persons dead or alive, is coincidental and not intended by the author.

Cover design: blogshank.com

Contact the author:
anthonycamber.com
twitter.com/anthonycamber
facebook.com/AnthonyCamber

For the present and the absent

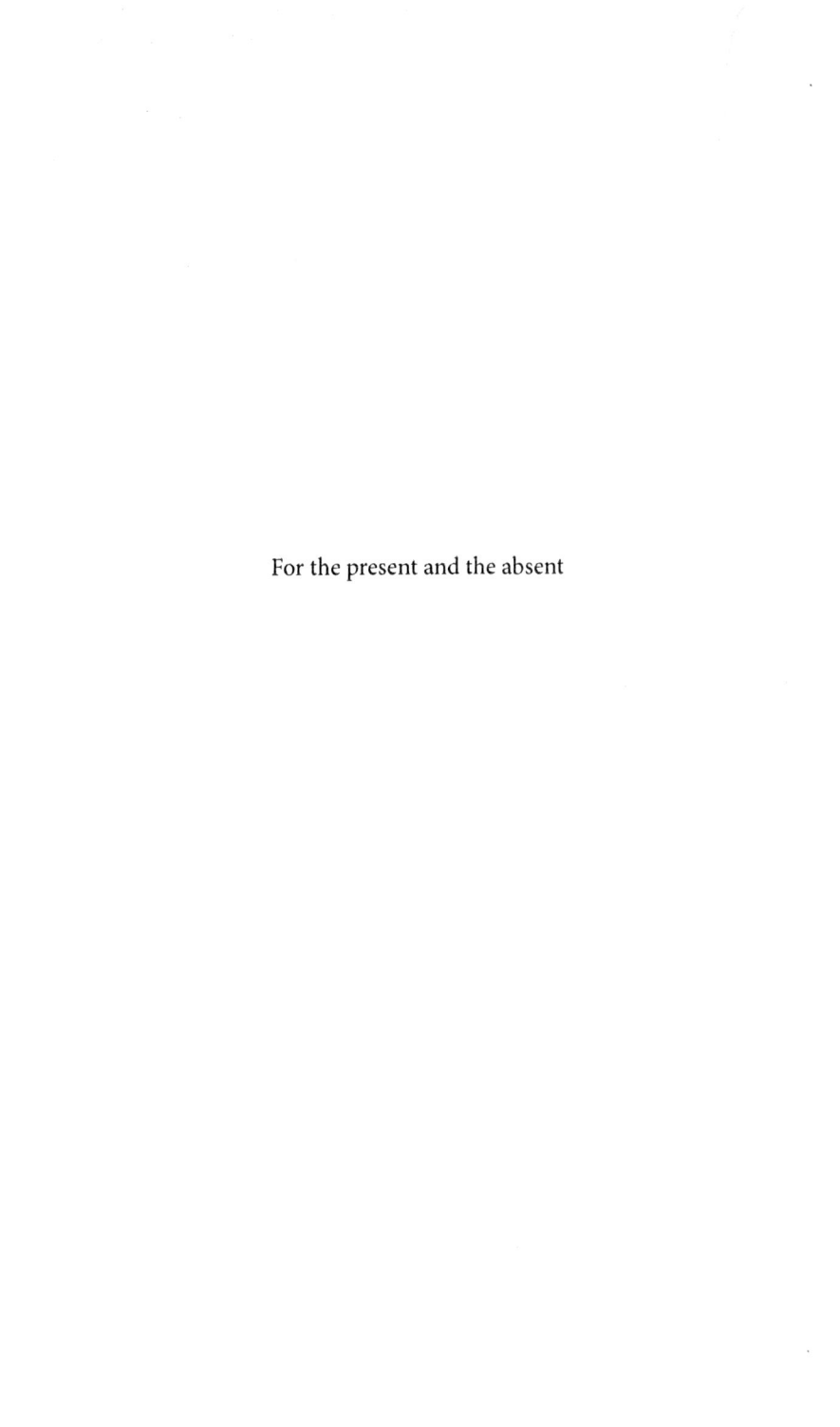

one
The Gambler

"*Mea culpa*, Amanda, *mea maxima culpa.*" I grovelled before the Master, my best sincere face bolted on.

She grunted from behind her desk. Her voice was like frogs boiled in whisky, and her words, as ever, left the English language impaled on a blunt pike weeping softly. "You very well may justice your imbroglio in that manner, but I mark it zero of an excuse."

I hesitated, then decided I dare not ask whether she had heard me correctly. It was too great a risk: I might have found myself bundled promptly out of college, with bags to follow. I used the opportunity to practise contemplative silence and engage in some guilt-stricken head-hanging.

"I declare it of terrible disappointment, Dr Flowers. Overwhelming in terribility. This is the second occurrence upon my carpet." She tapped a red biro onto the doodle-enhanced blotting paper in front of her.

I nodded apologetically, as genuinely as I could fake. Indeed she was correct, it was the second time I'd been summoned into her dark subterranean lair at the far end of the Admin dungeon, for an hour stretched upon her verbal rack. The first time had been in distressingly similar circumstances, following some late-night carousing with a young gentleman not of this college in which New Court's nineteenth-century fountain had played a vomitous part. On this new occasion there had been no urgent ejection of curried beer and no acid-stained stonework, but there would be a deal of tilling and replanting by the college gardener. And there was, most assuredly, a young gentleman not of this college. For the avoidance of doubt, a different gentleman.

"This is a college solar-powered with enlightenment, and as such I am not in place to dwell unduly amongst the, uh, *particulars*," she said with a gently fragrant distaste and a biro twirl.

"I can assure you, Amanda—"

"But, Dr Flowers. *But*." She peered uselessly over her purple spectacles and slotted the biro back into the plastic pot on her desk reserved for red biros.

I held my breath expecting Empress Palpatine's electric wrath to crackle from her withered hands and yet nothing, it seemed, was to follow the *but* — except fiery coffee breath and the undamped shudder of her chins. She steepled her fingers and bounced them against her upturned mouth, the lipstick and nail varnish forming a twitching purple moustache. Purple was *her colour*, she'd declared, hence her apocalyptic trouser suit: throbbing purple trimmed with the yellow of a thousand strangled canaries, and evidently rescued from a damp skip outside a holiday camp.

I shifted buttocks, awaiting a sign — sparking black smoke from the ears, or the disquieting smile of a mass murderer about to unsheathe a glinting blade. Nothing. I busied myself estimating train times the hell out.

"Dr Flowers," she said finally, formally, ominously, with hands together as in prayer. "You must fathom that it is unacceptable for a fellow of the Holy and Glorious College of St Paul, no matter how festooned with industrial garlands and salopettes he may be, to gallop unhindered across pristine, golden sands."

She'd lost me at *festooned*, if I'm brutal. I hadn't encountered her quite as indecipherable as this before. I pumped myself up to bleat some well-rehearsed mitigation but she raised her hand and

I deflated to a mild squeak.

"Spencer," she said more softly, in the sense that topaz is softer than diamond, "your peccadilloes are, need I subtract, well known and fully usual in this place." She raised a nail to a familiar portrait behind her, like ET pointing the way home. "Our founder was, I might say with some little exaggeration, similarly persuaded. Believe me when I speak I have no interest whatsoforth in precisely *whose* dillo, or indeed dilloes, you peck. It has all, is all, and will be all, seen before."

I glanced up at a corner of the office, where a dim red light located one of college's uncountable CCTV cameras. The masochistic chunk of me rather wished to see the recording she and — I was sure — several others had undoubtedly viewed many times. The sober chunk of me wished for a gin. Amanda could provide the ice: yank on an earlobe and a nostril would emit cubes.

"This college has shoulders of breadth and our bosom accommodates every spice. We take pride in our, as it were, pride. We celebrate our diversions. Our history welcomes careful drivers."

"Then I don't see—"

"The brazen flowering of nature unkempt, Dr Flowers. The infinitely unmitigated lack of discreetfulness. The casuality."

I winced.

"I welcome indeed your regret, twice bitten though it is. May I ask if you and he are—" A narrowing of the eyes. "—courting?"

I swear by almighty jeebus I saw the portrait stifle a powdered giggle. Our benefactor, our founder, minced theatrically down upon us through two centuries of dust and nicotine on oil. James Drybutter: a fop, a *macaroni*, a gentleman's gentleman and a gambler of some skill and much fortune. He formed and funded the college as a haven outside the capital for like-minded fellows to further their education along multiple independent and occasionally perpendicular axes. But despite his success in the sport of kings, Lord Luck deserted him (regularly) in the bedchamber and upon his early and rampantly syphilitic expiry we were indeed well-endowed.

I decided it was safest to assume Amanda meant *courting* in the sense of *a relationship*, rather than any of the euphemistic alternatives that leapt readily to mind.

"It is early days," I fibbed, raising a hopeful smile and what I prayed were convincing eyebrows.

Technically, it *was* early days. Technically, I was only recently in hard-won possession of his phone number. Technically, he had told me his name, although technically, it might not have been his actual name, and technically, I hadn't informed my phone, so technically, I didn't remember it.

This off-white lie placated her sufficiently and spring came unexpectedly to Narnia. "Well then, I am— pleased," she said brightly, but with the merest tickle of a pause before *pleased* that entirely inverted the sentence. "You must— bring him to a thing."

I must not. "I— shall."

I shan't. "Splendid."

And it was agreed: I must on no account be seen with the offending gentleman again. This was entirely acceptable to me. Stumbled upon by our dear ancient Praelector *in flagrante* in the throes in the bushes — the *autopilot du vin* having thrown us off course to a bumpy and soily emergency landing — my companion had hopped off at some velocity leaving me to face the purple symphony alone. As first dates go, well, let's say *he wasn't a keeper*.

The non-invitation had apparently exhausted Amanda's supply of pleasantries, and dark clouds crackled once more around her Cruella do.

"Be that as it be," she began, finger-rifle aimed at my heart, "for your first infringement I decided a warning would suitably deter you away. It is now globally apparent to everyone, of particularity the poor innocent Praelector, that I must react through proactivity in response."

I nodded through the jumble. "I understand," I replied, engaging wobbly lower lip at ten percent thrusters and staring again at my ageing and still slightly muddy Converse.

"I cannot be seen to allow you to escape away from your actions, as it were, scot-freely." (Which reminded me that Scott was the name of the scarpering gentleman in question. I resolved, once released from my shackles, to add him to my phone as *Scott — git.*)

So, this time I was to be punished. What would the punishment reveal itself to be? It was evident that I wasn't being tossed through the collegiate door. But perhaps a fine? She had eight hundred years of Cambridge precedent to leaf through. A ducking? Was I to be paraded through the major streets in my unfortunates? Something unseemly to do with a lady? My mind raced.

Amanda selected a new biro from the pot of red biros and began tapping again upon the blotter. I wondered if the tapping was a kind of kinetic energy transfer device — a mental elastic band powering her clockwork brain. *Wind her up and watch her go.* At any moment I thought a cuckoo might spring from her ample Klingon forehead and announce the hour.

Lest I be misunderstood, I wasn't being misogynistic about the batty old dear. It was unrelated to gender: I simply didn't rate her or, as it happens, like her or get on with her very much if at all. Despite my initial high hopes upon her installation she had proved herself unable even to doggy-paddle once out of the calm waters of college and fellowship and exposed to the stiff south-easterly of the university.

Of course some — though by no means all — of those in college chummed-up in furtherance of their careers on an almost hourly basis, fawning and whinnying and genuflecting as she cantered around barking claptrap and dispensing her *mal mots*. I chose to remain aloof and downwind, a pawn of a different colour, attracting her attention only on unfortunate occasions such as this.

I glanced around her dungeon office as she marked time on the blotter. It was a low, narrow rectangle suffused with the charm and warmth and strip lighting of a disused railway station waiting room. Underground and thus absent windows, its walls were hung with excessively enlarged black and white photographs of college: late pixellated regency from all angles, like a bank of screens in the office of a murderously short-sighted security guard. If I stared too long at them my eyes crossed — "magic eye" images, *sans* magic.

Amanda's elaborately carved and decorated thick oak desk, dominating one end of the room, proved the rule that the size of a desk is directly proportional to the self-importance of its owner. A carefully shielded laptop reflected from her glasses, showing occasional hints of shapes in motion and text perhaps describing my fate. Undoubtedly in purple, and probably in *Comic Sans*.

Behind the Master's head the portrait of our own, dear queen — the founder — hung framed in golden flames to distract attention from its shortcomings. He and she gazed upon the crumbliest of nineteen-eighties furniture, all ash greys and buttock-numbing straight lines — the college refurb budget not stretching this deep into the Admin dungeon — plus a drab, pinewood drinks cabinet calculatedly too distant for her to feel obliged to offer her visitors a sniff of its innards. The room wafted with instant coffee and undertones of ozone, the latter from an obsolescent laser printer skulking and venting like a cornered skunk.

The tapping stopped, and Amanda's bloodhound eyes fixed me with a rheumy, purple glare. "You are an intelligent man, Dr Flowers."

"Thank you." I looked away. This was unquestionably a trap.

"You are an intelligent man whose natural predilections facilitate the occasional poorly chosen decision, while in combination with the nihilistic demons of the devil drink."

That covered all men, give or take the *intelligent*. "We are all ultimately slaves to our genes, Amanda."

"Please don't blame your mother."

"I wasn't—"

"I'm talking now," she interrupted, and then was silent again. Seconds ambled past. I opened my mouth, she raised her biro, I closed my mouth. Finally: "I have decided my choice."

I began to think she'd been spending too many hours in front of reality TV squirrel-cheeking E-numbers, and that she now resolutely believed every meeting had to end with minutes of suspense and a sad piano, followed by a sweaty loser trooping away to weep into the shoulder of a gurning co-host.

"I fully furnish you with a challenge. A pistol of your calibre should be extending himself, not, uh, well…" Her hands waved. "I want you, simply and plainly and straightforwardly, to make St Paul's risen in the grand eyes of the public's gracious consciousness." Arms toward the ceiling, worshipping the artex.

"I'm not sure I understand. You want…?"

"I want a— I want the college to have an elevatored profile." She leaned forward conspiratorially. "You realise, of course, of the budget cuts?"

"Of course. Squeezed hither and yon. Less money overall, and also fewer applicants thanks to higher fees."

"Exactly. More fees, less applications, fewer cash."

I suppressed my stabbing instincts.

"And the eyes and wherefores," she continued, indicating the camera watching us, "these consume above their weight. Our dear Bursar weeps at the leakage in that direction. I fear floods bothly with nary a sandbag of the vicinity."

I thought for a moment. "You would like me to be a fundraiser? Do we not already employ a fundraiser? Kevin, nice man, unhealthy moustache?"

"I announce that Kevin has been made, regretfully, redundant." The biro drooped.

"You made the fundraiser redundant. To save money."

"Redundancy, regretfully, was the only activity course to avoid redundancies."

I spluttered. "I'm sorry, Amanda, your reasoning escapes me."

"Dr Flowers," she soothed me with the most condescending of looks, "the sunlit uplands of academica are but an alien jungle to cold, hard accountancy and the vivid fluctuations of the markets. This is dusted and done. Please, allow me progression."

I shrugged.

"I desire you to raise funds, but not through fundraising. Fundraising means a fundraiser, and we no longer have a fundraiser because we made him, regretfully, redundant, and we cannot replace him with a fundraiser, since that would mean he had not been, actually, regretfully, redundant and he might become, actually, regretfully, litigious."

That, actually, regretfully, made some kind of sense. This approximation to lucidity was alarming and unexpected.

"And so, Spencer, it is profile that we must raise, *profile*," arms heavenward once more, "in the sure and certain hope of the resurrection of funds. For profile begets publicity, and publicity begets interviews, and interviews begets conferences, and conferences begets cetera, begets cetera. And all these things will begetting students and donors."

"I see. And you are offering me the opportunity to help."

She removed her spectacles and folded them slowly on the blotter, and then parted her lips and bared her teeth in what I took to be a smile. "In my mind's eye I don't recall I can believe saying the word *offer*. Or the word *opportunity*."

That'll teach me to bum in a bush.

I began to contemplate how I might submerge this entire festering gizzard under the tottering pile of work I retained for such purposes: but she hadn't finished.

"Think not of this as a third chance, for two wrongs do not make a muckle. This is a matter of *gross* importance, a matter of death and life. I want your focused intelligence thereupon, the, uh, *laser insight* I hazard to recollect from a certain interviewee's *curriculum résumé*."

I raised my eyebrows.

"Ah yes, indeed, so might you express in that fashion. Not, as it were, bonkers yet."

She stood quickly, then fumbled mole-like on the desk for her spectacles.

I realised the grilling had mercifully ended and rose to leave. "I'll mull it over this weekend," I said, scrambling to lower expectations while the opportunity allowed.

"Mull? I expect a severe deal more than a good mulling."

She squeezed with a grunt between desk and wall to the proletariat side of the office and ushered me, all bony hands, towards the door. Shoved and hustled along by Voldemort's gran and enveloped in her sweet odour of decay I became quickly nervous, anticipating an exit via a fifty-foot cartoon cliff drop.

Here it came: "Monday afternoon, two o'clock. There is a committee. You are its new chair. I congratulate, there is no salary. Work begins. You must, I would suggest, encourage and fully, be prepared."

"The… the fundraising committee? But, that's—"

"No, Dr Flowers. *No.*" We stopped at the door. Her proximity was overwhelming, like a great-aunt's distorted needlepoint face salivating over your cot. "Of the fundraising committee there is regretfully no further sign. *Timpani allegro*. There is, in complete and legal contrast, St Paul's Immediate Action Now. Or SPAIN."

"Isn't that—"

"SPAIN, Dr Flowers. *SPAIN.*"

I saw no point in arguing further. I wanted to escape before I had to draw breath. But I had one question: "May I ask… does the new committee have the same membership?"

She laughed, the flavour of laugh that means *I'm not laughing, and by the way neither are you*. "Sat you upon the fundraising committee? I trust you are respectfully answered. Good evening, Dr Flowers."

I was summarily ejected into the ancient, grey, windowless corridors of the Admin dungeon, deep under Drybutter's Court at the southernmost tip of the college. It was early on a dank Friday evening in the grim fag-end of October and I stood alone under oppressively low wattage, breathing and blinking and processing. Through the closed door behind me I could hear Amanda shuffling back behind her desk, the dragon returning to rest upon the pile of dwarven gold. There was a clatter and a curse and then the muffled bawling of Lulu began to snake around me, a virtuous siren warning me away from the rocks.

There went my weekend, I thought. But first: booze. The idea relaxed me, releasing the tension from my shoulders. I rubbed my face and headed along the corridor.

As I made my way out of the dungeon I crossed the path of a lanky young gentleman venturing towards the bone-strewn duelling ground from which I had just escaped. He was new in college — a fresher I supposed, given his unfashionably regional blond locks and saucer-eyes. He wore a laptop bag upon his back, perhaps as some variety of shield against Amanda's attacks.

"You might protect your front portions also," I suggested with a smile and a vague wave.

He gave me a bemused, lopsided grin that I believed would fare him well among the college cockerati. "I'm sorry?"

"Posture, confidence, use your height advantage, watch your

flanks and— may I ask your name?"

"Beardsley. Jay Beardsley. I have an appointment with Professor Chatteris."

"Well, Mr Beardsley. Chin up. Set your jaw. Always keep her in your sights. And above all," I leaned in with a hand on his shoulder, "never let her appoint you to a committee."

I went off in search of gin.

two
The Interloper

"Conor, lad, I want you at the Union," the editor had said on the phone. "Got a tip-off, looks legit. Could be a demonstration, or maybe a ruck, full-on handbags. The gits there get pissy about cameras but flash 'em your pearlies and a bit of yer old blarney and squeeze out a couple if it kicks off." I'd called him a cock-erney arsehole under my breath for ruining my Friday night, and hung up. It was always either Geoff or his Evil Henchman Simon sending me out on one pointless little goose chase or another, and ruining the chance of a night of booze with the boys. I doubted they'd forget me, I was hardly a stranger, but it was the principle of the thing.

After a couple of rounds of therapeutic swearing and a change of shirt, thirty minutes later I was heading north, dodging between headlights and bike lights and dead-eyed pedestrians leaning into the squally drizzle along Sidney Street. The warm and sultry lights of Sainsbury's were beckoning students into a last-minute beer grab before the traditional Friday binge. I slipped quietly through the swarming toffs like a Henley pickpocket and nodded to the *Big Issue* seller, who gave me a sly wink. Good source, that man.

I'd been to the Cambridge Union several times before — but only as a reporter. I'm not one of that bunch. It's a debating society, where arseholes who want to be MPs argue with other arseholes who want to be MPs and get lectured by arseholes who *became* MPs. Occasionally there are arseholes who became comedians, and sometimes these aren't the same as the arseholes who became MPs.

I took a right after the short colonnade of shops just before the Round Church and zipped along the path to the Union Society building. It's well secluded behind the church, a Victorian gothic red-brick beastie in a city of old, fancy, fiddly, stuffy stonework. It's the type of building that belongs to a man in a rubber mask in seventies *Doctor Who*, and usually gets blown up by Tom Baker in episode forty-nine. It's got a coffee shop for the tourists, of course — everywhere's got a coffee shop for the tourists. If you stand still in the street long enough someone buys up your franchise and sticks a cafetière up your arse.

But the Union's a pretty anonymous place. There's nothing outside the building to suggest two hundred years of history, or that its doors have calmly welcomed multicoloured arseholes of all politics and all beliefs, no matter how bat-shit insane. Everyone who was and wasn't anyone has pontificated here, on expenses, with an agreeable lunch. I wrote an article for the *Bugle* on its history once. The editor spiked it. Can't think why.

I ran a hand through my hair to tidy myself up a little, then skipped up the steps into the entrance hall and planted my face in the office window, cranking up my most ingratiating smile. In a rare moment of actual effort the editor had cleared me with the society in advance and all I had to do was sign in and show my press card to an old fella I'd seen there before: haggard, charcoal pinstripe suit, military ribbon. He was a member of staff, possibly since the place was founded. He didn't ask about a camera but peered at my bag through inch-thick lenses for long enough for me to notice, and for long enough for him to know I'd noticed.

"It's all standard equipment, your honour," I said. "Notebook, camera, bolt cutters, lock picking kit, big brown envelope of tenners, teddy bear with one arm missing, semtex."

I liked to put that one in last. With my accent, guaranteed a reaction.

He gave me a look and I mimed a gunshot with my hand. "Gotcha," I said.

"No photos, sir," he said. "Standing order of the Society."

"What about the semtex?"

He blinked twice, slowly, and smiled as if to a child. "That would be fine."

He buzzed me through the inner door into the main lobby and back in time about a century. Wood panelling, photos of dead people, a deep burgundy carpet, and a wide staircase up to a gallery. The smell of money, and booze, and… chips?

Ahead, three sets of doors leading into the chamber and used for voting: *Ayes*, *Noes*, and *Meh*, I guessed. I could hear the debate already underway, and hoped I hadn't missed whatever Geoff was expecting to happen.

I bounced up the staircase three at a time to the gallery, since the chamber itself was out of bounds to lesser mortals like me. I snuck through the upstairs *Aye* door as smoothly as I could with my big bag of bits. Nobody else was up here — I had my pick of the shit seats. They ringed the chamber, two rows of bare wooden benches behind a balcony you wouldn't dare lean against in case it was riddled with woodworm. The place must smell like a monkey sanctuary when it's full, I thought.

I didn't want any doors behind me so I scooted along a bench for a good vantage point on the right-hand side. The floor creaked, the seat creaked. Great anti-surveillance system: I might as well have let off an almighty fart and be done with it.

Once I'd settled I could take a good look at the stucky-ups below. The debating chamber, a century and a half old, had been designed to look like the House of Commons. Both had seen better days. Rows of benches, tired purple leather slowly cracking in a bitter attempt to escape the monotony, were lined either side of an empty space just like in the Commons. Photos of old debates, or so it looked, hung on the walls around the chamber. There were a couple of despatch boxes all miked up, and the speaker's chair at the top of some steps like a throne. Except, as I wrote in the report Geoff spiked, it was a president not a speaker. Like I said, arseholes.

Some poor little suited gobshite sitting by the despatch boxes looked like he was transcribing speeches and pretending desperately that his life had meaning. He was the secretary, I remembered. The sequence, if you sucked enough cock, was something like this: secretary, vice president, president, merchant banker, PR consultant, special adviser, MP, Baron Arsehole of Taint-in-the-Midden, supersized pension, and houses in forty-nine countries.

The debate: *This House Believes That Music Be The Food of Love.* Jesus wept, I wanted to shake them all by their hundred quid haircuts and teach them a lesson about the real world. The first speaker was haw-hawing in favour, with one old Etonian hand on the despatch box and the other barely avoiding a Hitler salute, and looking like a twelve-year-old in his dad's DJ trying not to piss his mum's M&S knickers. A bunch of other no-chins were lined up to follow, for and against, on either side.

It was all little boys and little girls playing talkie-talkies with their lives mapped out, from here to the Cabinet table in twenty-five years or less or your money back.

What the hell was I doing here? I thought. *A tip-off*, said the editor. *It might kick off.* Kick off? This place wouldn't kick off if you smacked the Queen in the nose and kneed her in the bejesus. But god help you if you breached the etiquette. Try to make a point of *order* when it should be a point of *information* and you'd be skinned and flailed and you'd never get into the Athenaeum or the Carlton or the MCC old bean, no matter how many fifties daddy threw.

Anyway. Apart from that, Mrs Lincoln, how was the play?

Hypothetically I should have been writing notes for my piece: who was there, who said what, how the vote went, a quote or two about the result, as if any bugger cared. But I knew none of that would get printed. Geoff didn't want a straight report, or even a proto-toff version of the parliamentary sketch, though god knows I'd have loved to write that. If nothing punchy happened, and it never did, I'd be lucky to get an inch on page ten. Barely enough space to name the penguins flapping away down there and which zoo they belonged to. Better off writing *toss all* in forty-two point and moving right the hell along.

For half an hour I sat there, hands on balcony, chin on hands, bored out of my tiny mind and with the lazy, by-the-numbers rhetoric sending me to sleep. I did try to keep one ear on the debate hoping at least to hear a naughty word, as there's nothing funnier than a posh twat trying to talk dirty. *Blahdy terrible, Tarquin.*

No dice.

My gaze began to wander along the rows of students, arranged like muppet rejects below me. Every few minutes a Statler or Waldorf junior would jump up with a turgid or ho-ho-humorous or otherwise inane interjection. Some sat texting or tweeting or facebooking or cockblocking or whatever it is students got up to. Most were content to sit quietly and listen to all the drivel, rhubarbing when whisked up by whichever penguin was on the quack. God, it was dull. At least with cricket there's a chance someone might get a ball in the nads or in the face. I hoped that's what Geoff's tip-off was all about. A nutjob swinging a cricket bat, that'd be a story. Not the sterling-flavoured monotone that was currently sending me to sleep from the arse upwards.

This was not why I became a journalist. This wasn't journalism — this was babysitting. I became a journalist to investigate, to track down crooks with twirly moustaches and see them banged up. I'd learned my trade back home in Dublin and ended up here, all bright-eyed and cocky at the *Cambridge Bugle*. When Geoff hired me I asked him whether this place had any, you know, *actual crime*, and he bluffed and scoffed and sweet-talked me into it in his fat cockney barrow-boy way since it was a new paper and, basically, I had no money and he had a small carrot to dangle.

I'd quickly learned that he wanted me for all the boring shite, all the grunt work. I trod the court beat and dutifully wrote pieces about cats up drainpipes and similar non-stories fuelled by puns every ten words. If I was a good little boy, and ate all my greens, and didn't sulk, I might get the occasional obituary to flex my muscles. He and his deputy Simon nabbed the juicy stuff, whenever there was any, and the rest of the paper was packed in with topped-and-tailed agency copy and adverts. It's amazing how many column inches you can fill every week with photos of grumpy pensioners pointing at cracked paving slabs. And of course they buy a copy for themselves, and a copy for their neighbour, and a copy for their bemused grandson in a more sensible city, and that's how the paper was still going, to be honest.

It must have been about nine o'clock, when even the speaker — sorry, the president — was unsuccessfully stifling a yawn, that someone new came through the upstairs *Aye* door and found a seat in the gallery by himself, on the left-hand side, about as far away from me as he could get. A few of the muppets in the chamber below looked up and saw him.

He gave one a small wave.

I perked up.

Very slowly I sat back, hoping the seat wouldn't creak, and started to unzip my camera bag, one z at a time. There was nobody around to stop me. I removed the camera as slowly and casually as I could and, keeping it well below the edge of the balcony out of sight, powered on and removed the lens cap. For once I remembered to check that everything was set to automatic, so I wouldn't sit there swearing at the twatting thing and trying to make the photos not-entirely-black and not-entirely-white.

Zoom, focus, snap, snap, snap, that's all I'd need.

If anything did, by some magical fairy chance, kick off, then I'd have photographic evidence and without any question a front-page lead. I knew I could remember enough of what might happen to write it up: it'd be mostly photo, anyway, and I could do interviews afterwards. And if the copy wasn't long enough I'd upsize the headline and the by-line — especially the by-line. That's what you get if the journalists sub and lay out the pages themselves, Geoff, you cheapskate. Of course, if the story was any good Geoff would change a few words and ruin a gag and put his own name at the top, and I'd be granted an *Additional Reporting By* in nought-point text and lump it or take a hike. It wouldn't be the first time. It'd probably be about the twentieth.

Someone once defined insanity as doing the same thing repeatedly and expecting different results. That was writing for the *Bugle*, in a nutshell. First day: here's your desk, here's your computer, let's measure you up for your straitjacket. By now I'd long given up making a fuss about hijacked by-lines — Geoff and Simon had skins thick enough to snap needles. I just focused on clocking up the experience, pocketing the money, and cultivating the kind of simmering resentment that usually ends with the words "and then he turned the gun on himself".

As the current speaker droned on — he was making some half-arsed gag about music being the food of doves, or something, and *how my sides were splitting* — I kept my eyes fixed on the new guy. I decided to call him *the interloper*. Everyone has to have a name. He had short, dark hair, and wore a white shirt under a navy blazer. He looked white, but possibly a little stir-fried. Hard to tell from where I was sitting. Mid-twenties by the look of him, a few years or so younger than me. Too old to be an undergraduate, for sure. Maybe a postgrad? He was leaning forward, forearms resting on the balcony with hands clasped in front of him, looking intently at the toff whining away below. A little stressed, maybe? Or was I projecting?

This had to be the guy, I thought. He was probably the one who'd tipped off Geoff. I realised I should've asked Geoff more about the caller, but then again he was the old hand — if it was important he should've told me.

I decided the interloper had almost certainly seen me and figured out who I was, which was why he'd sat directly opposite me, and he was busy winding himself up to kick things off as promised. He had that shifty fake-relaxed look about him, the one you get when some lad notices you've been checking him out — that *oh, what an interesting ceiling* look with a nervous whistle. The same one a straight guy gets when his girlfriend asks him to hold her handbag.

I had no idea what dastardly act the interloper had planned. If he'd told Geoff, Geoff hadn't spilled the beans to me. He wasn't likely to pitch a tent there and try to occupy the Union, not by himself, and no amount of pepper spray could make a decent, photogenic difference from up here. A banner, or a flour bombing? I couldn't see any bag. That ruled out the cricket bat mayhem too. Was he going to piss all over them? My editor might still use a picture of that, give or take a censoring blob. He was restless, and shifting, which didn't rule out a full bladder. I felt sure *something* was brewing.

I took a chance and raised my camera to the balcony. Not high enough to be seen from below, but high enough to focus on the interloper. It was an SLR, digital of course, which meant I had to look through the viewfinder. I attempted a subtle, slow slouch, no sudden movements to alert anyone in the chamber. Down, down, down, approach, squint, zoom, focus…

The interloper was looking directly at me.

OK, I thought. This was either very good, or very very bad. I froze.

He aimed a nervous smile towards me, a dainty wave. More than a touch of the gays about him, if you knew the signs. No flamer, just what my grammy would call *theatrical* or *a little light in the loafers* with jazz hands and a fey little kick back. He'd pass in a crowd as long as you didn't throw him a ball. A *Waitrose balsamic* kind of guy. His face definitely showed more than a hint of eastern promise in his past, maybe a scandalous interracial one-nighter a few gens back in the far east. It worked, I thought. I decided I probably *would*, under different circumstances, and not, you know, while being caught papping him in the upstairs gallery of the Union chamber.

It was then that I noticed the silence.

And, through the viewfinder, I saw the interloper point at the president's chair.

I sat up slowly and saw my zoomed-in lens overlapping the balcony edge. Shit. Below, a sea of amused muppet-toff faces gazed up at me. I could almost hear the show's deep sax intro in my head. *It's time to play the music...* or face it.

The president was standing, holding the order paper, and staring at me. "Can I help?" he said.

Both sides of the chamber erupted in laughter and clapped for the ritual ten seconds, just enough for a light nasal browning without descending into outright rimming.

There was nothing I could do but brazen it out. I called out: "No, no, you guys carry on with... whatever it is you were doing." Not so much of a laugh. "Mutual masturbation, wasn't it?"

Someone coughed. It was *almost* a laugh. On a good day, one-to-one, it might've been a cough-laugh or a laugh-cough or maybe as much as an honest snigger. But not this time.

"I think, sir, you ought to leave," said the president sternly.

The secretary dutifully wrote something down, as if this were Nuremberg and they'd just passed sentence.

I cut my losses, packed up my camera and shuffled quickly to the *Noes* door, glancing across to the interloper whose expression was, I'd say, unreadable. Which was odd. Angry I could have understood, ruining his big night. Amused I could have understood, if his goal was to make me look like an arsehole, which I absolutely did. Unreadable suggested… I didn't know.

I rushed down the stairs two at a time, past the voting doors in the main lobby through which I could hear the debate continuing — with a joke or two at my expense, no doubt — and clattered through the inner doors to the office airlock.

"Got a deadline, sir?" Mr Pinstripe said.

"I'm lucky if I've still got a job," I replied as I banged through the front doors. I thought about calling back "Count to ten and then duck," but reckoned I'd caused enough trouble.

Outside, the rain had eased and the temperature had dropped. I could see a few washed-out stars battling through the glare as I escaped the grounds of Hogwash onto the damp city streets. Under the colonnade, leaning against a jeweller's shop window, I rang Geoff before anyone from the Union did: no sense prolonging the torture.

He was an unhappy little cockney bunny.

I had no photos and no story. If anything, I was the story. I paced back and forth, explaining, excusing, apologising, arguing. It was a stupid debate, nothing was going to kick off, it was just some bloke waving to his mates, his source was a flake, but hey, I wouldn't claim for those hours because, well, oops, and all that.

I was about to launch into a pointless but hopefully distracting plea to print my spiked history piece when the interloper appeared beside me, face still a blank canvas.

"Hang on, Geoff. Two seconds," I said, and muffled the phone against my jacket.

"Quite some exit there," the interloper said. Hint of posh, a bit like Donald Pleasence only not so much of the serial killer. Confident. Intense. Eyes of stone. Didn't look like he'd just pissed over a balcony.

"Shitty tip-off," I said. "It happens. You test it out, make an arse of yourself, and move on." I shrugged, and stuck out my hand. "Conor. Conor Geraghty. Your Majesty's Press."

He gripped my hand and shook firmly. "Oh, I know who you are."

three
The Barman

My college room enjoyed all the splendid comforts of home: to be precise, gin. Compared to the Master's bunker I had just left it was grand and palatial. It had windows, heat, the lot.

The accommodation nestled deep and high in the poky northern corner of New Court, about as far from the Admin dungeon as collegiately possible: T Staircase, room two. It had been in my possession for a few years but it was not my *home*, merely the ramshackle office for my day job as a Director of Studies — hence the gin.

I was honoured to be the present keeper of the place, the latest in a long line stretching back over a century. Once, before one or other of the wars, it had been the office of the college astronomer, or at least of a fellow with a powerful telescope and a hobby requiring many hours outside in the dark. Another occupant, according to the oral history of college passed between the generations, began to supervise undergraduates dressed only in a toga in dubious homage to our classical forebears. A fierce winter and a window disinclined to form a seal reputedly brought that experiment to a noble and yet rapid end.

I sympathised with that distress: the room was not a friend to the right-angle. The walls to left and right, half oak panelling, half crumbling plaster in an unforgiving cream, toppled very slightly inward and could induce a vague claustrophobia in the unwary or unsober. An attempt to disguise this tilt with floor-to-ceiling shelving helped somewhat but succeeded mainly in reducing the room's effective width. At least the wall's thickening with obsolete reference books and barely thumbed biographies obtained a certain amount of sound-proofing, for those within and those without.

My desk by the white-rimmed sash window was varnished beyond redemption and littered with dusty old toys — not those kinds of toys — plus papers to read and to ignore and the inevitable laptop front and centre. Add a brace of chairs, a sofa of unknown provenance and a disintegrating kettle to keep the paracetamol company, and the room could fit no more. Oh, there was the ubiquitous camera, of course, snug like a spider in the corner above the door — upon which hung a turkish rug of multicoloured wools and cotton, delicately woven, a story for another time, perhaps.

The room's least appealing feature was its rather unpalatable view onto the lifeless, foggy plastics of the bus terminal, and consequently and constantly it throbbed a sulphurous orange from artificial light no matter how lead-thick the curtains. The benefits, however, were occasionally many: on a warm summer's afternoon with the sash fully open, and in the glorious, brief moments when the ad-stained buses held their belching and stood silent and cold, I could absorb the sprawls of half-naked sun worshippers dotted about the grass of Christ's Pieces beyond, full of cheer and drink and tossing balls and frisbees and whatnot, and I could feel the breeze, hot upon my gently procrastinating face.

Sadly, my day was usually too damned occupied with work and panicked students and the blessed like to gaze too long at the unattainable outside.

I do confess the room was, on drunken occasion, pressed urgently into service for unofficial, personal purposes, witness the farrago with the Master over *Scott — git*. It was no accident I suspect that the sofa could easily transform into a bed of sorts whether my eyes consented to focus or not. But despite what Amanda might believe it was not my habit or my preference to bring gentlemen back to the room. I owned a very pleasant flat in a quiet area of town. Unhappily, it was a more distant area of town than I sometimes cared to stagger *post prandium*.

I returned to the room after Amanda's press-ganging and sat harumphing at my desk in the orange-dark willing an obvious, easy idea to pop quickly into life so that my weekend wouldn't be banjaxed utterly. The clock ticked stubbornly towards seven, at which point the gin switch in my brain would spark. All I could then hope for would be some lurking subconscious imp tackling the problem while the thinking portion disengaged. A few minutes of cogitation now might at least satiate what very little conscience I had on the matter.

Sadly, no life-saving plan was forthcoming as the hour chimed. No amount of riffing on the words *gin, git, tick, clock, cow, murder, escape, train*, and so on, triggered anything meritorious. I granted myself permission for a light starter drink, a *boozette*, since it was after all a Friday and pace was of the utmost importance, and then I called Claire.

"On a scale of one to ten," I began as soon as she picked up.

"My dear, he hasn't left yet." The *he* to which she referred was her husband, Ken: a chubby businessman, ruddy-cheeked and rarely present, even when present. Ask him his wife's birthday and he'd struggle, but he could rattle off Powerpoint keyboard shortcuts like Add Pointless Transition and Insert Shitty Clipart like a nerd on speed. He was forever jetting upon one urgent, sweaty business trip or another, and it seemed one such other was beckoning. I'd once called him a travelling salesman — why yes, alcohol *was* involved — and his cheeks had purpled for a nanosecond before the corporate smile reasserted. Aside from that momentary lapse he was always pleasant enough with me, and I suspect somewhere beneath the layers of blubber was secretly happy for his wife to have some unthreatening and convivial company while he counted ceiling tiles in airports and increased his circumference.

"Can you not decant Ken into a taxi and scuttle down here?" I said.

There was palpable tutting. "Spencer, you know I barely see him. Anyway, it's only just gone seven. Why now?"

"On a scale of one to ten," I repeated.

She paused and sighed. "How many?" I could hear the husband muttering darkly in the background, probably cursing me up and down as he packed his bag with hoovers or dusters or whatever it was he sold.

"A good 9.2, maybe 9.25." I'd decided the scale was asymptotic, never hitting or breaching ten, otherwise I'd exaggerate wildly into the thousands. I'd secretly reserved the full ten-point-oh for planet-sundering events such as births, deaths, and obtaining a boyfriend.

She sighed again. "I bet it isn't. I bet it's low eights. There hasn't been a nine since the play with Anita and that thing with the understudy."

"Oh yes, the understudy with the underwear. He was... a challenge. No, I'm telling you, it's unquestionably above nine."

"What is it, then? I'm not coming unless you give me some kind of reason."

"Gin. Gin is a reason."

"Gin doesn't score above nine, my dear. Gin doesn't score anything, we agreed that."

"It's Professor Chatteris. Lady Macdeath. I was caught, well, rather knob-handed I'm afraid."

"Again?" She laughed, and I made out her muffled voice passing the story on to her husband.

"Claire! This is serious!"

"It's not even low eights, it's somewhere in the fives at most. Hang on." The phone muffled again as her husband spoke. She relayed it to me: "We should get you a chastity belt for Christmas, apparently."

"Sadly negated by the lock-picking kit I already own. Listen. Being caught, fine. I tongued toes and made the right grunts. But she's installed me as chair of some nauseous committee. I'm supposed to conjure up a grandiose plan to raise the college some cash."

"Can't you just—"

"Monday. By Monday. I am dangerously inflamed. You need to come and help me drink through it."

The teens in their t-shirts and mini-skirts tailgating each other toward *The Regal* ignored the ghostly drizzle wetting St Andrew's Street as I stood impatiently outside the college gate an hour and a half later. The ritual Friday night metamorphosis from shopper's thoroughfare to drinker's crawlway had begun and the porter on duty, Arthur with the amusing wig, had as usual rightly enacted the *Friend or Foe* protocol once reserved only for wartime and drag night. The century-old oak gates were closed and locked, with their inset door set to open only via college swipe card or special knock.

I hopped from foot to foot waiting for Claire. The gin deflected the cold but was losing its tussle against the bladder. I distracted myself counting the alternating pink and grey stripes painted into the stone around the gate. A small college shield was fixed above: its design showing two golden stags rampant by a central oak, within a border of pink and grey like the gate. Rather fussy and busy to my eyes. And the motto: *ex glande quercus*, from acorn to oak.

The street lights tinted everything toward the sulphurous. The rain sucked away the vibrancy. A camera watched.

"Finally!" I said as Claire surfed on a tide of teens around the corner from Emmanuel Street and then waded against the flow towards me.

Five years my senior and tapping upon the peeling and lightly scuffed door marked *forty*, Claire was a lady of means — her husband's — and always appropriately turned out. Tonight she sported an allegedly slimming black jacket with some green and black patterned nonsense wrapped around her neck. Her hair, as usual, was hither and yon.

"Where have you been, scruffbag?" I said.

"Sorry, my darling. I had to, you know, see Ken off. Properly." She smiled coyly.

"Oh, please! You two still—?"

"Spencer! Of course!"

We exchanged mwahs, both cheeks as ordained. "But, you know, he's pretty much spherical these days and you're, you're looking forward to Christmas. I'm not sure I get the physics. How does it all—?" I made two fists and cracked them together.

"Oh dear, you did start early, didn't you?" she said accurately, patting my hand. "I have lost weight, in fact, thank you for asking."

"You look ravishing, Claire, I'm sure."

"I do. And you seem to have mislaid your axe and a forest, as well as your razor."

"One can hardly wear black tie on a permanent basis. The checked shirt is, I am told, very *a la mode*." It was a mix of reds and blues and purples, under an admittedly tatty blue fleece. College dress code extended to *attractive and decorous* and placed no further burden upon you, and as ever some students delighted in testing its boundaries.

"Well," said Claire, "I shall alert you if I spot a beaver. Now, where are we going? The usual, I suppose?"

The Barman

I nodded sheepishly.

"Fine, if we must," she sighed, and took my arm.

It was only a short walk at the slowest of paces, no more than a couple of minutes. I explained my present predicament as we strolled, hesitating on occasion to focus my attention upon any gentleman proportioned, scrubbed up and tailored within acceptable margins of error.

Our destination was Bar Humbug, hidden along a narrow passageway where it could attract a more select clientele. By night it was unofficially rechristened Bar Bumhug: Cambridge's most cocktail-friendly homosexual establishment, the watering hole of choice for those who are, those who might be, those who aren't but like to dabble, those who aren't but like to be dabbled, and unsuspecting tourists. By day it lowered its rainbow colours and used its more pedestrian name to draw in any passing trade, so to speak. As the sun set the lights were dimmed and the music grew feistier, and the shirts lost a button or two. It was usually busy and often packed, and any straights caught in the glare either promptly reversed and screeched away or were subject to trial by tequila. Some were found very guilty indeed.

My man Eddie was tending bar, as usual, with two of his imported minions. I say my man, we once enjoyed a minor dalliance. Brief, and yet something more, I thought, than the typical soulless encounter. He had an arresting effervescence and he amused me: but we had nothing in common. He was a fair distance along both the chunky and camp axes, not my usual preference at all. It could never have worked. I'd have drunk the place dry. Eddie never warranted a *code ten*, but our thing, whatever it was, was sustained enough for me to feel moderately protective during the lubricated dust-up the early hours inevitably brought.

My own drunkenness was never unduly troublesome. As Claire said often, I was verbal enough while sober and my bile was reserved only for those unable to distinguish "your" from "you're". The effects of alcohol manifested themselves in me purely via excessive and uninvited touching. The touching occasionally had its advantages, though, leading to further touching.

Pleasingly, Eddie had plonked a G&G&T on the long, scratched chrome bar — one of the few straight things there — almost as we stepped over the threshold, and it was still early enough to navigate the few metres to it without slicing through too many cosy groups. The usual vultures had, however, already begun to circle and to mark their territories: the haggardly optimistic, the over-dressed, and the under-dressed. Their prey — the twinks and the twonks — herded together for safety, with an occasional shepherding lesbian.

Dotted about the place were the weirdos and their hangers-on, such as the odd man beside us with the wispy salt-and-pepper beard wearing an exotic waistcoat and hat with detailed and expensive-looking embroidery — some kind of Arabian or Afghan contrivance, I shouldn't wonder. He always propped up the bar. There was often also an exotic creature possibly deposited straight from a shadowy Romanian castle, who stood large and lumbering with piercing blue eyes, and with whom I resolved never to make eye contact lest I fell into spinning hypnowheels and woke up in Bucharest minus my wallet and a kidney. Nevertheless I was proud to consider myself amongst their weird number: I imagined I was known as *the posh loudmouth groper with the fag hag*, or similar. Entirely appropriate and indeed rather desirable. I preferred life as an outlier, not an indistinguishable generigay gasping for air amidst complex interconnecting social strata I neither knew nor cared enough to truly comprehend. And, yes, I was easy too.

"You, sir, are a life-saver," I said to Eddie as I claimed my drink.

"It's a gift," he replied, brushing his little finger against a dark eyebrow. "Pay me back in kind later if you like, darling."

I knew he was joking. "I suspect you'll have a rather better offer by then."

"Ah, bless you, sweetheart. And what can I get for the other lady?" He looked at Claire. "Same again?"

"Please no," said Claire. "White wine. I'm tiring of gin. I keep imagining myself an old crone in a Hogarth."

"It's the teeth, I imagine," I said, and she slapped my arm.

An hour passed quickly, first at the bar and then hidden around the corner beside the hat man, in a cosy leatherette cubicle that after severe staring was finally vacated by a trio of hair product addicts aged twenty going on twelve, with their comedy multicoloured umbrella drinks. I had enlightened Claire on every sordid detail of the banished *Scott — git*, and on how St Paul's appeared to be in rather a precarious position.

"Tell me the ideas you've had already, then, my dear," said Claire. We were on our second bottle — I'd migrated from the gin. It was the house red, concocted from vintage rattlesnake venom mixed with sawdust, but at least it had the correct colour.

"Plan A," I said, holding up one finger. "Drink myself into a stupor, kill everyone with knives and run away."

"That would certainly raise the college profile, darling, but I doubt the money would start flowing in."

"I could just kill Amanda. Nobody likes Amanda. Mind you, I think she might be some variety of robot not yet familiar with English. I might stab her and wires and springs and flames and dictionaries would gush out."

"Let's cross murder off the list, shall we? What other options do you have?"

"What I *don't* understand," I said forcefully, "is why Amanda hasn't strong-armed the Archivist into coughing up some grade A gossip. His little red-eyed battalion can spot a lapsing hetero at a dozen paces. He must have all manner of *actionable materiel* at his disposal behind those blessed doors of his."

Now as far as I was concerned, a gentleman, especially a gentleman seeking the very roundest of education, had every right to a free sample should he so desire. I'd even throw in a fourteen-day trial with no obligation. And of course, the occasional *walk along Brighton pier* wasn't illegal and hadn't been for several decades — and St Paul's had had its entirely deserved reputation for two *centuries* without excessive intolerance from either town or gown.

Hypocrisy was another matter. When poor dear Oscar was picking oakum, and St Paul's, in a funk, admitted only the butchest of the butch, a far-sighted bursar — whose own college exploits if proven might have toppled several unmentionable establishment figures from their marble pillars into the Thames — took it upon himself to institute an extensive record-keeping operation. Should a student of another college visit St Paul's to see a friend for afternoon tea and a nosh and later, perhaps many years later, raise a tabloid mob against unnatural vices, he might well wonder if some evidence of his behaviour were still extant, ticking, in our archives.

"Maybe there isn't any gossip," said Claire. "Not everyone is as open-minded about such matters as you might think — or want, dear. And anyway, didn't a lot of your type go to Oxford?"

"We have a sister college. Reciprocal arrangement. I'm told we had one of the first dedicated leased lines when the academic networks grew up, you know. Lots to share. *Lots.*"

She turned eagerly to me. "You've seen it?"

I shook my head. "Insufficient clearance. I hear stories, of course. The Archivist, bless him, has been known to loosen his lips after the third or fourth port. Gets a twinkle in his eye and asks someone to name a year. 'Oh, yes,' he'll go, his hair dancing about, 'A very good year, that,' and then he'll lay down a clue or two. I couldn't *possibly*, of course. What happens in St Paul's stays in St Paul's."

"Except when it's useful for blackmail purposes."

"There's a tiny asterisk after 'stays'. All the way down the page in small print it says 'your career may be at risk if you do not keep up repayments'."

Claire refilled her glass. "There you go, then. Speak to the Archivist first thing in the morning and you'll have your money in no time."

"But don't you see, Claire?" I pressed my glass against hers until she refilled that one too. "Amanda might be one wheel short of a unicycle but she's well aware of the Archivist. You know the PM writes to the underground sailors telling them what to do if they can't receive the *Today* programme three days in a row? Whenever St Paul's appoints a new Master, the first thing they do is meet the Archivist. Then it's a mug of sweet tea and an hour alone in a darkened room."

"She already knows the gossip but won't use it, that's what you're saying?"

"Nobody knows for a hundred percent what the Archivist told her. Probably just a broad sweep across, no photos. I would expect a worked example involving a long-expired historical figure, purely to set the level. I rather strongly suspect the Archivist wouldn't trust a freshly minted Master with contemporary information unless it was immediately to be deployed, torpedoes away, *bellum collegium contra cockpot*."

"Perhaps Amanda thinks it too crude a tactic to use simply to beg for money." She took a long swig. "We women are more sophisticated thinkers than you. Not so phallocentric. I learned that in *Merchant* with Miriam, you know."

"Reserving the nuclear option? It's possible. It would certainly suggest the college is not in imminent danger of ruin and rack. Begone, foul accountants, ho, or something."

"Maybe she's just out to get you, Spencer." She laughed.

I sat back, finding the thought entirely plausible to my increasingly addled mind. We had, after all, locked horns on more than one occasion despite my proclivities being hardly of note in the span of college history or in its present. In comparison to those long-ago times before the college was forced to admit heterosexuals, I was borderline celibate.

I decided to apply some logic. "Either she's after my rather attractive hide or she isn't. If she is, the best thing I can surely do is not fail, because then the Chatteris beast is defeated. If she isn't, and the college is indeed broke, then it is my sworn duty to save it for tomorrow's homos. The homorrows."

"That seems prudent, darling. Ideas, then."

We spent another bottle brainstorming. Most of the suggestions required upfront investment, which wasn't available, or too great a risk, or both. Even on his most successful days, would our founder Drybutter have wagered the college on the Derby? The ideal solution would involve the minimum of expense, the maximum of publicity, and a legally watertight side-effect of income. We couldn't stand bellowing on street corners with those awful buckets: that was fundraising, which Amanda would not countenance.

"How about some kind of college competition?" said Claire.

"Competition? You mean, sport? Vertical exercise with scorecards? Claire, have you *seen*—?"

"Not necessarily sport. Some contest between the colleges that you could win. Synchronised bumming?" She laughed.

"While I have no doubt it's a competition in which we would triumph — I refuse to say 'come first' — I suspect the university might raise a dusty eyebrow at such ungodliness. An intercollegiate contest *is* attractive, though. We could butter the cost around the collegiate toast. We might even be able to locate a sponsor of some wealth and gullibility and spend precisely not one solitary."

"And to bring in the press, you could find a famous face and get them involved." She placed an excited hand upon my arm.

"Back to the Archivist, then. We want an A-list celeb, A for anal. B for—"

"No, no need for that. Make it something to do with charity. Celebrities love charities."

I thought for a moment. "Yes. Yes, I think we have the glimmerings." I began to fumble drunkenly over the outlines of a plan. "Celebrity face, of the persuasion or not. Charity. Sponsorship. Colleges in competition. That works for me. I pronounce us winners."

I tapped a drum roll on the table and flicked my glass as a cymbal.

"What kind of competition, though?" Claire asked.

I waved my hand at her. "Oh, goodness, that can wait. We've made some progress. I no longer feel homicidal, which deserves some kind of celebration. Would madam, by any significant chance, care for another bottle?"

Without waiting for an answer I hauled myself up and inched through the now-packed bar — past the silly-hatted weirdo who'd shifted barely a buttock since we'd been there — and sought the attentions of Eddie the barman, who was looking a mite more attractive and less dressed than the previous bottle. He acknowledged me, nodding toward the patron to whom he was currently attending. I smiled at them both— all three— both. I'd seen that gentleman here before numerous times and I remembered we'd spoken briefly — well, I'd dangled an innocuous flirt and he'd batted it subtly away, no matter, hardly worth— He had what I called an autumnal mane, almost leonine: auburn, tinting enticingly towards red under any kind of illumination. A light beard, more than stubble but less than tramp, and pleasingly trimmed, I suspected all over. Irish, I thought, or one of those places. He appeared to be accompanied by someone, a damnable shame, I decided, unless… Perhaps I could later encircle them both and demonstrate the *Flowers manoeuvre*, patent pending. Anyway. His name whispered from somewhere: Conor.

four
The Question

I nodded at the baldie beardy drunk around the corner of the bar trying to queue-jump to his forty-ninth bottle of wine. My smile said *take your turn, buddy, you're in no danger of drying out just yet*. Meanwhile he was so busy making googly eyes at Eddie the barman he didn't notice his standard-issue checked cuffs soaking up half a Stella spilled over the chrome. Classic college bell-end, I thought: probably never held down a proper job, probably called himself *boi* on all the usual sites and chopped ten years and ten kilos off and talked about *trust*.

A few months ago he'd tried it on with me at Humbug. We'd exchanged mumbles and then he made a surprise lunge disguised as a trip over an invisible manbag. I'd deflected him onto an overmedicated friend of mine I particularly despised, and they groped off together like a ride on a Ghost Train. Two birds, one stoned.

The baldness of the guy I could deal with. The age difference was not an issue either. He was just a twat.

The bar was pretty packed that night with town gays and gown gays mixing it up. It was always like that: the big nobs wanting a crack at the servants, and the workers fancying a bit of the high life. Nothing wrong with that unless you make a habit of it and your profiles start laying down the law on salary expectations, or pedigree. *Postman seeks peer for special delivery, please supply references (Debrett's).*

It was a decent place though, especially when full to popping, the hardwood floor scuffed by a couple of hundred pointy shoes. A great long aircraft carrier of a bar with mirrored shelves stacked with every shaped and coloured bottle you could think of, and cute staff that knew how to handle them. I couldn't be arsed with all that juggling shite but some punters liked it.

Plenty of space to spread out and hawk your wares if that's what you were into, or to talk and be talked about — high silver-coloured tables mostly, with low surfaces and comfy chairs around the corners for the old folk and the lightweights. It had wide glass doors along two sides that opened up in summer and doubled the size of the place. At this time of year the glass was pulled shut but you could still go out with your booze, for a fag or a flirt, if you passed inspection by one of the bouncers.

The barman finally delivered the goods, a couple of cocktails, and shouted out a price.

"Let me buy these, Mr Geraghty," said the interloper above the noise. He was called Seb, he'd revealed on the walk here from the Union. It was the only thing he *had* revealed. It wasn't what you'd call a conversation, more a monologue from yours truly towards someone auditioning for Mount Rushmore.

Three letters wasn't a great deal of return on my Friday night investment. Since the initial greeting — and the promise of a story — he'd withdrawn into a silence, a cocoon. Perhaps, I thought, it was because I'd suggested we come here. Maybe he wasn't *one of us* after all — as if that would stop me testing the boundaries after a couple.

I graciously allowed him to pay. It was the very *least* I would let him do.

I shouted in his ear: "I doubt the editor would let me expense mojitos. I'm lucky if he lets me expense bribes."

He looked at me oddly.

The Question

"Joke. We're not like that any more. I'm as honest as the next guy sifting the bins."

Still nothing.

"Look, I'm trying my best here," I said. "You could at least smile politely, I'm not very good at spotting when I'm being patronised."

He got his change and nodded at the barman. "Shall we find somewhere quiet?"

"My place?"

"Don't be so nervous, Mr Geraghty."

"I don't like it when people call me Mr Geraghty. They either want my money or my da, and I haven't seen either for several years."

The crowds had us trapped at the bar. I held up my glass and began to squeeze through and around, apologising and smiling and placing my free hand wherever I felt it would make most difference. Seb trailed behind mutely, but I was getting used to that. We made it outside through Checkpoint Charlene and parked ourselves under the heat lamps where we could talk — if not privately then at least without yelling.

I placed my mojito on one of the high chrome tables and went to grab my notebook from my bag. Seb stopped me with a soft hand on my arm.

"Please, Mr Geraghty. Or Conor, if you prefer. This is off the record." The hand remained a fraction longer than necessary. Game on, I thought.

"Off the record doesn't mean I have to commit everything to memory. I'll need to write stuff down, even if I don't, you know, take down your particulars. At least, not yet." I gave him a grin and put the notebook on a dry part of the table.

"I must insist. Nothing in writing, or I walk away."

"How about if I write in code, like pig latin or polari or esperanto or something?" I flipped open the notebook. "I don't actually know esperanto, which might be a bit of a stumbling block, but I'm a quick learner."

Seb's eyes dropped and, briefly, I saw a reaction: disappointment. "Then I have made a mistake. Enjoy your mojitos."

He made to leave. I grabbed his arm. "Listen, Seb, if that's actually your name, I'm a journalist. I might be a crappy one but it's my job and part of that is to write shit down, otherwise it fades away, replaced with a memory of a nice arse or something. And funnily enough my editor *really, really* hates arse poetry. So it's either the notepad or *once upon a time*. Write shit down or make shit up, what do you want?"

Seb stopped, and considered, and his arm relaxed a little. "If not off the record, then, perhaps, off duty? A chat about many things, about why we are both here. Think of us as new friends, getting to know one another. For the moment."

Hello. Promising.

He met my eyes. "Please."

I held on for a second and then let go of his arm and put the notebook away. "Fine, have it your way. You bought me a mojito, I'm off duty for this round at least."

"Thank you."

There was a brief silence.

"So, you come here often?" I said.

Finally, he smiled. A true smile with some eye crinkle, a bit of tension loosened.

"That's better. You have a decent smile. I'm not nervous, I'm Irish. If there's a gap I fill it. Not that sort of gap. Not always, anyways. Are you going to say anything or do I have to talk all night?"

Seb quietly and deliberately sucked hard on the straw in his mojito. The ice shimmered and shifted and I saw him begin to relax as the alcohol bit and worked its magic. I took a long draw of my own, and struggled to keep my stupid mouth zipped. Rule

The Question

one: STFU.

"I confess I was unsure," he began hesitantly, "whether it would be you at the Union or your editor Mr Burnett."

"Geoff doesn't do Friday nights. Or any nights. We're not that sort of paper. We're barely any sort of paper."

"I wondered whether he might want the scoop for himself rather than delegate it to you."

"Ah, well, there are scoops and there are scoops. And this wasn't a scoop. It was a *potential* scoop, just a tip-off. Believe me, if it grew into something he'd be undelegating the hell out of it."

Seb stared at his drink and mashed the ice with his straw. Someone behind me was smoking a cigarette and boasting, and if the lit end got any closer to my face he'd be boasting about my elbow in his kidney.

"Come on," I urged. "I'm off duty. No notepad, no wires. I sit naked before you. Don't go all shy on me now."

"It is not a matter of shyness, Conor." He met my eyes again: dark, intense, black sambuca chasers.

"What then? Don't make me use the word *inscrutable*."

He blinked, then smiled sarcastically and flipped me the finger — and that's when I knew I was getting somewhere. But he said: "To be honest: there is no scoop. There is no story."

I didn't have an itch but I scratched the back of my head anyway. "You know, I could've stayed at home tonight. Watched a bit of news and *Corrie*, put my feet up with a zombie book. Maybe a glug of whisky in my tea to make the pain go away. Instead I was sent to, frankly, the dullest debate since Jeremy Kyle did curtains, and got kicked out on my arse for some minor photography. And then you *dragged* me here to this hell-hole—"

"*You* dragged *me*, I think," Seb interrupted.

"True, but—"

"And you *are* here every Friday."

"That's as maybe. Wait—"

"And now you wonder why you have never seen me here."

"Yeah, so how—"

"I thought you wanted me to do the talking?"

Neither of us spoke for a few seconds. I frowned at him. "Who are you?" I asked.

"Your round, I think."

"Oh, no," I said. "I know that trick. I may be naïve and innocent but you can't pull that one on me. I've seen the movies. Cut to me at the bar, picking up another couple of mojitos, turning round, and *poof!* you've disappeared. And then a hot Swede comes up and delivers a line *really badly* about whether that drink's for him, and I fast forward a couple of minutes to the good bits. Or maybe I'm getting confused with something else."

"I am perfectly happy to buy another round."

"Right, now you want to own me," I said with a grin. "It'll take more than two mojitos to own me, mysterious guy who calls himself Seb. About three more, for future reference. Listen: if you go to the bar, I'll give you the money."

I dug out some cash and kept as close an eye on Seb as I could while he went for the drinks. He might still make a run for it, I knew, in fact I thought it was pretty likely, but I could see both entrances to Humbug and had a decent speed on me, mojitos or no. I kept trying to fool myself I had the upper hand, even though the only piece of dirt I'd squeezed out of him so far was about a certain Mr Conor Geraghty. *Got a great story for you, Geoff: reporter gets kicked out of Union and is played like a banjo. No, no source on the record. Fired, you say? What a coincidence!*

I lost sight of him amongst the crowds at the bar — many familiar faces, who might also know Seb, which would explain how he knew I was always at Humbug when I'd never seen him. Or maybe I just hadn't noticed him.

The sound system notched up a few decibels: some new manufactured anthem or other.

The Question

I pulled out my phone to attempt some research, but I had nothing to go on. I had no photo to send to any sources for identification, not that I had many sources. All I could throw at the internet was "Seb" or "Seb Cambridge" or "Seb Union" and they wouldn't get me anywhere. If anyone at Humbug did know him, I had no idea who. As for that guy at the Union he waved to, Kermit or Mr Snuffleupagus or whoever the hell: not a damn clue.

I imagined myself sprinting down the alley after Seb screaming *just tell me your name* like an infatuated teen crushing on the high school jock.

He finally reappeared from behind a bouncer — walking, not running, and even better carrying a tray full of mojitos. It looked like he'd bought the third round to save time, and I fancied him even more. Thankfully he hadn't snagged a fresh catch of hangers-on. I knew what these guys were like, hooking onto any unaccompanied man and flapping about begging for scraps. I knew what they were like because I was pretty much one of them.

"I took the liberty," he said, placing the tray of minty goodness on the table.

"Are you trying to get me drunk, Sebastian? It is Sebastian, isn't it?" It was time to push for some answers while I could still hope to remember them.

"One day you will make a fine investigative reporter," he said.

"But not today, is that what you're saying? Hey, I'm starting small. It might be Seb short for something wacky like Sebarnacle, or it might be your initials, or any number of unlikely things."

"Sebastian."

"Great. Last name?"

"In good time."

"I can't write a story with just your first name. You're not Madonna, or Kylie, or Diana, or Rupert."

"Remember, you are still off duty. And you have no story. Nothing you are going to print, anyway." He chuckled.

"Right. Well, cheers for that."

A fresh infusion of mojito livened me up a little, and the smoker behind me moved on so I wasn't so murderous. Time to set out the facts, as he'd gone quiet again and I couldn't stop myself.

"OK, here's what I know. It was you who called Geoff, but you weren't sure whether it'd be him or me at the Union. It was me that pitched up, and you seem to know all about me, which by the way I'm finding simultaneously scary and highly arousing, so that leads me to think it was me you *wanted* to appear and not Geoff. I have no idea what you were planning to do at the Union, but whatever it was wasn't the real point of the exercise, which is some kind of scoop you're not telling me about that's to do with me. How am I doing so far?"

Seb had listened carefully, nodding along, with his hands wrapped around his glass. "Pretty good. Mostly correct."

"What I don't know is why you're all coy and defensive. Is it the ginger?" I rubbed my beard. "For the right guy it comes off, but then doesn't it always. In any case it's not properly ginger, not offensively ginger."

Seb tugged at his cuffs. "To be honest, I had no demonstration planned at the Union." He looked at me with the barest hint of a smile. "Had your editor appeared, then simply I would *not* have appeared. Had you not… embarrassed yourself, my intention was eventually to move across the gallery to speak with you."

I frowned. "That's a very strange way to ask someone out on a date. A smile and a hello usually does the trick, and frankly with me both of those are optional. I'm not exactly picky. Why didn't you just sit right beside me in the gallery? Would've saved me a hell of a lot of face."

"I wanted to see what you would do."

The Question

"What I did was bollocks it all up. Was that good? Did I pass?"

He grasped his glass and spun it slowly on the table. "Not exactly. You were rather slapdash. Hasty. Reckless."

"That's me. Those three words and more. You should hear what Geoff calls me."

"But I think you will do," he said, sucking on the straw.

We spent the next couple of mojitos on nothing more than smalltalk. It was mostly me doing the talking. I didn't get his surname, his home town, his college if he was at college, his job if he had a job, or anything. The notebook still in my bag was empty *to the brim* with facts about Seb.

I couldn't decide whether he was quiet because I wasn't — and the more mojito'd I became, the quieter I wasn't — or because he was just one of those types. That was the more likely, I figured. I reckoned he was the sort of guy who'd be the first to spot flames curling out of an upstairs window over the road but the last to say anything. Not in a malicious way — he'd be quietly heroic and emerge smoke-damaged and coughing with a baby and a puppy, and then vanish into the night hand-in-hand with a fireman. But me, I'd be setting records clattering down the fire escape and into the nearest pub, going *look at the size of his hose* and forgetting I was a reporter.

So I told him all about myself, of course, about growing up in Dublin, about my father's vanishing act, my journey of unrelenting self-discovery that somehow led to a season ticket to Humbug, all the usual sort of bollocks. He probably knew it all already. He probably had a manila folder somewhere with all my movements for the previous six months — and worse, the guys I'd slept with. There weren't that many: I was pretty much Captain Bravado.

The evening grew late, tipping toward midnight, and the

massed ranks of drinkers began to disperse or be dispersed slowly to their pits or wherever came next. The wind gradually left our sails and for the first time I felt the chill of the night, despite the lamps.

We went back inside the bar to finish off our drinks. It was still too loud for any kind of decent conversation and, more to the point, anything other than the grossest of flirting. And several mojitos in I'd given up on discovering Seb's mysterious story: other things were on my mind. When he suggested a walk, I couldn't agree fast enough.

"Where are we going?" I asked him.

"I live by the river."

"Cool," I said, though that didn't narrow it down much. I didn't care.

As we left the bar we had to jump out of the way of some kind of octopus woman, all arms, storming out. I didn't recognise her. She looked like Helena Bonham-Carter in a kind of a Grim Reaper make-over. She swept along the alley ahead of us, people leaping out of her way in case she snuffed them out with a touch. I think I heard her say the name *Spencer* — that was the baldy drunk with the beercuffs. I had to laugh.

Some part of my journo brain was still awake as we walked. The cogs turned silently, analysing the route. We walked south along the Roman road, the city's spine. Most likely that cut out the posh colleges — the ones with all the cash and the river views. That still left dozens of others, though, and he might have been a student living out of college anywhere in town. If he was a student at all.

"May I ask you a question?" Seb began.

"Is it the top or bottom thing? You're forward after a few glasses, aren't you? I'll have you know I'm strictly—"

"No, not that. This is an ethical question."

I wondered where this was going, as I wondered where *we*

were going. We'd barely reached M&S, and we were being passed by drunk kids bouncing off each other and heading to a club. A couple of hi-vis types in caps — cops or pretend cops — promenaded just ahead of us.

I looked at Seb. "I'm not sure how ethical I am after a night of mojitos, but try me. I might surprise myself."

A short pause. He was inspecting the pavement as we walked. "How do you feel about your editor?"

"Geoff? He's too old. Never met a pie he didn't like. And I can't stand Londoners."

"I mean professionally."

"Oh." It was going to be one of those deep-and-meaningfuls setting the world to rights, was it? "Is this a trap? Is this all a big ruse to root out disloyal staff? I'll proudly sing the corporate song if I have to, I think it's about dustmen and trousers."

"I do not work for him. I want to know what you think."

I wasn't sure the alcohol had affected him at all. He was a little more talkative, perhaps, but he wasn't mulleted. Neither of us was walking in a zig-zag.

We crossed the road by a packed taxi rank, turning down an unidentifiable offer from a taxi driver and avoiding a couple of beery cyclists taking the scenic route home.

I used the time to consider what to say. "He's a shithead, I guess. A greasy fart in a lift. All the empathy of a blocked drain. Does that help?" I looked for Seb's reaction: nothing. "I'm not really doing the job for his benefit, if that's any better. I need the money and the experience, and I'm getting a trickle of both. First sniff of a better offer and I'm all *sayonara, suckers*."

He nodded and said nothing for a while. We turned between Christ's and St Paul's, onto Christ's Lane: a narrow old passage paved with cobbles, with high stone walls on either side cast into sharp relief by balls of yellow light inset along its length. I could hear music and laughter from a first-floor window on the St Paul's side, and there was a sweet smell wafting down that might have gotten someone into trouble.

"They sometimes call this little alley Romans," I said to break the silence. "It's a Cambridge theological joke. If it helps, I don't think they're meant to be funny. It's something about epistles. Not entirely sure what, I haven't been a good Catholic boy for several years now. These days it's usually called St Paul's Back Passage, what with the college's reputation and all. Well deserved, too."

"Yes, I know."

"Did you go there?" *Bam!* with the journalism.

"No." *Woohoo*, a negative fact.

There were another few seconds of quiet, which I was beginning to recognise meant another question bubbling up.

"Has your editor ever asked you to… embellish a story?"

I made a kind of hissing sound. "You're asking the wrong guy. No point trying to embellish what I'm allowed to do. *Yesterday a pussycat with a history of drug-dealing and prostitution was run over by person or persons unknown but believed to be linked to the Mafia and on a bicycle.*"

"But would you?" asked Seb, voice raised a little. "Are you loyal to him — or loyal to the truth?"

"Jesus, this is getting heavy. Ask me again when I'm sober."

I could see him becoming agitated, a little more expressive in the gestures. It might have been the alcohol finally kicking in, I guessed.

"What about phone hacking, email hacking, dirty tricks? Does he get you to do those?"

I shook my head as we passed the bus terminal. The trees along both edges of the path through Christ's Pieces were lit by strings of bulbs bobbing into the distance, thick constellations between the branches. I kept my eyes open for bikes without lights, the little shits.

"Hacking? That's all big boys' stuff," I said. "We're a tiny, tiny

The Question

paper. We tell the truth. I *think* we tell the truth. I try to. It's as dull as Hull on a wet Thursday in November, but it's accurate, give or take a stolen by-line. Accurate, you know, as long as I'm allowed my notepad." I mimed scribbling. "If you ask me, the dodgiest things we do are the puns in the headlines. We spend more time on these than on writing the shite that follows them."

Silence again, which I filled before a new question could be asked. "You know, at the risk of sounding defensive, we're not all horrible people. Sure, I wouldn't give Geoff the time of day if I didn't get paid for it, and the red-tops with their brown envelopes and private investigators on the sly, they've done bad things. But it's not what I do. Not what I want to do. I want to make life better, investigate the arseholes and get 'em put away. I'm one of the good guys, I promise you. Now, are you gonna tell me what this is all really about?"

A quiet voice: "Yeah."

"Off the record."

"Yeah."

"Then fire away. I'm all ears, apart from the mouth."

He took a deep breath. "Do you know much about your editor's past?"

I stopped and turned to him. "Would you stop talking about the pissing editor and get on with your story?"

He shushed me, a hand on my arm again, and walked on. "I am, I am. This is about him. Burnett. Do you know what he did before the *Bugle*?"

"A reporter on Fleet Street, is all I know. Does he have something on you? A little dirt? Is that what all this no-notepad stuff's about, you want to tell the story properly? I can probably arrange—"

"No. You are correct, he was on Fleet Street, twenty years ago. He was an investigative reporter, just like you want to be. He broke stories, like you want to, and sent people to prison, like you want to."

"Why do I get the feeling there's a *but* coming up."

Emerging from the trees, we walked a few yards to a zebra crossing. There were still a few taxis trailing up and down. Were we heading towards Midsummer Common, I wondered? It looked very much like it.

Maybe, I thought, he just *said* he lived by the river. Maybe he was planning to lure me to the riverside, break my back on a narrowboat and toss me in. Maybe the story might be about me after all. The pavement ahead peeled right, towards the river, and I consoled myself drunkenly with the knowledge that if he did bump me off there'd be a massive front page photo of me, albeit below the masthead where you don't *really* want it rather than as one of the columnists' mugshots along the top, the duck shoot.

Seb took his time, apparently gathering his thoughts. I kept my mouth shut, and shivered.

"My father had a business. It was moderately successful, not yet global but expanding. It had won an export award. A bright future awaited us, so we thought. And then your editor decided this could not be allowed to happen. He uncovered some financial irregularities — correction, what he *thought* were financial irregularities."

"Ah," I said. I saw where this was going. I imagined a small silver key in his back, winding him up and up as he spoke.

"He didn't contact my father. Why not? *Why not?* It could all have been stopped there and then. Misunderstanding, or something. An apology, no hard feelings. But no, oh no. As far as we can tell he didn't contact anyone from the company at all. Not a word! No phone call, nothing!" He was angry now. "Based on barely more than supposition and a source even the— *even the Metropolitan Police* considered unreliable, he and his editor went barrelling ahead and just printed the story. No regard for the truth. No regard for the effect on the business. No regard for the family." He punctuated the sentences by chopping the chill air ahead of him. Someone across the street looked over at the noise.

We skipped across a set of traffic lights and through a metal gate with a narrow cattle grid, its dark paint peeling off with the passage of thousands of bikes and feet. This was Midsummer Common, dozens of acres of grassland criss-crossed by paths, and with Narnia-like street lamps at the intersections. It was currently occupied by a herd of cows somewhere away in the mist. Only in Cambridge.

The river was getting closer. We skirted the eastern edge of the common, on a path curving slowly to the right as the common narrowed, and then took a fork aimed directly towards one of the footbridges over the Cam. We'd be passing not far from many of the college boathouses across the river, where some of the fittest and most lycra-hugging arseholes of their generation trained and rowed. Not that I used to walk along the footpath occasionally on the off-chance, of course, and *never* with my long lens.

"So what happened?" I asked, hoping he'd unwound a little.

There was no let up in his anger. "What happened? What always happened. Businesses were ruined. Lives were ruined. There was a cascading effect." He mimed tumbling over and over. "I was young at the time, protected. It is only recently that I learned the whole truth. The board sacked my father, of course. They could do little else against the publicity, day after day after day. He tried to clear his name. No chance of that. Your editor and his friends kept on and on with the story despite the lack of evidence. They grabbed at anything to destroy him. They dug up an old girlfriend and made people think they were having an affair. Nudge-nudge, no smoke without fire. Those stories. Bitter, vicious lies."

I nodded. He needed to get this out.

"It was relentless, and groundless, and devastating. The family, my family suffered greatly. The pressure. The constant cameras, the intrusion. At our windows, at the front door, on the bonnet of the car. It was a witch hunt. I used to have nightmares, all banging and flashes and arguments and tears, whirling around."

He stopped for a moment, and looked at me, and took a breath, and became quiet again. "My elder sister took an overdose. Luckily we found her in time. In fact, I found her — she was supposed to be babysitting me while our parents were out talking to solicitors. And the stress of it all, well, ultimately, it ended my parents' marriage."

Well, that put a great big fucking downer on the evening, right there.

"So you see," he said with a cold smile, "I'm not a great fan of Geoff Burnett."

It was my turn to be silent.

He finished the story, slowly, quietly. "And afterwards, well, my father was reinstated eventually because he had done nothing wrong, of course. But it could never be what it had been before. It was not long before he left that company and started something new, not so *corrupted* with memories I suppose. Something quite successful, which is good. I grew up with my mother, as did my sister."

"How is she now?"

"Fine. Both are fine. My sister is married, with a little girl. My mother says she is far too busy now for marriage." He let out a short, sad grunt. His foot connected with a pebble, deliberately or not I couldn't tell, and it skittered along the path and escaped into the grass.

I made the right noises but I wasn't sure what I was expected to say — what I *could* say. I could hardly apologise on behalf of all journalists — or even just Geoff, had I wanted to — for any wrongdoing perpetrated by others while I was playing kiss-chase. And that's assuming everything Seb had told me was true.

"Listen, I'm sorry, but—"

"What's it got to do with you?"

"Crudely, yeah." I gave him a sympathetic smile.

We were approaching a footbridge, which arced low over the Cam to slice through the boathouses on the other side. At the steps, Seb stopped and turned to me. "We were a happy, contented family until Geoff Burnett came along. I would very much like to organise a little payback. I want you to help."

Hands deep in my pockets for warmth, I shrugged and shifted from foot to foot. "Hey, I mean, I sympathise, but what the hell can I do? Your beef is with Geoff and I don't want to be piggy in the middle. If I'm honest I'm only in this right now for the mojitos and the afters — and since we're standing still in the cold I have the sneaking suspicion I'm gonna be eating dessert on my own tonight."

Seb laughed sadly. "I apologise. I had no intention to lead you on. I want you to help because you say you want to right wrongs. You want to fight injustice. You want to put away the bad guys."

"Yeah, but not the guy who pays my cocking wages."

"So justice has a limit, and the limit is your wallet, is that what you are saying?"

"I'm saying—" I let out a frustrated breath, a cloud of steam rising into the night. "I'm saying you don't get far in journalism by attacking the man with the spike, is all, even if he is a shithead."

"Look at it this way. Who better to establish your credentials? You want to be an investigative journalist? Investigate."

"It's not as easy as that. There's a contract, you know, *reasons*."

"Of course. There are always reasons. And all it takes for evil to triumph is for good men to do nothing."

"Is that from *Hollyoaks*?" I said, giving him a grin. Then I looked up at the stars for a second or two, and sucked in a lungful of air, sharp and cold. "Look, I'll see what I can do. I'm not saying no, I'm not saying yes. I have a bit of due diligence to work through. Make sure you're not some kind of lunatic, that sort of thing. You've got to admit you haven't given me a huge amount to go on, though."

He held out his hand and I shook it. It near burned with heat, the passion of a wronged soul. "Sebastian Greatsholme. Spelled G-R-E-A-T-S-H-O-L-M-E, pronounced Gresham. Pain in the arse. I might change it one day — if I meet the right man. I shall be in touch."

five
The Potential

"Was it something I said?" Best puppy-dog eyes at Claire as she ranted all over me.

"Oh, Spencer!" she growled, wrapping the god-awful scarf around her neck. "I'm tired and I've drunk too much and I'm afraid my patience is exhausted. You're a spoiled child. I don't see why I should have to change your nappy. It's no wonder Amanda can barely tolerate you. In her position I'd probably be the same."

"Don't talk about her, that mangy old— Tonight is for dancing and flirting and loving and tomorrow is another hangover." I *might* have been a little tipsy, perhaps one or two over the eight. I'm not entirely sure how I managed to upset Claire so, but she clattered to her feet and effected a vibrant and stentorian exit at a stomp unexpected in one usually so delicate. I suspect it likely I made an unfortunate remark about her little salesman fellow, probably occupying a double-seat on a red-eye to Taiwan at that very moment to pick up more door-to-door throwaways.

I granted myself a silent five minutes, huddled in the cubicle with what drops remained of bottle n, before a swift visit to the below-ground toiletry facilities for activities that were purely above board.

I returned to find the cubicle hijacked by two young things ascending each other's learning curves at some velocity. No matter. In any case it was well past time for a leisurely sweep around the establishment to see and be seen, to sniff and be sniffed. It was always a similar pattern: the same faces with the same greeting rituals, the same vapid smalltalk. *Yes, it's nice and busy tonight. No, I haven't seen so-and-so. I do hope the weather clears up. I fear punting season is at an end. Have you heard about such-and-such? I understand X is seeing Y, and Z is climbing the walls.* I was not a gossipy queen, except in that I was (a) a bit of a queen and (b) a bit of a gossip.

Cambridge had a relatively small cabal of homosexuals for its size — at least, counting those that frequented Bar Humbug. There were many others who never dared venture out of St Paul's or whichever lesser college they attended, and there were rufty-tufty towny types who preferred to take their alcohol from a much straighter glass and drank with the dirty heterosexuals. Consequently you could stride into the bar and know almost everyone there. Not *know* know, necessarily — not biblical knowledge, though one or two theologians worshipped there occasionally — but anything from basic facial recognition to flighty acquaintance to drinking buddy to closest chums of all sorts. And then there were the sainted *Others*, the strangers. I'm not referring to the weirdos — like my good self — with caps and hypno-eyes, but the gentlemen recognised by no-one. The *fresh meat*, one might say.

My grand pinball tour of the bar was never explicitly designed to identify these types, but it was a pleasing side-effect. On a busy Friday evening thumping with multicoloured young persons' music there were usually one or two strays to be found loitering. Sometimes these were naïve, unaccompanied straight boys, smelling of something advertised on television, who never stayed long unless a few umbrella specials revealed they were secretly neither naïve nor straight. Occasionally we were visited by hetero couples, the male inevitably clinging tightly to the other to assert his sexuality, and anxiously avoiding eye contact: these *Pussies of the Jungle* were always worth a slow, deliberately accidental touch or two to make them all skittish and jittery, eyes wide — and there's me thinking that *we* were the friends of Dorothy.

And then, as this night, we might see some obvious college gentlemen testing the waters, polar bear cubs perhaps out on the ice for the very first time. Usually a small, tight group, rarely alone. This time, three: a confusing number, as any two might be paired already and it was not always evident which. What *was* always evident was the unofficial queue of regulars trying their luck. A succession of doomed redshirts.

I liked to think this was modernity's homage to the centuries-old tradition of presenting débutantes to the sovereign at court — which was, of course, merely a device to insert marriageable young ladies into the eyelines of eligible stallions. Our miniature establishment had even evolved an order of precedence, of sorts. *Your Otherly Majesty, might I present the Usual Suspects, beginning with Count Hypno-Eyes of Bucharest.*

I did not consider myself unduly predatory. I was a mere amateur, a part-timer in the lower leagues who occasionally enjoyed a rewarding run in the cup. Lack of success did not prick my drunken ego: I didn't consider myself a miserable failure if I staggered home alone after Eddie or one of his boys sluiced us onto the streets. Where an opportunity presented itself, I indulged. It is true that the more I had imbibed, the more indulgent I became. Upon the calling of Time and the raising of the minger lights I could be less than fussy. A cavalier in search of a roundhead for hand-to-hand combat and heavy petting.

Of the trio of *Others* comprising that evening's little group, body language and instinct indicated two were coupled: a hand on the small of the back, sustained eye contact, whispered nothings. The third stood fractionally apart, still engaged with the twosome but with one toe dipped into the frothing 'mocean of the wider bar.

On my promenade through the room I tackled another regular about who they were — who *the singleton* was. He shrugged. Ah well, I thought: *carpe diem*, before any other bugger does. *Set phasers on stunning.*

He seemed to grow taller as I approached, or perhaps I shrank at his beauty: olive, mediterranean, sultry, knee-weakening. He smelled of late Spring, of a garden at full thrust. Sober me would wilt and shrivel, his burning glance scorching into my heart, his black surfboard fringe dashing my lifeless body onto the rocks. I locked onto his deep brown eyes and roused the most confident and attractive smile from my armoury.

"Wotcha," I said. *Wotcha? Dear jeebus.* "I'm Spencer. I don't think I've seen you here yet. Not that I've been stalking you. Are you newly gay, or just here on the off-chance?" *Oh, arse,* I thought, *I've turned into Amanda.*

He glanced at his friends and grinned. "I'm sorry?"

Warp core breach imminent, Captain. I stuck out my hand: in for a penny. "Spencer." *Say nothing else, your foot's in too deep already.*

He was British, and therefore obliged to shake and respond in kind: "Laurie."

"Are your friends called Lift and Pavement?" *What in the devil's name am I saying?*

"I'm sorry?" He laughed. I fear this was *at* rather than *with*.

I ploughed on, treading a fine line between lecture and unconsciousness. "Laurie brought to mind the road vehicle, the lorry, and then truck, the ghastly American equivalent. And then other godforsaken Atlantic variations, like elevator for lift and sidewalk for pavement, and then my mouth just blurted them out you have very sexy eyes."

"Spencer, right?"

I nodded. First goal achieved.

"I hope you're not driving."

"I've never driven a lorry in my life."

"Ah, very good." A gentle chiding. "I've heard them all, you know."

"Heard them all what?"

"Never mind." His smile warmed me pleasingly.

I thought it was going rather well at that point. We'd scaled that initial awkward hump and were hurtling towards an intimate conversation of some length, should the dice fall my way. I launched into the usual conversational gambit and attempted at all times to maintain eye contact.

In the next hazy time period I discovered many things. He was a post-graduate student specialising in early Romance languages, who'd spent eleven months circumnavigating the globe and teaching English along the way for subsistence. He was a keen and accomplished chef, helping out in his parents' restaurant during vacations. His fringe would fall over his eyes were it not for his defensive eyebrows. And I was a fool and a wastrel and we had absolutely nothing in common, bar the obvious.

I blustered haphazardly, the drink sploshing about my brain. "That's all rather exciting. As for my own self, I'm preparing to embark on a major marvellous project at St Paul's designed to practically rocket our profile into the broiling stratosphere and take us sprawling to the next level in funding income achievement."

"Sounds interesting. What are you doing?"

My hands began unaccountably to wave. "A, er, celebrity, charity, competition, er, thing. Lots of charity and mystery celebrity, wrapped up in an enigmatic competition. Hush-hush, early days, need-to-know, shush, that sort of solid business."

"Charity competition? What, like a race? I did the London Marathon for charity a few years back."

"A race? A race! Yes, a race." Subtle was not the word. Paralytic,

paralytic was the word.

"In Cambridge? Whereabouts?" Bless him, he seemed genuinely interested.

I touched his arm, his drinking arm, and a quantity of beer escaped. "Careful," I said, "they make you lick it up. Whereabouts? Now then. This has yet to be confirmed, but we're looking at, we're looking at, all over. From St Paul's, to, to, which college are you doing again?"

"I'm at St John's."

"Yes, St Paul's to St John's, that seems fair. And back again. No! Not back again. Somewhere else." I pointed at his two friends, silent and smiling admirers of my delicate flirting technique. "You two, Pavement and Sidewalk, or whatever you were. Colleges." My finger now alternated rapidly between myself and Laurie. "St Paul's, St John's, St John's, St Paul's, then where? Speak up. St, St, John, Paul—"

One of them looked at Laurie, and me, and said: "George and Ringo?" All three laughed.

"St John's, St Paul's, St George's, St Ringo's. Yes. That's it. And we're getting all four of them along, except the lookalikes. No, except the— hang on. No. Which one's St Ringo's again? Is it the little fiddly one by Darwin?"

"He's joking with you, Spencer," said Laurie. Rather kindly, I thought. "There's no St George's, no St Ringo's. You should probably go home now, I think you've had enough to drink."

"Yes, we should go back to mine. I have a bed and everything—"

"No. Sorry. I have a boyfriend. Go home, drink plenty of water, sleep it off."

He gave me what I could only interpret as a *go thither* look.

My crest fell, shattering into a hundred and one pieces to be lost in the crowd along with my dignity. I attempted a blurred smile, nodded, muttered an inconsequence, and withdrew. *Curtsey to the sovereign and retire, and do not turn your back.* Self-destruct sequence initiated.

I decided to call it a night.

My autopilot set me on course at half impulse power from the bar to my room in college. At this level of alcohol consumption my flat half-way across town, with its proper bed, and hot and cold running water, and curtains that successfully blocked the light, was light years beyond sensor range. The tiny part of my consciousness still battling against the onrushing booze knew this and lamented that I would awake in a small number of hours thumping and banging and in a foul mood ready to heft skywards through the window any undergraduate presenting the slightest of grammatical squeaks. As chance would have it — well, no, as careful planning had it — I kept Saturday's diary always mercifully free of such unfortunate potential.

I have no idea what time it was when with the usual grudging assistance of the night porter I tumbled through the college gate on St Andrew's Street into Drybutter's Court. Colloquially and commonly, Drybutter's Court was known as Bottom Court, in contrast to its northerly neighbour Top Court, properly Prince Albert's Court. West of these two lay my room in New Court, which spanned the remaining half of the larger rectangle that made up the college as a whole. New Court's unofficially assigned nickname, Versatile Court, had sadly yet to catch on.

Bottom Court was the earliest part of the college: a cosy, almost claustrophobic enclosure of three-storey late-Georgian architecture in pale Portland stone, edged with cobbles and deep, tempting flower beds. Its central lawn, as ever, was impeccably tidy. Prince Albert's Court to the north had a more Victorian feel to it, as one might imagine: a pompous curtain of fussy, neo-gothic stonework around a much larger rectangle of grass. New Court was a dull late-Victorian addition, prim and proper but with a saucy fountain at its core daring undergraduates to cross the forbidden greenery for a closer, more educational examination.

Unlike many other colleges we had no adjoining grassland outside the rectangle, no sprawling playing fields. We shared sporting facilities with other colleges and generally kept ourselves to ourselves. The college was always closed to tourists, at least these days. One main gate, on St Andrew's Street, and one wider maintenance gate around the rear. Secure, private, monitored.

As was my habit upon returning from Bar Humbug I urinated freely and copiously in the flower beds I perceived to be most directly above Amanda's office in the Admin dungeon, below Bottom Court. There were, of course, toilet facilities near my room, had I cared to use them, but I did not.

Humming drunkenly through the low archway linking Bottom and New Courts, I nearly ploughed directly into the poor Praelector, who recoiled in aged fright.

"Heavens above, Flowers, have a care, have a care," he said.

"Praelector! Dennis! I'm not in the bushes tonight, sorry!" He was the chap who'd discovered me with *Scott — git* and landed me in Amanda's bubbling pot. He was the longest-standing college official, supposedly sixty-nine but with a birth year that crept up annually and had done so for all the years I'd known him. The unofficial estimate was eighty-five, giving rise to the recurring and eternally changing college joke about a calendar year being sixty-nine eighty-fifths of a St Paul's year.

For a man of either age he was skeletal of frame, and nary a grey hair on his head remained, but he was surprisingly robust behind the standard augmentations of his vintage: round-lensed spectacles of thin silver, and an unobtrusive aid in one ear. He always had a kind word — about most.

He chuckled, sweeping his ever-present gown around him. "Still up and about with your shenanigans startling people, eh?

You know startling's not good for me. Not at my age, at my age, you see?"

"Sixty-nine, Dennis? Barely more than a tiny little puppy."

"It'll be my birthday soon, I'm sure, I'm sure."

I wasn't so sure. "Already? Well, when the time comes, we should have a party," I said, noticing the alcohol had switched on my touchy-feely arms. I consciously restrained myself. "Externally catered, of course. Unless you want a cake with melted polystyrene as an ingredient, in which case college would be fine."

"No fuss, no fuss," he said. And then conspiratorially: "How'd you get on with the Master?"

"Marvellously, if she's listening," I said. Then a whisper, close up: "I should come over for tea. We'll have a splendid natter about the old— the old times. She told me you were upset and all a-quiver."

"If only, lad, if only. My quivering days are long gone. Sorry I had to drop you in it. She rather strong-armed matters. It's the cameras, the cameras." He stabbed up at a metal sphere nesting in a nearby eave.

"Oh, it's absolutely fine, all my own fault," I said. "No hard feelings."

"No, I don't get those any more, either." His head drooped.

I laughed. "Then why are you up so late, my dear Praelector? A touch of the Drybutters?"

"The wretched SPAIN thing. Research, research, as ordered."

I drew back. "You too? Amanda led me seriously to believe I was to be the chair. Shouldn't I be doing the ordering?"

He thought better of something. "I'm saying nothing. I'm saying nothing."

"Well, I order you henceforth to your bed. And no naughty business."

I was too far gone to be overly concerned about the Praelector's words. The ubiquitous cameras straddled both the Archivist's and the Master's domains, and although *officially* they were for security and long-term insurance, *unofficially* and most obviously the Master kept the closest of tabs upon both her favourites and her least favourites. Regardless of all that bumfluff, I was already utterly aware that Amanda's hands would be on SPAIN's tiller however the formal roles were dealt. All I could do was puff hard on the sails and try not to vomit over the side.

My college room was silent, cold, orange and spinning. The walls leaned in ever closer. I weaved to the window and drew the useless curtains to darken the orange, and then attempted to identify the cleanest glass in my vicinity: it was the most recent to contain gin, unsurprisingly. I necked the few drops it contained — never one to waste the magical elixir — and clutched it the few metres along the creaking, distorting corridor outside to the shared kitchen: narrow, drab, cluttered, lit by an unforgiving neon strip, also spinning, but with a cold tap that worked and a hot tap that was several years past its prime.

I hung on desperately to the miniature stainless steel sink as I filled the glass, downed its contents, and repeated a few times until my stomach overflowed. Were I tremendously lucky I might stave off the worst of the upcoming throbbing, and my head might not explode brain all over the sofa bed like neuronic popcorn. I thought back to the bar, to my embarrassing failure even to connect loosely with Laurie and his companions, even to hold the mildest of conversations, and the dawning realisation of precisely how tremendously, ball-wrenchingly terrible it had all been.

There was Claire, too. She, at least, had prior experience of my excesses and I knew that the rift could be patched by promising to attend her *Coriolanus* or whichever was next to be ticked by her am-drams.

And as I gulped more water and stared into the accusatory

plughole, I realised that amongst all the nonsense my mouth had emitted was the idea of a charity race. And more: John, Paul, George and Ringo, thanks to Laurie's friends, the couple, Lift and Pavement. What if, I thought, we *select* two colleges to substitute for the non-existent St George's and St Ringo's? What if we held a race from St Paul's, to the others in turn, and then back? And what if we could repeat the event each year?

There's nothing worse than a drunk with an idea. It's either genius, and survives the sharp glare of morning, or more likely — far more likely — it evaporates, dream-like, into a random assortment of meaningless words, a smear of inedible tripe on a cracked white plate. The only way to know for sure is to write it all down, sleep, rise regularly to pee or to throw up or both — though preferably not at the same time — and then once dawn smacks your retina around the chops and the hangover muscles its way in, attempt to examine it with some dispassion. And then screw it up and toss it in the bin, because it's always unadulterated rubbish. But you'll never know for sure unless you do it.

Back in my room, a fresh glass of water by my side, I flipped up the lid of my laptop and cursed ferociously at the unfiltered sunlight melting my face. I hammered on the *Decrease Brightness* key until the nuclear intensity subsided, then blinked away the tears, fired up a word processor and began to mash the keyboard, swiftly and inaccurately.

six
The Choice

The newspaper office was shut on Saturday morning — which for me was a very late morning — the paper being a crappy little two-bit local weekly rag with a shoestring budget. But I went in occasionally on a Saturday if I thought it might buy me a bit of time to work on something juicy during the week — usually spiked or nicked — or if my alarm didn't wake me up due to a heavy night for one reason or another and I needed to make up the time. So it wasn't too out of the ordinary when I pitched up at the building we shared with a bunch of other shitty little companies and used my amazing toothy charm with Colin the security guy, plus my ID card and my key, to let myself in.

Once upon a time a place like this — well, not exactly like this — would be full of copy-girls and ink and cigarette smoke and the mating calls of typewriters. It'd smell of Johnnie Walker Black Label and grease and Old Spice and Chanel No. 5. You'd wade through discarded copy and comps to get your ritual bollocking from a slicked-back sub-editor for shitting all over the house style. The editor would survey his alcoholic, cancer-riddled hacks from a sound-proofed, bullshit-lined office. Everybody would have a cut-glass English accent except the cute blond country boy in the post room who you'd have a secret crush on and know, at some point, you'd see in a cottage somewhere with burning cheeks lurking beneath his fedora. And then you'd run away together to

The Choice

Jamaica and set up a news agency and drink rum every evening on the beach watching an enormous sun melt into the horizon. Or maybe that's just me.

These days the *Bugle*'s office looked like any other arse-scrapingly tedious open-plan workplace. Plasterboard walls you could push a blunt pencil through. A couple of computers, a couple of big displays for them, and a grumbling monster of a printer for checking, which only Simon knew how to feed. A *Health and Safety at Work* poster dangling on one drawing pin that nobody had ever read. A laminated set of instructions on how to give CPR to an ethnically diverse set of fatties, all of whom had mysteriously grown felt-tip moustaches. Windows that defied all attempts to let in air in summer or to retain heat in winter.

If you wanted an atmosphere you opened the drawer with the whiteboard markers and huffed till your eyes spun.

Geoff's desk watched over the room. To his right, Simon's domain: haphazard, disorganised unless you were Simon. To Geoff's left, mine and Manish's area. Kiddy corner, they sometimes called it. We were obliged to keep ourselves nice and tidy, or else. It was part of our "apprenticeship" apparently, along with the crappy wages and the bullying. I think we were allowed one piece of unfiled paper per year of service, which was fine, since paper was for old people.

The editor's desk lay silent and brooding, and locked down tight. I didn't go near it: I was hardly going to tip it upside-down in any case. There wasn't going to be a padlocked box inside a combination safe inside an unlabelled file drawer, marked TOP SECRET: PEARLY TWAT'S EYES ONLY. He'd keep all the dirt on his computer in a folder marked *stuff* with all the porn, like everyone does.

I wasn't here for that anyway. I was here to investigate the hell out of Seb's story. I wanted to pull at the threads, to see if there was information Seb wasn't telling me. Did his father really leave to set up another business? Was it legit? Where was his mother? What about his sister? What does Seb do for a living now? Were there any baby photos I could embarrass him with?

I knew in my gut it would all check out — he was a clever man and I wasn't exactly daft myself, and he knew I wouldn't blindly take his word for it. This wasn't a trust exercise. I was potentially putting my meagre pittance of a salary on a gossamer line. Geoff would fire my arse soon as look at me. There were plenty of more compliant Geoff juniors out there gagging for the gig if I accidentally fell out of the window that didn't open.

Armed with Seb's unusual surname and my infinite Google-fu, plus a quick dance through some news agency archives we must have subscribed to when Geoff was half-cut and more compliant, the information trickled through nicely. It wasn't clear what Daddy Greatsholme was doing now other than sitting on piles of cash: he'd been spending most of his time running and funding impressively lucrative hedges and other shrubbery. There was less on the family side and virtually nothing about Seb specifically, but the internet confirmed that he did, in fact, exist, and he was the guy I was speaking to — and it wasn't those parts of the internet that make themselves up, either. A quick phone call to a college friend, with access to the archives Geoff was too skinflint to cough up for, second-sourced a lot of it.

The big fat cockney bastard unknown in all this was Geoff. He was a git to be sure. That's partly the job of an editor: spike that story, sub out that gossip, drag you away from that tea to fill that gaping space with yet another story about those dreary punt wars. It didn't make him evil, or vindictive, although he was.

I despised the man. But was it right to pursue him for a dodgy story two decades old?

Was it wrong not to?

I stayed in on Saturday night, which triggered three texts from people asking if I was ill or off the market, and I spent Sunday hibernating and drinking pints of strong, sugary tea. I needed some kind of plan for Monday.

The traditional *Bugle* extended Monday pub lunch was an opportunity to chew over the gristle of the weekend and its dull football results and maybe pitch a story or two for this week's edition. Geoff would always sit at one end of the table with his enormous team, all three of us, along the sides: it was an editorial meeting with beer and Thai food.

Geoff had a face etched on leather by an unhappy child: circular, with round eyes, round nose, and a thin wonky line for a mouth. By all accounts he'd chubbed up a bit over the years and now looked like a thuggish younger Churchill. *fight 'em on the beaches or I'll kick yer teef in*. The hair had all but disappeared two newspapers ago, he'd told us. On his right, as ever, Psycho Simon, not that anyone except Geoff ever called him that if they valued their testicles. Geoff and Simon divided the plum stories between them and played good cop bad cop whenever the law or related shite needed laying down. Simon had an east-end Goebbels look about him, wired on intravenous espresso. Always with a cigarette or a substitute in his mouth.

Opposite Simon sat Manish: the other junior, dogsbody, tea-maker, court-sitter, RTA-attender, doorstepper, and whatever else Geoff and Simon didn't want to get off their arse to do. I'd started at the paper before Manish — a whole week before — and regularly gave him the benefit of my greater experience. For some reason I'd never once persuaded him to make me a cup of tea. He was of south Asian stock, via Birmingham. Now I was no heavyweight but he was stick-thin. He'd made the classic mistake of telling us that his nickname at school had been Twiglet, and so Twiglet he'd instantly become. Hell, if I had to deal with the *ginge* and the *top-o-the-morning* shite day in, day out, he could cope. We took the piss out of each other all the time, which he *claimed* wasn't flirting.

After an hour of curry and planning we'd reached the *any other business* part of the meeting, which was the cue for the bashful little Thai waiter who wouldn't meet my eyes to clear the plates away and deliver the second pints. I decided it was now or never and with a decent hit of endorphins buzzing through me I gulped down a mouthful of beer to gird my ever-fruitful loins.

"Hey, Geoff, tell us about the olden days back when you were thin," I said. "You do any vice stories? Ever had to pull your trousers up, make your excuses and leave?" I wanted to keep it oblique, chummy, *knobs-up-muvver-braahn*.

Geoff gained a far-away look in his eyes. "Once or twice," he replied finally, and I worried for a moment he might tell us more than I wanted to hear. "Back when I was young and virile. And could run." He laughed. "What was 'er name, Psych? That Madam in Chelsea?"

"Which one?" replied Simon. "There was the House of Feather, Jill's Union, the Iron Lady, Chocolate Mansions..."

Geoff laughed again. "I knew you'd remember 'em, you perve. Customer one day, next day outside in a car with a notebook and a photographer."

Simon raised a hand. "Vile slander, that is. Contact in the vice squad. Cost a few quid but she was worth it."

"Yeah, like the prossies."

"See anyone famous?" asked Manish with a half-burp, his fist against his mouth.

Great thing about a table of journalists: everyone starts asking questions, taking the heat off you.

Geoff grunted. "Not 'alf, Twiglet. Couldn't publish, though. The old moneybags' briefs slapped an injunction on us. Can't say a dickie about it. Not till you're all grown up, anyway. Nothing to do with the injunction, by the way — you'd blab. Kids always do."

Simon added: "It'd be all over the bloody Twitter."

They were a right little twosome. Not in that sense: it was more Fat Ant and Dec than Elton and David. Of course they knew all about me liking guys — I'm not sitting in anyone's closet. If Manish turned up on a Monday morning bleary-eyed and bragging from a dirty weekend I sure as hell wasn't going to play little miss prim and proper. If it got them uncomfortable and shifty-arsed, it was all the better. I gave not one single toss.

I kept prodding at the editor. "What about, I dunno, businesses? Did you bring any of them down?" I asked.

Geoff turned to Simon and cocked his head in my direction. "Jeez, all these questions, Ginge thinks he's a proper journalist." Back to me: "Keep it up kid and we might give you a fag-and-sherry." He supped his beer.

Manish jumped in again. "What's a— what?"

Foam moustache. "Think about it, son. A fag and a sherry. What all the 'undred-year-olds say when you ask 'em why they're not dead yet — you know, the 'to what do you owe your longevity' bollocks."

Simon, as so often, had a different take. "No-one ever answers 'sitting around watching *Countdown* and Swedish hard-core pornography' do they?" He added a grumpy cackle that evolved into a wet belch.

"I don't know," I replied. "Do they even allow porn in retirement homes?"

"God I fucking hope so," said Geoff. "The missus is not gonna bleedin' last."

I tried to reverse the conversation gently out of porno sidings and back onto the main line to self-destruction. An appeal to the ego seemed like it might get us chuffing along the right track: "So, you didn't bankrupt anyone then. You know, I thought—"

"Yeah, course!" said Geoff, sitting up and preening. "Businesses go tits-up all the time, but yeah, we 'elped a few out. Only the ones that deserved it though. There was that one, what was its name..."

Simon again, with a tight smile: "GH Instruments?"

Geoff picked at his fingers. "Not the one I was thinking of. But yeah."

"GH Instruments?" I said. "Never heard of them. What did they do?" I knew exactly what they did.

"Fiddled the taxman," said Simon. "Claimed they didn't but the proof was all there in black and white." He swept the back of his hand across the rough table, miming the evidence.

"What kind of proof?" I was trying to strike a casual pose between *tedious-lack-of-interest* and *keep-digging-you-shithead*. I was pretty much aiming directly for *keep-talking-so-we-can-stay-in-the-pub*.

"From the auditors," said Simon. "We had about a—"

"Enough of all this crap." Geoff slapped his hand abruptly on the table. "This is supposed to be an editorial meeting not a bleedin' history seminar. We're not sitting around a fire toasting muffins and smoking dope. Drink up, you've got five minutes. I'm off for a slash."

I wasn't sure what I was expecting. A signed, tearful confession to wrongdoing was never on the cards. I guess an evil glint and some hand-rubbing would've helped. There was no indication of remorse, or regret, or shame. He seemed happy. Entirely happy. In fact they both did.

I spent the afternoon back in the newsroom beneath my headphones listening to something heavy and obnoxious, while laying out crappy shop adverts in the grid and trying not to punch Geoff in the nose.

The clock ticked finally over to five thirty, and I logged out and went straight to Bar Humbug leaving a trail of dust behind me. The two pints at lunchtime had been and gone and needed replacing in spades while I thought about what to say to Seb.

Eddie looked at his watch and smiled as I walked in. The guy with the furry hat was in his usual seat. He must've been installed there permanently by law as part of some cruel and unusual punishment.

"Bit early for you, darling," said Eddie. "Looking for an exposé? Cornelius here will give you an exposé, won't you dear?" He nodded at the guy in the hat.

I made a noise and he understood: pub-grunting is a universal language. He was professionally sympathetic until I crossed his palm with a fiver and Cornelius the hat guy's waving arms demanded his attention.

I found a corner of the bar with a high stool and a table and did the arse-dance to get myself comfortable. The last of the daytime crowd was drifting away into the cold — home for their tea and their soaps. Their cosy family school night in, little Timmy whining about homework, and his son with a switchblade threatening to cut him if he didn't do it. Happy families.

My own childhood was a haunted forest of arguments. Arguments between my mother and my father, until my father had had enough and slammed his way out. Between my mother and my two elder brothers, until they got girlfriends and had arguments with them instead. And between my mother and me, starting the day I came out to her aged thirteen and ending two years later when I moved in with my grammy.

I was the third of two children.

Grammy had run a middle-of-the-road B&B in Dublin near a theatre. She'd seen a thing or two, and sometimes more than two. She'd put me in her attic room with a lock on the door and told me to use it. And I used the bejesus out of it. Occasionally I'd see a critical eye on her at breakfast and we'd have *A Discussion*, during which she'd wash the same plate forty-nine times and I'd tell her everything was just hunky-dory in fairyland and she didn't need to worry about me. I did my homework, I did my share of the housework, more or less, and I ate all my peas except for the ones I gave to her little Westey when it sat up and begged like one of the boys from school.

And sometimes at school I got beaten up, and had a cry, and she was there for me, and she didn't argue with me.

She was there waving at the door when I left for college. She wasn't there for my graduation. Nobody was there.

Ancient history.

I couldn't fix my own childhood, and I couldn't fix Seb's either. I wasn't sure whether he'd ultimately gain any solace, any happiness, from kicking Geoff up the metaphorical arse. I knew why he wanted to do it, though.

Seb strolled into the bar almost exactly thirty minutes after I did. I showed no surprise, just raising my near-empty glass a fraction and allowing myself a small grin. Perhaps his source was Eddie, perhaps the hat man, perhaps some ninja hiding under a banquette blending in with the grime and the faded white paint, just out of the corner of my eye.

Seb bought a soft drink, causing all manner of fake outrage and eyebrow action from Eddie, and took the stool beside me. Compared to Friday he'd downgraded the dress code to catalogue casual. One of the expensive catalogues. Pale blue cashmere and mustard chinos: he looked like a damp beach.

"What a coincidence!" he said, knowing I knew.

"Good to see you again," I smiled. "If I'd known you were this loaded I'd have let you buy *all* the mojitos."

"I did offer."

I could only agree.

I expected at least a few minutes of banter before we got down to business, but he had other ideas. He looked me in the eye: "So, Conor. Three days. What have you learned?"

I bought a few seconds of thinking time by downing what

remained of my drink.

"I'm a mere junior reporter," I said. "I don't have super-mega-ultra-clearance on the top-secret database held in the evil journalist castle just outside Slough. I've learned enough, though."

"Will you help me?"

It was at once the trickiest and easiest of questions. To say *yes* would turn me from a simple and/or naïve journalist seeking the truth into a vigilante, a cowboy gunning down other cowboys in the not-so-wild west. To say *no* would mean I wasn't interested in the truth, or the short-term or the long-term effects of the stories I hypothetically wrote, when Geoff gave me the opportunity to hypothetically write them and didn't then cross my name out and write his in instead.

I stared at the ceiling. Behind Seb, Eddie was thumping the coffee machine with a cocktail shaker and inventing swear words. I could do that instead, I thought. I could work behind a bar. Flirt with customers, pour pints, learn how to juggle. A much simpler life—

"Let's make a deal," I said finally. "I call this the *Give Him Enough Rope* deal. Together, we'll come up with a story, somehow, I don't know how, that's going to tickle the interest of the dynamic duo back in the office. And we'll make sure it's juicy, lucrative and one thousand and one percent toss. And we'll see if Geoff sticks his little round head into the noose. If he does, there you go. We pull the whole rug out."

"And if he doesn't?"

"Let's hope he does."

Seb studied his glass, a piss-weak concoction of lime and lemonade overdosing on ice. He spun it slowly round, examining it like a delicate artefact just unearthed from the ashes of Pompeii, except a little wetter. I was biting so hard on my tongue to stay quiet I expected a chunk of flesh to flop into my pint glass at any second.

He looked up and took a breath. "So what's the story?"

seven
The Meeting

A purple nail dinged thrice, dully, upon the rim of a full mug of coffee. Silence fell. Amanda dinged twice more, irrelevantly, and called the committee assertively and messily to order. Naturally she performed these actions unilaterally, pre-delegating to herself the responsibility that should rightly have been mine, or so I had been led to believe. My smile wavered not one smidge. My rigid back was unyielding.

I was glad this time to be encountering her above ground, in a bright, high-ceilinged, wood-panelled conference room in Prince Albert's Court — Top Court. The Bandolinum Room, named after a racehorse upon which our founder successfully wagered a great sum, overlooked the easternmost fringes of the bus terminal. Hardly the most glorious and historic of views for contemplating the very future of St Paul's, should it even have one. And yet I knew that should events surge against me I might easily offer my excuses and catapult myself through the window onto the roof of the X5 and thereby make my getaway to Oxford, via St Neots, Bedford, Milton Keynes, Buckingham and Bicester. I imagined the free wifi extended to the roof.

The conference room's long, cheap table was cobbled together from several smaller pinewood affairs — possibly detritus recovered from failed businesses — and simply mashed together in an unlikely fashion like poor council house tiling. As college was not blessed with vast wealth and space the table was often reconfigured for use by private firms wanting a sniff of toff and by dubious student societies, and thoroughly sanitised afterwards. Its current layout could sit at least two dozen, were chairs required. The SPAIN committee thankfully comprised only four people: me, our dear Master Amanda, the delightful codger and Praelector Dennis, and our Bursarette Helen. We huddled around one corner of the table, various papers and beverages spread before each of us.

Amanda cleared her throat, or a kettle boiled, I was unsure. "Let me begin opening the proceedings by offering a warmly welcome to Dr Flowers, this committee's *chair nouveau*," she said, gripping tightly to a red biro.

"Thank you, Master," I began, with a nod. "May I first—"

"I find the role of chair full of stifle and pompy, and thus ceremonially disbalanced and not to be stood too heavily upon. Do you not concur, Dr Flowers?" She sacrificed a gulp of the blackest coffee and her eyes blazed.

"Do we have an agenda?" asked Helen, a rather small and squeaky and relentlessly cheerful lady who catered regularly at hockey matches but remained unhappily single. "I scoured my inbox but saw no trace. Is there an agenda, Dr Flowers?"

"I'm not aware—" I managed.

"The agenda is the cartwheel of the savage rodent," said Amanda, and Helen's shoulders drooped. "We have merely one singular pressing upon us, upon which Dr Flowers shall now enlighten us upon."

I leaned forward and opened my mouth—

"Praelector," Amanda continued, "am I to disbelieve that you have not discovered anything notelessworthy?"

Poor Dennis was rather startled to have the whip cracked so promptly, and jumped from an early doze. He fussed with his papers, moving spectacles up and down his forehead and up and down his nose, groping for focus. "My dear, my dear, according to my investigations we have few rooms of prominence remaining in college unsponsored. Bids for the naming of the boathouse gym, as anticipated, as anticipated, oversubscribed immediately upon announcing unfettered usage during full term. This, I report sadly, is the only bright spark. I fear the alumni, the dear Old Paulines, have already been squeezed quite dry, quite dry."

Amanda glared at the Praelector and the biro-tapping began. I thought it wise to insert myself verbally between Dennis and whichever death ray Amanda was about to unleash upon him. "Amanda, if I might…"

"You, as it were, might," she said slowly above her purple spectacles, and I took that to be agreement.

"I have taken the liberty of preparing a small document outlining my proposal," I began, distributing four stapled sheets of grammatically correct, typographically pleasing, skimmable, bulleted, readable text to each of my colleagues.

A jet of pure white steam erupted from the top of Amanda's head and I expected at any moment a thunderbolt to despatch her *X Factor* coffee mug to the winds. I sensed she had not anticipated this move. And in truth neither had I, upon waking late on Saturday afternoon with my head attached to my desk by industrial-strength drool. My typed scribbles were, as expected, bordering on incoherence in significant part and I had wishfully inserted the notion of the *Chatteris Batteris*, a chase through the city centre involving the Master and an uncountable number of baseball bats. It had been a simple matter to tidy up those issues and I spent the remainder of the weekend fleshing out sufficient detail to answer all the probable questions, and cursing the word processor, and recovering from backups, and the like.

"As you will see," I told the committee, "I am proposing an annual charity event open to students and non-students alike, to be called *Band on the Run*. Participants may run or walk between

St Paul's, St John's and two other colleges: these are to be selected randomly before the race and designated honorary St George's and St Ringo's colleges. The course naturally finishes back at St Paul's: it is thus a giant quadrilateral, and would differ each year to add variety and interest. Each participant has a numbered bucket, and collects for a charity of their choosing. It is not a timed race: the aim is to raise money, not to complete the course quickly. I anticipate the appearance of a miscellany, a smorgasbord, of costumes: pantomime horses, musical pastiches — most especially the obvious quartet — and black tie, for example. No restrictions on dress other than the usual proprieties, with speedos most definitely permitted and indeed encouraged. And whichever participant raises the most money is to be presented with a small trophy and proclaimed the year's *Fifth Beatle*."

"I see," said Amanda glacially. Other brows furrowed, scurrying through the details in the proposal.

"Annual publicity," I continued. "A good cause — many good causes, in fact. Ideally with a celebrity aspect to the proceedings, although this might prove difficult in year one unless the Master can incant some devil words and summon Lulu. I do certainly anticipate a very many hectares of goodwill and a consequent raised profile, as desired."

"I see," said Amanda again. One tap of the biro.

"Dear boy, dear boy," said Dennis, failing to suppress a smile, "splendid concept. Is there not, though, an issue with the boys in blue, in blue?"

"Section 5.6, Dennis." I directed him to the appropriate clause. "A three-stage process: informal, formal, archival. Given college, uh, experiences of which I am aware, and assuming many of which I am not, I see no great issue in persuading the authorities of our case."

"I see," said Amanda again, her face advancing through the traffic light sequence and her biro tapping increasingly frequently.

The Meeting

My chin remained firmly up.

"I'm a teensy confused," said Helen. "How exactly does this raise any money for the college? Charities, yes, and very much tick V.G. But for St Paul's?"

I nodded thoughtfully, then indicated to the Master. "Amanda assured me that fundraising was a role designated for a fundraiser, and I am regretfully, legally, not a fundraiser."

"Oh," Helen said quietly.

"So," Amanda began, tap-tap-tap, starting to bubble and froth, "you do before us bring this, this—"

"Fully thought-out proposal," I said, attempting to rein in any hint of smugness.

A rolling boil. "—with buckets of charity, with musical running—"

"The theme is in truth merely a conceit, linking us and St John's and two others in a simple and I suggest lightly humorous fashion, to help create a university event rather than a college event, and allowing for an uplift in publicity."

A mess all over the hob. "—and winners, and trophies, and how in the *Boom Bang-a-Bang* shall we afford it?"

I was rather taken aback by her angry clarity and I recoiled, blinking. "A-a-appendix A," I stammered. "It is fully costed, admittedly with several assumptions."

She scrunched bitterly over the pages to find the data, muttering silently and occasionally tossing out an epithet of some indelicacy.

I continued. "I did, perhaps, think that this committee might discuss how best to fund the event. We could share costs with St John's, obtain sponsorship…"

The bursar swept her calculating eyes over the figures, displaying no obvious signs of distress. "I would need some quality time alone with my spreadsheet, Master, but on first glance—"

"Glance, Bursar? *Glance?*" That appeared to be the sum total of her response.

"On first glance the figures do not appear unreasonable. As to funding..." A mousy shrug.

The fidgeting and babbling from Amanda gradually sputtered and burned out, the purple candle snuffed, during which Dennis successfully dropped off, and she calmed sufficiently to form what passed for a coherent sentence. "I shall of course require to ingest myself of the completed and unabridged contents, Dr Flowers. To allocate sufficient of my remaining minutes such as to appreciate, as it were, the fullest of intents."

"Of course."

"Suffice and in summarisation, Dr Flowers, I say that I am— impressed." There was that negating pause once more, such a welcome return.

"I am— grateful," I replied.

"And in full and final settlement my decision is No."

"I beg your pardon? You just informed us you were going to read it! Did you not?" I was suddenly unsure.

"Read it, indeed shall I. And yet, No, Dr Flowers. *No.*"

Dennis was with us again, in great part. "Goodness, my dear Amanda, such haste, such haste."

A laser scorch from the Master. "The essence of time is upon us, Praelector, such as of you might be fully aware."

I fought on. "At least let Helen run the numbers—"

"Helen's numbers runneth over, as doeseth this meeting."

"But—"

But *nada*. To be precise: energy expended, lots; agreements achieved, few. When Amanda closed the meeting, allegedly my meeting, and shooed us away like snot-squirting young tykes, I stomped out and down and out into the greying, brooding afternoon of Top Court where I stood breathing heavily, hands on my hips, hunting for a bush to strangle.

The Meeting

Dennis appeared after a minute or so, chuckling, unfazed, and put a hand on my shoulder. "Eight o'clock, lad, eight o'clock. Tea at mine. Frightful woman, isn't she? Don't turn up drunk, drunk."

The temptation to dive immediately into the gin was overwhelming and, I realised, slightly tragic. I had promised Dennis I would arrive promptly and unmunted, and so I dared not tempt myself even with one sniff. *Nunc est* most definitively not *bibendum*. The blessed bottle, pride of place on my desk, remained virgin and unmolested as Monday afternoon dragged its carcass on.

I ate early in the college dining hall, a high-ceilinged echo chamber ringed with portraits of Masters past and cameras present. I chose a bench apart from all others, deliberately so. For company would lead to *just one drink*, which wouldn't be just one, or indeed just. I reacquainted myself with the unfettered taste of water, drunk this time out of choice and not a desperate necessity. The college food was as it always was: on the bland side of insipid and only identifiably edible given the accompanying crockery and cutlery. I should have asked the morlocks of the kitchen to blend it to a dirty brown mush so I could take it away and spoon it in at my leisure, like a meatshake.

Eight o'clock begrudgingly agreed to arrive. Instinctively I grabbed a bottle of emergency wine as the traditional gift but quickly thought better: tea it had been proclaimed, and tea it was to be.

It took a minute, no more, to cross to the Georgian stone of Bottom Court and climb C staircase to Dennis's rooms. I had been here frequently, though regrettably and ashamedly not recently. Three knocks and the door breezed open, Dennis ushering me cheerfully through with a twinkle and a cravat.

Unlike me, Dennis lived in college — and college lived in him. He had been here, in these few rooms, longer than anyone could remember. He'd arrived a fresh-faced undergraduate, either in the dawning of the nuclear sixties or the sunset of the warring forties, depending on which birth date you subscribed to. And somehow, he'd never left. Each room was cluttered with the trinkets and thingumabobs and hoojums accumulated over a lifetime at St Paul's, learning and teaching and serving and goodness knows what else. He was a fixture, a heartbeat.

"The kettle is well on, dear boy," he said. "Peppermint, I think. Very calming. That's your chair, sit, sit." He waved at an old plush velvet armchair he'd evidently discovered moments before under an angry pile of something dusty. His own chair — more worn, more faded, long-dimpled with the memory of his flesh and bone — lay with easy access to books and a remote control, and angled toward a large, new, impossibly thin television wedged into a corner.

"New toy, Dennis?"

He fussed around in the tiny kitchen. "One has to keep up with the news."

"You could use a computer for that."

"Ha!" He emerged with two mugs of peppermint tea, one of which I extracted from him quickly before it spilled. He looked over the round lenses of his spectacles. "I fear I like computers about as much as I like A-M-A-N-D-A." He spelled out her name with a childish glee and tipped his head towards the spy camera mounted high above the television.

"Ah, yes," I said, sipping and sitting. Peppermint was the tea of my long-gone undergraduate days — now rushing dangerously back as I let my eyes close — when essays were short and without consequence, when the booze lasted forever and the hangovers didn't, and when a crisis was an unwashed top and an opportunity was an eager bottom.

Dennis eased himself into his chair with that comfy noise those above a certain threshold involuntarily make. "Oh, that dreadful woman. One doesn't like to tell tales out of school, but — *fucking bitch*, is that what they say?"

I burst into laughter. "Oh Dennis, I knew you'd cheer me up. If I were an undecidable number of years older, or you younger…"

In truth I worried that he was rather too blatant in his treasonous anti-Amanda talk given the camera and the chance we might be overheard: but he was unbothered by it. Perhaps, I thought, he believed himself as untouchable as our founder Drybutter. It was an unsettling theory.

He chuckled. "Nothing ages you more than the calendar, dear boy. Sixty-nine seemed as good a place as any to stop that nonsense. Now I find my contemporaries no longer dwindle, they simply move on and are replenished by ever-bountiful nature. The harvest heralds new growth. And here I still am." His habit of repeating words withdrew as he relaxed, and that in turn relaxed me.

The conversation was warm and drifted fore and aft, but always reeled gently back towards the present difficulties: Amanda and the college funds. Dennis agreed that my race idea was appealing. He did, though — kindly and carefully — wonder exactly how the college might directly gain, financially. I admitted my hands had rather waved over that in the hope of pixie dust to conjure up a solution. I felt sure, though, that there would be some kind of beneficial effect.

Tomorrow's first job, he told me, should be to shuffle on my knees across the city and prostrate myself before the gods of St John's: for without their blessing the entire enterprise was, to use his words, *up the shitter*. I should, he said, proceed merrily on as though Amanda had approved the proposal, despite her earlier words.

The evening drew finally to a close. I set down my mug and made leaving noises, but Dennis had a surprise in store.

"Before you scoot home, my lad, we have a short journey to make," he said, rising to his feet. The twinkle was back. "To drop in on a colleague. He's expecting us."

The Archivist worked out of a suite of rooms in the Admin dungeon. It was no secret that he employed many assistants, undergraduates recruited to his cause and universally known as elves, who rotated in and out on shifts to lighten their fiscal loads. The elves saw much, and knew they were seen much, and it did not affect them much. This current generation at least clutched personal sharing to their very public bosom, although the adage *what happens in archive, stays in archive* was steadfastly and rigorously adhered to. Naturally there were stories, especially of pranks perpetrated during an eager fresher's first *elving*, as it was called: these usually involved impersonations of celebrities or, shall we say, volume of numbers.

It was said, but never publicly stated, that the Archivist's empire expanded beyond the college boundary and under St Andrew's Street and Emmanuel Street, such was the volume of data to retain.

A fog of rumour and legend surrounded the Archivist himself, whose face was well known but whose name was never uttered. The title was enough: should any local politician fly a policy kite in dangerous proximity to college power lines, mere mention of the Archivist might cause the wind to drop.

The current Archivist had held his position for many years and was nearing the compulsory retirement age of sixty. The late nights and constant scanning of video streams, especially in more recent data-rich years, took its toll.

"Professor Sauvage, Dr Flowers." He gave us a polite and curt welcome at the entrance to his domain. He used the Praelector's formal academic title, embers of a long-softened Mancunian harshness rekindled by the French pronunciation.

Identity checks efficiently and thoroughly completed, he showed us to what appeared to be a small office. It was stark, bare, minimalist. No pictures on the walls, no photos of family on the smooth, compact desk. No stray papers at which one might sneak a revelatory glimpse. No bank of screens tracking miscreants like myself from court to court.

It was, I realised, an office-cum-interrogation room. I looked in vain for a mirror, behind which might stand a camera and two elves in white coats with clipboards. We were surely observed in any case.

"Do please excuse me, professor, doctor," he said, careful to refer to us in protocol order. "My shift begins in six minutes and forty-seven seconds and I must prepare. But we may talk briefly." As was traditional the Archivist took the night shift, nine till nine. He habitually worked through a light exercise regime to limber up for the long evening ahead.

I felt slightly uncomfortable sitting in a plain wooden chair, alongside Dennis, as this short, sinewy man bent and stretched for our entertainment, his mop of white hair billowing as a willow in a strong breeze. We were disrupting his well-rehearsed routine, and a man's routine is his castle.

"Flowers here wants a favour, Archivist, a favour," began Dennis unselfconsciously, and patted my arm.

I looked to him, confused. "Favour?"

The Archivist said nothing.

"Our friend Amanda," the Praelector continued.

Perhaps a glimmer of reaction from the Archivist, or simply a muscle twinge as he pulled and stretched his left foot back and up toward his buttocks.

"Archivist, I shall be blunt with you," said Dennis. "The snowfall becomes heavier and begins to drift. Do you have anything that might clear a path?"

The Archivist switched feet. "Be very careful, Professor."

"You see what is happening. It is hardly unexpected."

"And what would you have me do?" The Archivist froze. "This

is not via proper channels."

"Proper channels be damned!"

"The protocol is well-established. I cannot break it and you know well why this is so." His dark eyes, shaded and ringed by years of night shifts, years of screens, years of cataloguing and recording, regarded Dennis sternly.

"Not even—"

"Not even." A second more, and he restarted his exercises.

Dennis turned to me and forced a smile, bleak as midwinter. "Worth a go, worth a go."

"Forgive me," I said, "but might someone explain? Channels, protocol? Snowfall?"

The Archivist and the Praelector exchanged a look. The Archivist nodded with, I felt, a slight reluctance.

"The screens," said Dennis. "She has... some access to the cameras. Perhaps too much, my lad."

"You might think of it as an addiction," said the Archivist, grunting as he bent over. "Like pigeons pecking constantly at a button that once delivered seed."

I could see Amanda pecking away in my mind's eye. Unpleasant.

"There is such a thing as too much data, Dr Flowers. Within these walls we manage it through shifts and careful monitoring of the elves."

"Who watches the watchers? You do."

From his expression, a weary smile, it was not the first time that phrase had been uttered. The phrase *elven safety* also came to mind but I wisely kept it there.

"Indeed," said the Archivist. "We believe with the Master the influx of data combined with a pathological desire to know *everything* and, of course, her general floundering in the role, triggered a kind of scrambling. Hence her increasing infelicity with language. The snow, falling, drifting."

The Meeting

"And I suppose," I said, "it explains her selecting me, of all people, to resolve the funding crisis."

"Oh, no, my lad," said Dennis, "that's entirely personal."

"Then I confess I don't have the faintest idea why we are here. Why me, especially."

The two men looked again at one another, the look of a joke shared.

"Oh! Were we about to attempt to blackmail Amanda?" I said, and they both laughed.

"There is no such thing as blackmail," said the Archivist tightly, pulling an arm behind his head. "Black implies an absolute. There is no black, there is no white—"

"—All is grey, above, below and beyond," the two men completed together.

My back shivered with a touch of the freemasons. I must have looked confused. Dennis touched my arm again. "Don't worry, lad. Old saying. We are all complex creatures, and none of us is perfect, is perfect."

"I am afraid I cannot help you on this occasion, Dr Flowers." The Archivist dabbed his face with a branded college towel. "And now it is time for my shift."

He made a signal to what appeared a bare wall. Evidently not: in a few seconds we were joined in the room by a young man, a student — an elf. I recognised him as the undergraduate I had encountered just after the Master had forced SPAIN upon me. He saw me and gave a shy smile. I was glad he was making himself useful here.

"Please escort these gentlemen out," said the Archivist.

The elf led us out of the office into the entrance hall. I saw three other doors, leading somewhere unknown: secured, reinforced, with some form of scanning device guarding against unauthorised entry. Retinal scan? Hard to be sure in the gloom.

eight
The Contact

"A word, please, Mr Geraghty," said Simon after my first Tuesday morning coffee. What he meant was: a bollocking. It's never just *a word*, especially if he's not taking the piss and calling me *ginge* or *mick* or something. The little mini-Kray. Nelson's bell-end. *Oi oi saveloy* my Irish arse.

All bollockings were officially administered in private, in the fire exit stairwell off to one side of the office. Everyone knew full well, though, that every whisper echoed and amplified up and down and was about as private as a celebrity sex tape — and that was the point, of course. It was the newspaper equivalent of executing a recaptured Steve McQueen-alike at a prisoner-of-war camp: against all the rules but, well, *how else will these savages learn?*

I donned my flame-proof suit and gave Manish an any-last-requests wink, and then followed Simon through the fire exit to the naughty steps. But he surprised me by not stopping: he headed straight down, two flights, and out past the beautiful arrangement of discarded cigarette butts into the car park. I screwed my eyes up against the damp sunshine and smelled wet dirt, but frankly it could've come from me or Simon or anywhere. Was I being fired? Driven to a building site to make friends with a cement mixer? Taken for a swim in the river inside a bag with some labrador puppies? Or a good old-fashioned beating?

I waited for him to say something.

"Fag?" he asked, and grinned, pulling a pack from his back pocket. He always said that. He knew I didn't smoke.

"Out and proud," I replied as always, with a clenched fist in salute, as he lit a cigarette and took a long drag. "What's this about, Simon? Before you start: anywhere but the face. I have a beautiful nose. You can break my arm if you like. Just the one, mind. I'd get a lot of sympathy from the boys for that. I could get them to sign the cast, you know, leave their mark."

"Yesterday," he said, scuffing along a couple of pebbles and blowing smoke after them. "All that talk about the— the past." I picked up a hint of Old Spice from him.

"What about it?" I tried to keep it light, relaxed. No sense in raising hackles, and neither was I about to go the full hedgehog. I kept my eyes on his fists.

"I admire your historical… interest." Admiration? This was a brand new flavour of trouble. "But don't forget the perspective, *mate*, will you?"

I waited in vain for him to give me some of that all-important perspective, while I tried to remember whether he'd ever called me *mate* before. It was a deliberate *mate*, though. It wasn't an *alright mate* mate, or a *you've had enough mate* mate. It was more a *you looking at my bird, mate?* mate, a "mate" suffocated by camouflaged quote marks.

"Sure," I said finally, straining every muscle not to say *mate*. "I was just being sociable, is all. You know, like the humans do."

He toe-poked a pebble skipping under some random's Volvo and gave me a dead smile. "I know you were, son, I know you were. Remember the five Ws: who, what, when, where, why."

"I try." I tapped my head. "They're right up there with the seven dwarves and Elizabeth Taylor's husbands."

"Glad to hear it. Right, ginge, clear off." Muffled, fag between the lips.

"Not even a clip round the ear?"

He waved me away. That was all a threat, to be sure, but simultaneously not a threat. I went back through the fire escape door feeling like I'd just come out of confession with a dodgy priest with a combover and he'd told me to say three Hail Marys and sit on his lap.

Manish was buzzing when I got back. "What happened?" he whispered as I sat down at my desk beside him. "I was waiting for the screams."

"Just a minor kneecapping. Used to happen all the time back in Dublin growing up. I got through about forty-nine different knees in my time. When you're an experienced journalist like I am you learn to take the pain."

"Yeah, sod off Weasley."

"Twiglet."

"Seriously, though."

"Oh, it was all a bit of friendly banter. Mostly him saying keep your nose out and me going *don't cut me!*"

"Keep your nose out of what?"

I thought he was about to get out his notebook and start taking shorthand. "Nothing to concern your pretty face."

"That's sexual harassment, that is."

"Take it to the papers."

That lunchtime I scooted into town, officially on an emergency mission to find a last-minute card for a non-existent aunt about to topple off the perch back home. In truth, to visit a source. As usual at this time of day, he was at his pitch outside the supermarket opposite Sidney Sussex College and had probably sold half a dozen of his "very last copy" of that week's *Big Issue*.

"Conor, mate!" he said, arms outstretched, as I approached. This was a *could do with a tenner, mate* mate. We shook hands tribally, two chiefs meeting on a savannah with dust and grit and

The Contact

Sainsbury's bags spiralling around us. His dog, a bull terrier with a dirty white coat, sat serenely upright behind like a wise elder of the tribe tied to a bike rack.

"Hey Charlie."

Charlie was my age, my height, but looked old and broken. He had lank, unwashed hair in tangled dreads, greying from black, or at least it looked black. A scuffed anorak hung limply around his shoulders but doubled his bulk. He didn't talk about his past, or his present. His apparent cheerfulness always subdued me.

"What can I do you for, mate?" he asked.

"I'm looking for some gossip, Charlie. New and exclusive gossip."

"A scoop, eh? After a bit more moolah?" He leaned in and I smelled old newspapers.

"Something like that." I instantly felt bad. "Need to get into my boss's good books."

"I got nothing for you, sorry mate." To some passers-by: "*Big Issue*, sir? Madam?"

"Shit. Are you sure?"

"It's been really quiet. Not sold one in two hours, have I?"

I took that as a hint and dug into my pockets. "I'll take a copy off your hands, Charlie. Least I can do." I handed over the cash and with a flourish he presented me with that week's edition.

"You're a gentleman, Conor," he said. "Listen, probably nothing, but I just remembered. You know Quiff? You must know Quiff."

It was a new name for me. "Quiff?"

He fished out another one of his last copies of *Big Issue* and failed to attract the fanny packs of a gaggle of Americans.

"Yeah. You not know him?" he said. "Dunno his first name. Sometimes comes and spreads a little love around, know what I mean? Full of stories. Said something's going on at one of the colleges."

It didn't sound that promising — something was always going

on at one of the colleges. Usually in Latin and with a procession. But it was all I had, and time was ticking, and I didn't want to give Geoff or Simon any more reason to dislike me.

"Worth a punt I guess. Where can I find this Quiff guy?"

"Where he always is, which is why you should know him. Humbug. Stupid big hat."

My face must have lit up.

"Ah, now you know who I mean."

I thanked him and gave him another couple of quid — always keep your sources well hydrated — then hurried off to Bar Humbug, less than a minute's walk away. I'd never spoken to this hat guy before, except perhaps the odd *excuse me* or a strangulated mumble in the piss queue. He'd always seemed part of the furniture, almost a sideshow along with the juggling cocktail boys and the occasional drag act. I presumed he was *family* — but I never saw him leave with anyone. I never saw him leave at all, or arrive, come to that. Eddie had said his first name yesterday — Cornelius — and now I had his surname too. Gave me the upper hand. Useful.

Humbug was a confusing, unfamiliar place of sunshine and mothers and young kids bouncing off the walls. The nighttime Bumhug had become the daytime Mumhug, or maybe Mumdrug thanks to the supply of caffeine and chocolate. The coffee machine growled and coughed on a loop, and one of Eddie's tight-shirted little twinky helpers was in great demand for a de-stressing Manhattan or Cosmo — or anything, as long as it had chocolate sprinkles. It still had the soul of Bumhug, just with a lipstick sheen.

And at the far end of the bar, in his usual position watching over the world, sat the man with the furry hat I now knew to be Cornelius Quiff, cuddling some booze. Early fifties, I guessed. Thin, struggling beard turning to silver. Every day a little heavier. Enveloped in a fog of some manly fragrance I recognised but couldn't put a name to.

I sidled up to the bar not far from Quiff, hoisted myself onto a stool, and went full-twinkle.

"I guess I'd better get a coffee," I said to the barman. "First time for everything. Normal coffee, normal cup, normal milk, please. I'm a simple Irish boy with simple tastes, and I don't think I've ever come here and felt older."

The barman laughed. He knew me from the evening crowd. "Is different, yes?"

He was eastern European. Latvian, perhaps. Face like an angel after a few too many five-in-the-morning finishes. Not perhaps the land of DILF and money he was expecting.

Off to the left a small fat boy pushed a smaller fatter boy into a chair, and the tears and the wailing began. "Obviously not that different," I said, thumb aimed at the kids. "Switch on the waterworks and fall into the arms of the woman with the big breasts. No different at all."

I turned to Quiff and nodded a greeting. It felt mildly sacrilegious, saying a proper hello for the first time to someone you've recognised but skirted around for a year. Like the mind-whirling clumsiness and rictus grin when you finally meet someone after months of chatting online: you know that your relationship changes at that point, changes irrevocably. You just don't know how.

"It's Mr Quiff, isn't it? Cornelius Quiff?"

He seemed shocked at the need to speak, and coughed. "It is, yes, that's right." Yorkshire? Lancashire? All those northern English accents sounded alike to me. This was soft, light, camp. "Have we met?"

The barman slid over my cup of coffee.

I said: "Can I get you a drink, Cornelius?" Stick to the first name: keep 'em friendly.

He nodded gratefully and the barman didn't bother asking:

double vodka, lemonade, lots of ice. Liver a gift from the gods, I guessed. And wallet.

"I'm Conor. Conor Geraghty. You've probably seen me here more than a few times. What with the ginger and all that. It tends to draw the eye. Not that I'm complaining, mind you. That's a decent hat you've got there. What kind of a hat is it?" I took a sip of coffee. Black, strong, buzzy. I could see why the mums all came here.

Quiff's hands moved to his hat and adjusted the fit slightly. "It's a karakul. Afghan origin, this one. Keeps the heat in when the clocks go back."

"You've been to Afghanistan?"

"No love. Camden market. About five years ago?" He swapped out his empty glass for the fresh one I'd bought. "It's much more convenient than Kabul. On the tube, you know."

I laughed. "Well, it suits you. Very distinctive. You've got to stand out, haven't you? I'm the ginger, you're the furry hat. Could be worse, let's face it. Now listen, I have a confession: I'm not talking to you entirely by accident."

"Oh?" He sat back, upright. "You've sought me out? You're not the tax man, are you dear? It's all accounted for."

"I'm not the tax man. I'm the newspaper man. A journalist, for the *Bugle*. Should have a hat of my own, a fedora with a Press card in the band, but the boss is too cheap."

"It's not about the operation, I hope. I'm bored of talking about that flaming operation."

"It's not about any operation. We're not interested in operations unless something goes wrong. Did it go wrong?"

He shook his head.

"No, right, good. Listen. A mutual acquaintance gave me your name. He said you might have some useful gossip for me."

He giggled like a schoolgirl. "I always have gossip, young man. Not gossip you're likely to print though. It might get me into trouble."

I didn't want to prompt him, to lead him on. It was better that he volunteered it. "Not about this place," I said. "God knows, it has enough of a reputation as it is. I'm looking for something properly newsworthy. Something that could get me a front-page story."

"Don't want much, do you, for your double vodka? I'm not sure I have anything you could use."

"Come on now, this is Cambridge. Nothing happens here. A dog barking after ten o'clock gets on page two."

"I'm sorry."

"Are you sure? I could set you up for another if you'd like." I was gambling that Seb would pay my expenses without a second thought. "And there's plenty more where that came from. You might not get the decent stuff every time, mind. Times is hard, even in this town." *Take the bait, take the bait.*

"I'm sure I could manage another, if you're offering," he said.

I signalled to the barman, who'd been watching, and he fetched another glass. My eyes remained on Quiff, and my mouth stayed zipped. It was simply a question of who broke the silence first. I was happily tripping on caffeine. For once, I was determined it wouldn't be me.

"Well, there might be something," he said finally.

Buy a man a drink and you have a friend for the evening — but buy him two and he'll stay the night. I think that's how the saying goes. Not that I had designs on Cornelius Quiff, but I'd happily have given him a smacker on the lips right there and then.

He explained, softly and confidentially, how he'd *happened to learn* — by which I'm sure he meant *overheard* — of a problem in the money department at St Paul's College along the road. The place was running on empty. Cashflow negative, despite apparently sitting on a gold mine of top quality gossip themselves, and with some idea of a competition to raise money.

That sounded like a story Seb and I could make use of. It would mean talking with the poshos at St Paul's, but from what Quiff told me it was pretty clear who the source was: that guy Spencer, who was some arsewiper-in-chief up there. He was always in Humbug, falling-down drunk, and Quiff was always sitting-down listening. Made total sense.

So I'd need to get in touch with Spencer. As long as he didn't throw himself at me again it'd be fine.

I didn't have Spencer's contact details. I sure as hell wasn't going to ask anyone back at the *Bugle* offices to find them. I could have called the college switchboard and got all their tongues wagging overtime, but I needed to keep this entirely under the radar — for my sake and for Seb's. If we were to pull off the *Give Him Enough Rope* plan with Geoff, secrecy was paramount.

After paying for the drinks at Humbug — and remembering to get a receipt and keep it somewhere nice and safe — I spent the afternoon back in the office on the day job, the one that actually paid my wages, fending off excited questions from Manish about the non-existent aunt that I'd already forgotten about by then.

I waited until after work, back home in my hovel of a flat, before logging in to Gaydar. I wasn't a regular user. I figured there's more to life than tapping into a box and trying to figure out whether the guy you're talking to is twenty-five like he says or fifty-five, and the photos are all filtered and photoshopped and generally dicked around with anyway. But I knew Spencer had a profile there. I bet he could barely last ten minutes without having a sniff around.

The message was easy enough: "Spencer! How's it going? I hear you're having a few problems over at St Paul's. Wanna chat about it?"

I figured that was about as upbeat and ambiguous as I could get. He probably wouldn't remember I was a journalist. Chances are I'd told him when he was draping himself all over me, and the memory had never stuck and was flushed out of his kidneys about ten minutes later.

His reply came as I was in the kitchen fixing myself up some pasta. "Lovely to hear from you. A little local difficulty, all under control — who's been gossiping?"

He wasn't biting. I had to try harder. "I'll tell you over a drink."

Fifteen long minutes passed before he got back to me, the git. The paranoia was starting to set in: who was he grassing to? I'd said nothing incriminating, though, nothing that could derail the plan. He finally sent a single word: "OK".

nine
The Agreement

It had been a long day of hurried and occasionally fraught meetings across the city, variously informing and pleading and negotiating with all the relevant parties and some irrelevant but mistaken ones. As Dennis had suggested, I presented the race as all agreed with Amanda and kept my fingers crossed that her disreputation was well known and nobody would dare check with the woman herself.

The police were unusually compliant regarding possible road closures — especially at the urgent notice I had requested, just ten days or so — and merely asked for an early peek at the anticipated route, which I gladly promised. I told a rouge-faced desk jockey I planned to select the two random colleges midweek and assured him of my cooperation in every available respect. His reaction to my verbal stroking led me to suspect I might hear from him again in some alternative capacity.

The university authorities rolled rapidly over when I assured them no decisions were required on their part, and we would not sully the university brand or present the logo at a disrespectfully jaunty angle.

My colleagues at St John's presented a somewhat harder challenge. I had hoped they might agree to open their capacious purse and allow me to harvest a few of the more burdensome coins for the purchase of necessities such as printed sticky numbers and collection buckets for the race participants. The response was better than a defenestration, which was pleasing. They were, however, of the opinion that if they footed the bill for everything it was arguably their event and so they should reap the accompanying publicity whirlwind. Hard to counter with anything other than a glum face and a near-tearful goodbye. Happily they were content to be part of the event as a whole, or else one would be well and truly up scuttle creek.

When young Conor popped up in my Gaydar inbox that evening I was considering how best to approach local businesses in the hunt for freebies. From behind, with a pop on the head? Brazenly, with a politician's mile-wide smile? Where could one obtain a couple of thousand buckets anyhow? I realised that if anyone knew about such things, Claire's husband Ken most certainly would. I was on the phone to her, tendering the usual sincere apology for my behaviour on Friday night, then badgering about her little salesman. The upshot: little salesman laughter.

I almost missed Conor's second message, having drifted with Claire onto lighter topics and poured myself some well-deserved lubrication. The ginger gentleman was persistent and seemingly rather eager to meet. And who was I to turn down such an invitation? We agreed what appeared an unnecessarily cloak-and-dagger manoeuvre, a nine o'clock rendezvous on Magdalene Bridge. I considered telling him I'd be wearing a scarlet buttonhole and that he should call me Yevgeny, but sense and propriety prevailed.

Cometh the hour, *et cetera*, Conor was easily visible in silhouette on the crest of the bridge as I approached along the wooden boardwalk hugging the river's edge at Quayside. The evening was blustery and few others were out and about. As I got near I saw his hair, swept back, rippling like a bonfire on a moor as the wind whipped a froth along the Cam.

"Nice weather for ducks," he said on spotting me. In truth, the ducks huddled in and around the punts stationed here for the evening and they appeared no happier than us poor schmucks. He pointed a thumb at the pub just behind us: "Pickerel?"

An unusual choice of venue, but then this was an unusual choice of meeting place. I agreed, if only to escape the weather. The Pickerel was one of several pubs claiming to be the oldest by some arbitrary self-selected measure or other. It was sited almost by the bridge, opposite Magdalene College, and boasted low ceilings and long dark beams in authentic medieval style like all the neighbouring establishments. Were it not for the TV by the fire and the mobiles squawking and glaring — plus the modern clothing and the electric light and the fruit machine and painted slogans on the walls and all the rest of it — one might have felt transported back to Newton's simpler, more syphilitic time.

Conor bought two authentically modern pints of some kind of mysterious dark beer, churning in the glass like a dirty protest. I eschewed my favoured spirit to appear more genial, I suppose.

We curled around the back of a large table onto an angled upholstered bench, avoiding the worst excesses of the present day.

"I like this place," said Conor, wiping some beer froth from his upper lip. His accent was strong, his voice perky. "Cosy. It's an old man's pub, you know what I mean?"

"Do you prefer older men, Conor?" Too easy.

He grinned. "Older men have their advantages. They're generally not living with their parents, is one. That's a morning-after conversation you don't want. Younger's good too though. It all depends what's up here." He tapped his head.

"I can confirm I'm not living with my parents."

"I should hope not, man in your position. Bet you can't fit stairlifts in ivory towers anyway."

He was smirking, and I took no offence and smiled in return.

It coincided with a ball of noise from beside the television behind us: some team scoring against some other team, which was apparently vitally important for a reason I couldn't fathom.

I ventured a sip of the bitter and estimated it would take approximately two hours to work through. "No ivory towers at St Paul's I can assure you," I said.

"So how's it going there? Money troubles, I hear."

"Who told you that?"

"Is it true?"

I considered bluffing my way out of it, spinning a joyous yarn of sunshine and fertile pastures, of gambolling lambs, and of Amanda smiling beneficently from a platinum throne held aloft by olive-skinned rugby players in jockstraps. "We are investigating several options for improving our—"

"Come on, Spencer, cut the bullshit. Level with me. It might be to your advantage."

What a curious thing for him to have said, I thought. He was hardly in a position to write me out a cheque with several significant trailing zeroes there and then, unless he wasn't the Irish chancer, albeit a charismatically attractive one, I thought he was.

"I confess you have me confused, Conor. What's this about? Do you have a donation for the college?"

He nursed his pint for a few seconds: he was already nearly half-way through it. I was struggling, just a few centimetres in, wondering whether I should ask for a knife and fork.

"This is about honesty," he said slowly, and turned to me. "If you're honest with me, I'll be honest with you." His smile was bright, open, suspicious.

"I don't know what *you* need to be honest about." An unsettling thought smacked me. "Has Amanda sent you?"

"Who?"

"Amanda Chatteris. The Master."

"Of St Paul's? Now that's interesting," he said, sitting back. "We talk about honesty, and you bring up your boss. You nick all the money, did you?"

"No!" An angry whisper.

"OK, then maybe you're doing something behind her back? Maybe—" Forward again, on his elbows. "Maybe some kind of competition?"

"She *has* sent you." This was not, evidently, going the way I had anticipated. A commotion behind suggested a missed opportunity by a player decried as useless, which made me wonder why he had been selected to play.

"I promise you on my poor dead grammy's life, your Master hasn't sent me. I don't know why you're afraid of her, but she hasn't sent me."

"I'm not afraid of *her*." I took a large gulp of the beer and a malty taste burst upon my tongue.

"Then why are you trying to subvert her? Come on. The college is skint, you're trying to organise something to raise money, and for some reason you're afraid of her finding out the truth. And— and for some *other* reason, you won't use this amazing top-secret gossip you've got."

"We don't have any gossip," I muttered. Where did *that* come from?

He looked at me disbelievingly. "Really? You're really denying all this?"

This was all getting rather too odd for my liking. There I was, contemplating a light touch upon his knee to indicate a rising interest rate and an opportunity to make a deposit, and he's blathering about honesty and advantages and accusing me of all manner of inaccurate and nearly inaccurate things.

I took a breath. "Conor, I think there might be a misunderstanding, of sorts. I— I didn't think we were here for a discussion about St Paul's. I was most certainly not anticipating an interrogation about honesty, of all things."

"My message, I thought it was clear enough. Problems at St Paul's, I said."

"You did, that is true. I believed that merely to be a convenient hook for a more general discussion with a view to…" I trailed off with some eye contact and a Spock eyebrow. "Apparently I was mistaken."

"Are you flirting with me? Is that it? Oh, right. I hadn't noticed. Ah, the older man stuff. Yes. I get it now. No, this was a genuine attempt to talk about St Paul's. You know, I'm not saying you're not attractive, Spencer."

I shook my head. "Don't hide behind a double negative. You were the one discussing honesty."

"OK, you're right." He emphasised each word: "You're just not my type."

I suppose I had asked for that. Ah well, it was good to know in which cow pat I stood.

A whistle blew on the television. Those watching considered this a grave error and gave vent to their feelings.

"But the college thing," said Conor, "that I *am* interested in. And there really might be something mutually beneficial going on here."

I took another mouthful of the beer. It was really rather pleasant, if excessively filling.

What the hell, I thought. It would all trickle out soon enough: the buildings of Cambridge might be made of brick and ancient stone but — the Archivist excepted — gossip permeated the silent walls as if they were paper.

I told him about the Praelector's unexpected discovery of my accompanied self in the shrubbery and my subsequent trampling under the purple moccasins of Amanda, plus the charity race idea I had proposed and — against Amanda's wishes — was organising. I was reluctant to divulge too much about the

Archivist, merely suggesting we had unusually detailed visitor records that occasionally proved useful: and judging by his creeping smile, he was in receipt of my drift.

I did not hold back on my dislike for Amanda. In fact, the further down the pint glass I reached, the more vehement I became. Perhaps there was something to this beer business after all.

Conor digested the information readily. And then, only then, did he inform me he was a journalist.

One to beam up, Captain.

To say I felt foolish is an injustice to good, honest cretins. I was sure I had just destroyed everything I was trying to save, ensured the fierce white light of transparency would burn and boil away everything that made St Paul's unique, interesting — and safe. I would be condemned to hell, or Oxford.

My face lost its colour and I began to rise to leave, head down, limbs weak. But he stopped me. A hand on my arm. A reassuring look.

"Sit down and stop your flapping, you great arsehole," he said.

"You cannot print this. It would be the end—"

"I'm not going to print any of it. I told you: you be honest, and I'll be honest."

"I don't understand."

"I think it's about time I introduced you to someone."

"Wh-who?"

He knocked on the back of the bench on which he sat. Three short taps. Behind the bench was a wooden divider with a decorative carving along its top: and behind that, where I could not see it, was another table. The person sitting at this table rose and came quickly to join us. He was, I recognised in a few thumping heartbeats, the person Conor had been with at Bar Humbug a few days before.

He held out a hand: "Sebastian Greatsholme. Pleased to meet

The Agreement

you, Dr Flowers."

"Count yourself lucky," said Conor. "It took me all night to get that out of him."

There was uproar behind as the correct team did whatever it was they were supposed to do. Such are the different tribes of man. Together and yet apart, with and without. Travelling a common path to an unknown future, decided by a boot or a racquet or a bat or a brain, or simply upon a coin toss.

I shook the gentleman's hand.

Over the course of the next few hours — and the several gins that Conor kindly let me revert to, which Seb, as he wished to be known, generously subsidised — I learned what had happened to Seb's family, and how the pair hoped to extract some form of reparation via the medium of revenge. Gradually I became aware that this was not simply a mutual opening of kimonos: not some collective unburdening, a bloodletting or *soixante-neuf intellectuel*. Should I care to scratch their backs, they would be generous enough to attend to mine. I emphasised the reach and intensity of my particular itch and was reassured that even if Seb couldn't deal with it personally, his father could apply a topical cream of some ferocity.

It was a tempting prospect, becoming ever more so as the senses dulled. We groped and argued our way to a plan not without risk, and indeed overflowing with danger and foolhardiness. I was persuaded ultimately, my arm twisted that way and this, that the potential rewards would benefit college greatly in many aspects.

I began to feel in my somewhat gin-enhanced way the hand of our college founder, Drybutter, upon my buttock. I pictured him making, in Kipling's words, one heap of all his winnings and risking it on one turn of pitch-and-toss — a turn without which, perhaps, St Paul's would not have existed. Might this be my turn? Two centuries on, a chance of renewal? Might New Court one day be renamed Flowers' Court in my memory, my portrait on a wall? As long as I did not follow too closely in Drybutter's syphilitic footsteps I would not object greatly.

The agreed plan: we would forge a number of documents incriminating someone provably of good standing and, pretending they originated from the unimpeachable source of gossip at St Paul's, leak those documents to the editor of the *Bugle*. They would undoubtedly be shown quickly as false and lead to the downfall and calamitous ruin of the editor.

In return, Seb — backed by his father — would gratefully underwrite the costs of our charity event and also make a substantial donation to the college for use however we saw fit.

The plan as it stood had a number of what might charitably be called *unknowns*. In particular, which person to select to be libelled by the forgery. I, of course, immediately volunteered Amanda. This would diminish the risk for the college, I argued: if by some happenstance some aspect of the libel held and the falling skittles included both the *Bugle*'s editor *and* Amanda, this would indeed be a grand day for Cambridge and St Paul's.

But there was also the issue of the Archivist's reputation to consider: it was critical to avoid unduly tarnishing his good if unknown name.

The plan needed some application and refinement, we agreed, and we would labour over those issues while proceeding at pace with the *Band on the Run* event.

I had one question for Seb. "Why, might I ask, does your father not simply expose the editor? He has money, he has influence. Is that not a simpler and more sensible route?"

He was unequivocal. "Those who live by the sword, Spencer."

I promised the pair that I would sleep on it and give them a decision the next morning. When that came, dark and wet and pricked by the mildest of hangovers, I had determined to join their scurrilous adventure. There was no other route to fund the event, and despite the significant risk the opportunity to save the college, and to eject Amanda, was too great to pass up. I let Conor know that their conspiracy had a new member.

Amanda scowled as I entered her dungeon office at a skip an hour or so later. "My dear Master," I said, crossing the dirty grey carpet to her outsize desk. "I have some wonderful news for you."

She lowered her laptop lid, set down her mug of instant frog's legs and flicked off a low-intensity Lulu track. "Really, Dr Flowers? *Really?*"

Scandalously I sat before the chair of doom was offered. "I have located a very generous sponsor for *Band on the Run*. An anonymous sponsor." The three of us conspirators agreed I should not mention the separate donation to college funds in case Amanda promptly lassoed that and cancelled the race forthwith.

"I hope that this heralds not a Wednesday of my discontent, Dr Flowers. I informed you barely Monday of my negativity." I felt her yearning for a sweet caress of the biro pot. "Am I understanding that you have been, as it were, behind my rear?"

"With respect, Master," I said, attempting humility, "you assured me you would read the proposal. Given the compressed timescales it was apparent I must not delay preparations. Have you had the opportunity to reconsider and possibly repolarise your negativity?"

She pointed to my document, which lay on her desk, and neither confirmed nor denied. "I require one answer."

"Of course."

Imagine a long syllable, and double it: "Who?" It was like a barn owl, high in a tree, spotting a mouse and preparing to dive.

"The sponsor? I am afraid I am not at liberty to say."

"Dr Flowers—"

"Professor Chatteris, I must insist. The sponsor has agreed to underwrite the race on the sole and unbreakable condition of absolute anonymity. Even to college authorities."

My boldness unsettled her. It unsettled me.

She took a deep, rattling breath. "This is dilemmic, Dr Flowers. For how, tell pray, should we be receiving of the money? Via a darkened cash launderette?"

"We should, uh, be receiving of the items themselves, as purchased or otherwise obtained by the sponsor. I will inform the sponsor of our needs."

"I see. And then whom should I be tirelessly thanking upon my victory speech?"

I frowned in confusion. "Victory—?"

"Speech, speech, come the finishing elastic and the glorious crowning coronation." Arms raised in supplication to the ground floor. "When I might extend the bosom of the college around whomsoever and whatnot."

I had not considered that Amanda might want to deliver a speech. I had naturally assumed she would hover and skulk and interfere like Beelzebub's kitten mashing upon a keyboard, but, well, I'd thought I might appoint *myself* as Master of Ceremonies. In any case, in the ideal scenario she'd have been booted out of college in disgrace by then.

"We can… consider that in detail later, perhaps when SPAIN next convenes. But I am delighted to say that any speech you… or I might care to make will be blessed with a surfeit of press coverage, as will the race itself. I have elicited the support of a young reporter at the *Bugle*. I have hopes for a high-profile announcement in Friday's edition."

"I see."

There was no tapping biro, no steaming nostrils: just brooding, percolating silence — more unnerving by far. Waiting for the whistle in the trenches to send you over the top. Waiting for the jury to return its verdict. Waiting for the "but" after a boy says "I like you".

Amanda's face suddenly brightened. "Well done, Dr Flowers. You have well done."

It felt as if I had passed an examination of which I had been hitherto unaware. Cautiously: "Am I therefore to understand that you now approve the proposal?"

Above and away, I heard a distant rumble of thunder. "Yes, Dr Flowers. *Yes.*"

ten
The Change

Despite the rain and a threatening storm I bounced past Colin on security and upstairs into the subdued *Bugle* office with my usual level of witty charm, or so I thought. As I sat at my desk dripping and steaming, takeaway coffee similar, Manish leaned over and came straight to the point: "You seeing him again?"

"Seeing who?"

"Whoever it was put that shit-eating grin on your face." He did an impersonation of my smile, all teeth and wide eyes, with both index fingers pointing towards his face like neon signs. "You're not usually this happy."

I powered on my screen and logged in to the computer system, which whirred and chirruped, and like everything that old it took its time. My sweater doubled up as a towel on days like this: I wiped down my face and beard, and rubbed it quickly over my hair. "Of course I'm happy. It's a Wednesday. Middle of the week. Over the hump."

"It's pissing down outside and you're on green ink duty."

"I can think of no greater task on this fabulous morning-stroke-evening." I gestured to the gathering darkness outside. Green ink duty meant it was my turn that week to separate readers' letters into piles marked *sensible, funny, fawning, ranting, swivel-eyed, dangerous, libellous* and *Thora Hird*. That last one was all the letters from the old dears writing to us like we were their grandchildren, making sure we were eating properly. Geoff would throw away the sensible, the libellous and the Thoras and select a couple from each of the other piles, which I'd then have the joy of editing and laying out for greatest amusement value all round. The Star Letter was always, without exception, from the swivel-eyed pile — this was to encourage more letters. The Letters page was the paper-and-ink version of a hydrogen bomb, basically.

"You're a freak," said Manish, still teasing me about the smile. "I bet it's about what Simon said to you. I bet you were lying. Have you got a pay rise? Or maybe it was a proper full-on bollocking, a double-scrote. Can I have your chair when you're fired?"

I met Manish's eyes and gave him a smouldering look. "My, you're a handsome little fella when you're confused and fishing."

"Sod off, ginger." He turned back to his computer screen. Worked every time, a squirt of the old flirt-repellent. He loved it really.

"Twiglet."

Last night's mental three-way with Seb and Spencer, and Spencer's confirmation this morning, had left me buzzing and a little hyper. That was the real reason for the smile. I needed to cool it down a little, especially since Manish's spider-sense was tingling like a bastard. I waited half an hour, enough time for me to dry out and to catch up with the overnight news and for the eager beaver alongside to become absorbed by the week's selection of kitten photos or whatever chore he'd been lumbered with. Then I snuck up to the editor with my usual subtle approach.

"Hey boss, I got the scoop of the century for you." I slouched on an old plastic chair beside him, crossing my legs in a big 4.

He didn't look up from his laptop. "Oh, yeah, ginge? Is it *Top Ten Cambridge Arseholes* again? Some guff you got off the internet about lesbian traffic lights?"

"It's about St Paul's College."

"Look, kid," he said, clicking his mouse a couple of times. "Nobody wants to hear about how much of the Limpopo river some dead toff swam up in 1842."

I didn't take offence. Nobody who took offence could last long there. "This is an actual story, Geoff. Actual news. They're organising a charity race across town for Saturday week. I spoke to the guy in charge. He's an arsehole, of course. Wants a big splash from us to kick off the publicity." All these things were true, especially the arsehole part.

"Saturday bleedin' week? Another bleedin' famine, is there? What's the hurry?" He was typing now, an email. His little fat fingers hammered over the keyboard in a race against the red squiggly line showing up his typos.

I shrugged. "Academics, eh? Probably something to do with prime numbers. And I think the Latin Olympics might be coming up soon." These things were not true. "Oh, it has a *Beatles* theme. Maybe it's to do with that. Is there an anniversary or something?"

I suppose I'd describe his next expression as *Young Churchill farting on an angry wasp*, a kind of anticipatory relief and confusion, and he finally looked up from the computer and turned to me. "Aren't *The Beatles* a little *avant* sodding *garde* for that lot? Sure he didn't say Bach or Beethoven? Or some Russian pillock?"

I outlined the concept behind the race, keeping it rough and sceptical and throwing in a few ritual insults, and he nodded along. I left out the names: no Professor Chatteris, no Spencer. I didn't want to display too much knowledge. Which was unusual for me, I admit.

"OK, ginge," he said almost in defeat, "you can do the story, god help us. If it's gonna clog up the bleedin' streets all day we might as well let people know. I might even give you the front page, unless there's a broken window in Debenhams or a photo of a cyclist stopped at a red light. One condition." He held up a finger.

"Just the one?"

"Big photo. Busty blondes, t-shirts and shorts, jumping in the air."

I realised to a distant clap of thunder that he didn't know a great deal about St Paul's. I tried not to smile. "I— I really don't think it's that sort of college, boss."

"That's my condition. I bet you they'll be queueing up for the photo. Front page? Boobs in the air. You'll see." He mimed a smiley face with cupped breasts.

I held onto my jaw in case I lost it on the floor somewhere. "It's pretty grim out there today, they might not—"

"Even better! Wet t-shirts! Might be an experience for you, ginge. Might turn you yet. Maybe I should send Manish instead, eh?"

Now *that* I didn't want. "I'm perfectly comfortable with breasts, Geoff. Some of my best friends are breasts. I'll do it. Manish is barely out of school—"

"I'll get him thinking about a headline then. Starter for ten: *Boobs On The Run*. No! *Toff Titties*."

"That's— that's— I'd better be going."

When I'd heard of St Paul's College, I'd thought it must be all rainbows and croissants and skinny dipping — you'd pass through the front gate into a palace of testosterone. And to be fair it was a tiny bit like that. It still had the stuffiness of the university and a Latin boner, but all the suits fitted, and deodorant wasn't a radical new invention that needed another ten years of fragrant dead rabbits before human trials.

The first time I'd seen inside the college was soon after I'd arrived in the city a year before. Back then it was very early in the autumn term, what the toffs call *Michaelmas* term, and I was lured back to the college for a late-night party by a couple of postgrads who knew a couple of undergrads who knew about forty-nine other undergrads, as it turned out. We'd packed into some function room in some poncey court or other and danced in airless proximity for a couple of hours. It was like being vacuum-packed into a Sahara sauna. They'd called it *The Old Curiosity Bop* and I suspect a few guys had their curiosity well and truly satisfied by the end of that night. I'd left before then — it got all too *rah-rah* and *oops-a-daisy* for me. There'd been a guy wearing a top hat, and I'd wanted to toss a loose cobble at it and send it spinning, then dance on a roof with a chimney sweep from Malibu.

I presented myself at the porters' lodge just inside the gate on St Andrew's Street and signed in with a frazzled old gent behind a desk who introduced himself as Arthur and called me *darling*. He had shaped eyebrows and a dodgy wig and looked like the star turn at the Chelsea Pensioners' cabaret night. With a couple of biro sweeps on a photocopied map he directed me swishily to Spencer's room in the laughably named New Court, and then sent word ahead to let him know I was there. He used the phone rather than a carrier pigeon or a dirt-faced young urchin, I was glad to see.

When I'd skipped out of the *Bugle* office I'd co-opted the newspaper umbrella — the only one — which had a *Bugle* logo, and as I passed along the paths and through the stone archways of the college I saw whispered conversations behind the backs of hands from twosomes and threesomes rushing past me through the rain. I didn't think I was especially welcome, and I didn't blame them. I don't know, maybe they thought I was wearing the wrong cut of trouser for a Wednesday.

Spencer held a flimsy, ill-fitting door open for me at the bottom of his set of stairs. Off to the right a bunch of names, including his, were painted onto the stone wall under a heavily-serifed letter T, the name of this little block of rooms. And carved roughly into a shallow arc above the door were the words *ex glande quercus*.

I nodded a greeting and hurried through, shaking the umbrella back outside through the doorway and dropping it in a convenient stand. The stairwell smelled of chlorine, wet stone and a cloying smugness, and was being watched by a red-lit camera in a high corner. I knew I had to watch what I said: we'd be monitored.

"What's with the Latin over the door?" I asked.

"You must be new to Cambridge," he said with a mild sarcasm. "College motto, I'm afraid. *From acorn to oak*."

He led me up the stairs.

"It's carved throughout college, almost randomly," he continued. "We suspect a drunken classicist ran amok with a chisel in the dim and distant. It happens on occasion. The tripos, the boys — you know how it goes. Adds character, I think."

Two flights up Spencer took me along a corridor my brain told me was listing at several degrees, and opened a door into his... room? Office? Lair? It felt claustrophobic and oppressive: dry and dusty, wallpapered in books, and liable to crackle into unquenchable flame if a bell-end with a pipe merely thought about crossing the threshold.

Over a cup of Lady Grey tea — very much not my usual tipple — and sitting on a sofa I tried not to look at too closely, I explained what the editor wanted. Spencer, sitting at his desk, rubbed a hand over his near-bald head and didn't look happy.

"I'm afraid we don't really do breasts, Conor. There are, of course, ladies here, and they are fully equipped, I imagine. I would hazard— without wishing unduly to stereotype, you understand— I would hazard it unlikely in the extreme that any would agree to this request."

"There must be, you know, feminine ladies. Ones who don't play pool."

"Of course, of course. We do not discriminate. Modulo the

limitations of the Data Protection Act I believe I can also confirm we have resident one or two heterosexual persons of the opposite gender. We are an *inclusive* establishment, regardless of the popular sentiment."

"Great! Can't we get those together and do a big boob jump or something?" I found myself miming it, as Geoff had, and felt my face flush.

Spencer looked at me distastefully as he lifted his cup. "I see all journalists are cut from the same cloth, notwithstanding the stitching."

"I'm sorry. You need this front page, though, don't you?" He did, we all did — it would set us up nicely for the big one the following week — though I couldn't say any of that with the eye in the corner. *The price of freedom is eternal vigilance*, apparently, but I wasn't sure what Spencer had was what I'd call freedom. More like trading today's privacy for tomorrow's security. But I suppose it wasn't all that different from CCTV on the streets — except these cameras were exposed to a little more of the spice of life. The sofa felt suddenly less comfortable.

Spencer took a gulp of tea and set the cup down. "There is one possibility, though. Assuming the editor doesn't want anything too racy, too explicit."

"It's a page one story, not a page three."

"In which case I believe I might have a solution. Drink up," he said, and reached across the desk for his phone.

Half an hour later we were in another part of college — Spencer called it Top Court, with an ironic smile — in a small room tucked alongside the dining hall. I could only describe it as *bright brown*: wood panelling varnished to shite, below ochre walls and a bronze-coloured ceiling. One wall was covered completely in mirrors tiled top to bottom. The whole room shimmered with specks of glitter. We were in a kind of dog-shit disco.

And with us were four students, undergrads by the look of them: still with a fierce, knowing innocence and cheekbones that could slice cheese. Barely a muscle between them, and certainly not an ounce of blubber. Spencer had called them here. He lined them up and introduced them individually, and then, with a flourish: "And together, they're *Cream of the Crop Top*." The guys bowed and curtsied elaborately.

It was a student fucking drag act.

"Jeez, due respect, I'm sure it's great, but… Geoff will have my hide. We can't do this."

Spencer was dismissive. "You have yet to see them. It is a sight indeed to behold. I promise you, Geoff won't only not *notice*, he'll be positively overcome with desire."

The act busied themselves noisily with bags and clothing and *equipment*.

"It's madness! I've never seen a drag act you couldn't tell from a mile away! I'm gonna be laughed out of the cocking paper! Are you sure we can't lure a couple of lesbians here with a kitten and a copy of *Sporting Life*?"

"Trust me." He patted my arm. "These boys know what they're doing."

And they were doing it fast. I gave them that, it was a well practised setup. They were shaved glass-smooth already — face, arms, chest and legs always ready for a bit of action — and they dressed quickly, tucking and padding and slapping on the make-up like a whore in a hurry.

Ten minutes after arriving, the wigs were on and adjusted and we were good to go.

It was an impressive transformation, I had to admit. Close-up, you could tell. You could feel the breasts weren't right, you could spot the unavoidable physical differences. But, say, from a dozen feet, when they were jumping up in the air? The only ones who could tell would be the ones who would *never* tell.

The leader of the gang called herself Cody. Bright blue eyes, determined. Hungry, even: a man-eater. A pout of steel. Brash, confident, never short of a snappy response. Out of uniform, she'd been a mousey geographer called Jonathan.

Cody led the group out into the court and straight onto the grass. Even I, an outsider scurrying behind, knew that an undergraduate violating the turf was some kind of sacrilegious act.

"Cody, I don't think—" Spencer started to object, and Cody gave him a glare that stopped him like stone.

The rest of the *Cream* gathered beside her, all four girls with legs apart and hands on hips. Like a group of superheroes: *The XX Men*, perhaps. The rain, gentler now, almost a mist, dappled their luxurious real-hair wigs and their light t-shirts and college-pink shorts. I could already see a few faces popping up at windows around Top Court as Spencer fussed me along.

I hurried to sort out my camera. It was important not to let the girls become too damp: although the editor might have wanted a wet t-shirt line-up, the wetter this lot got the less female they appeared. I scurried around to make sure the light, such as it was, was behind me.

There was a whistle from somewhere high up, echoing across the court. One of the girls waved. Then chanting began: *Co-dy, Co-dy, Co-dy*, and she waved too, to cheers.

I was ready. I called them back into position, a not-so-straight line of four, and counted down: three, two, one, jump *snap*. A second shot, and a third. I got the girls adopting different poses mid-air, with whoops and hollering and yelling all around, people banging on window frames, clapping, calling out names. I felt like I was taking photos of a girl band: a beautiful, successful, powerful girl band everybody had heard of except me. I felt like— I felt like my father.

Except, of course.

"Have we finished?" asked Spencer. "Only, the girls are getting rather rained upon." The mist was coalescing back into small raindrops.

I quickly rattled off another five or six shots: different angles, different styles. Showing other parts of the court, showing the walls behind them draped with faces, with the girls stony-faced and arms folded, holding hands, pretending to run, anything I thought Geoff might conceivably buy. Then the rain began to splatter more heavily and it was all over: we darted back inside to the dog-shit disco with cheers ringing around us.

And in another ten minutes Cody and the girls had reverted to Jonathan and the boys and a smirking, flushed anonymity, and *Cream of the Crop Top* had been packed away into their overstuffed kit bags until the next time. The adrenalin in my body was leeching away into nothing and I was thirsty, and hungry, and damp, and feeling like something had changed.

We thanked the boys, and then Spencer and I sprinted through the cloudburst back to his room. "Quite something, aren't they?" he called as we dodged the growing puddles. "They sing and dance too, though that is in all honesty less refined than their overall look at present. They're making rather wonderful progress though."

"You know I had no idea there was a degree in drag. What is it, like a BSc in Sass and Shaving?" I had my camera bag under my jacket to try to keep it dry.

"BA, dear, not BSc. Oh, no, this is purely extra-curricular. We do very much encourage it though. We positively delight in our students graduating from St Paul's having emerged from whichever particular chrysalis they might have arrived in."

"Like, coming out?"

Spencer bounced through his stairwell door and held it open for me again. "There are many types of closet, Conor."

The high I realised I was in from the photoshoot lasted until I returned to the *Bugle* office, dried off again, and sat at my desk next to a curious and restless Manish to start pulling the story together.

"Oi, ginger." It was a muffled Geoff. He beckoned me over with one hand, the other stuffing a sandwich into his mouth.

"All sorted, boss," I said. "I've got some cracking pictures. Page one copy on the way. Have you come up with a better headline yet? I've had a couple of ideas—"

"Hold your horses, kid. Change of plan." Still chewing, he waved me onto the chair beside him.

"Geoff, we agreed page one—"

He swallowed. "Don't get shirty, sunshine. You're right, I said page one if you got the boobs. But I'm killing that story." He gave me the full-on Churchill face.

I got louder. "You can't, man, it's a good story. What have you got, a councillor falling off a chair? This is better than that."

He raised his hands to quieten me. "Listen. Who was it you spoke to at St Paul's?"

"The guy running the race. Flowers, Spencer Flowers. He's a good guy."

"Was he the one you called an arsehole earlier?"

I nodded reluctantly and tried to calm down. "He's an academic. Course he's an arsehole. But he's a decent enough arsehole. I've seen a few arseholes in my time—"

Hands up again. "Enough. And he's a bender like you?"

"Hey, if you're gonna get all hate crime on my arse there's a whole bunch of better words you can use."

"Is he?"

"What's all this about? There's not some radical homosexual page one conspiracy going on." Not *quite*. I was starting to properly bristle and my gay agenda hackles were on the rise.

"I've heard a few stories about this Flowers bloke. I thought you might have a bit more for me, some back-up."

"Yeah, right, because all the gays know all the gays. We all sleep with each other and use the big gay telegraph to tell each other our big gay secrets. Tell me, how *is* the Queen? You must know her, she's straight and old."

"You know what I mean, ginge. You've just come back from meeting this guy. You've said he's an arsehole — your words, mate, your words. So, how much of an arsehole? Word is he's out of control. Slagging it around. It gets a straight-up bloke like me a bit suspicious, don't it? Taking liberties with innocent young freshers is he?"

I took a breath. Now was not the time to get all *West Side Story*. For all I knew Spencer *was* taking a few liberties with freshers, though I doubted it. What I'd seen at the college didn't suggest that. He was genuine, decent. Proud of the girls and the boys. I reckoned they could look after themselves, no problem. In fact I could imagine one or two freshers taking liberties with him, if he'd let them.

What worried me was that Geoff didn't understand St Paul's, and more importantly St Paul's — and Spencer, and Seb — didn't need this kind of publicity. I was pretty sure Spencer was no saint, but I was also pretty sure that *nobody* was. Manish might have been slagging around more than Spencer. This kind of talk seemed… twenty years out of date.

"Geoff," I said as calmly as I could. "I hate to break it to you, man, but… I'm sorry, you've been asleep for a couple of decades. It's the twenty-first century now. Nobody gives a single shit any more."

"This isn't about all that. Fuck me, we hired *you*, didn't we? Don't start defending the bleedin' tribe mate. If he's in a position of power and abusing that trust—"

"Like you?" Oh, jeez.

"What's that supposed to mean?"

Roll back, roll back! "I mean — you're sitting there in a position of power right now. You mustn't abuse that trust by— by printing stories about some college arsehole that might turn out not to be true." Nice recovery there, Conor, you great cock.

The argument had gone on long enough to draw Simon slithering from his desk, the enforcer wheeling his chair across to run interference for his master. "This isn't about Geoff," he said. "This isn't about newspapers, what they do now — or what they *used* to do."

Geoff shrugged, palms up. "If the Spencer bloke's clean, he's clean, and there's probably no story."

"Back in the bad old days," said Simon slowly, scraping a finger on Geoff's desk, "it was a lot freer and easier in the business. We might print stuff then that we wouldn't now. These days, we have the internet. Things can be checked. Traced." A pause while he flexed the fingers on his right hand. "You'd be amazed what you can find in access logs."

"So," I said, "you've got something about— about this Flowers guy from some access logs somewhere? Is that what you're saying?"

Simon fixed his gaze on me. "About him? Oh, no. Not at all. Not about *him*." There was an emphasis on *him* that made me think of baseball bats and a broken nose. "Remember where your loyalties lie, *mate*."

"Tell us what you know about Flowers," said Geoff.

I walked into my flat that night and went straight to my laptop to open up Gaydar. A very quick message to Spencer: "Incoming!"

eleven
The Attack

It was the second consecutive long evening chewing the cud with Conor and Seb, and certainly not as pleasurable as I would have preferred. It was apparent I was now the target of the *Bugle*'s rabid ire, despite Conor's gallant efforts to distract them from my college record. Even a knight in shining ginger armour such as he was unable to wield his broadsword against his liege and his deputy liege with any degree of decapitatory success.

One sticks one's head jauntily above a parapet for just one millisecond and the wrath of the detritus of Fleet Street is arrayed pestilently against it, I thought.

Conor told me I was likely to be branded in print some flavour of *sex pest* with the stage-whispered subtext that I was preying upon the youth of St Paul's. Via some lollipop-based subterfuge, perhaps, or promises of grade advancement according to some tariff of services.

Frankly, nothing could have been more distant from the actuality. The students at St Paul's were far too tickled preying upon each other, and *ordering in* from sundry other colleges, to have any special regard for me. My rapidly decaying flesh and accreting gut held no allure when the first flush was, as it were, on tap.

A secondary but no less dangerous trouble for our conspiracy was the deputy editor: intimately allied with his *governor*, as Conor put it, the Riker to his Picard, and — were Conor's suspicions proved — aware of Conor's interest in the duo's dubious past. This complication hastened and altered our plans somewhat. We could not risk the deputy's investigations unravelling and foiling the intended revenge.

In Seb's disturbingly capacious apartments beside the river, away from the cameras of college and the twitching ears of Humbug or anywhere else in public view, we inched soberly, in all senses, towards a revised and accelerated attack. Over the course of the evening I became half-tea, half-biscuit.

Thus Wednesday night granted me fewer hours of sleep than I was accustomed to, and Thursday morning began with the insistent, shower-interrupting ringtone allotted to the Master's outer office — one of the poorly documented and less fiery of Dante's circles. I was instructed to present myself for ritual castration by the Forked Tongue of Chatteris at precisely nine o'clock.

The first four bars of *Yankee Doodle*, from the college clock high above Bottom Court, seeped mournfully through to the Admin dungeon as I knocked and entered the coffin-office.

"He is arrived," said Amanda from her desk, apparently to no-one: she was the sole occupant of the room, a small purple oasis of gibberish.

"Right," said a voice from the phone, and I understood. The voice had a pronounced East London accent, distinctive from just that single word: the "r" drifted toward "w", the "i" was more "oi", the "t" absent without leave. The editor, or his deputy: and yet officially I still knew nothing. My heart began to pound.

"Sit, Spencer. *Sit*."

I did meekly as I was told, clasping hands together in case they shook. I was thankful not to be hungover.

"I am telephonically engaged with Geoff Burnett. His position is as of editor of the *Bugle*, of which you are no doubt aware of."

"I am— an avid reader," I said, pre-deploying the negatory pause.

"Good to hear it, son," said Burnett, voice muffled and distorted on the ancient speakerphone. "You're in the next edition."

I feigned ignorance and trowelled on the guilt. "Indeed, the race. We are profoundly grateful for your publicity, Mr Burnett, as will be the many charities that benefit from the event. I hope your picture editor found—"

"Silence, Dr Flowers," Amanda commanded, perching upright on her distressed leather chair.

"Sorry, son, but a little bird has sung us a better story. Of course, in the interests of balance, we thought you might like to give us a few comments on the record."

"And what story might that be, Mr Burnett?" I said. "I can assure you my finances, and those of the charity event, are strictly in order." I kept my smile to myself.

"Your finances might be, kid, but your love life's a bit of a cock up, if you pardon the pun."

This I could hardly deny. I was awash in adrenalin, pushing the deliberate incomprehension further. "Are you proposing some species of — what's the word? — *make-over*, Mr Burnett? I am afraid there is very little anyone, even the most talented, can do with my hair these days. I must decline a hairpiece on religious grounds, and a transplant—"

The editor interrupted. "Spencer — can I call you that? Spencer, listen. I'll level with you. I don't much care for the likes of you smart-arses and god knows this town's chocka with 'em. Same goes for all the queer stuff. I tolerate it but I don't have to like it. Once it crosses the line, I don't have to tolerate it no more."

Amanda listened impassively, hands folded on her blotter and not even twitching towards the biro pot. I saw a narrowing of the eyes at the word *queer* but that was all.

"A line has been crossed, you say? Which line is that, Mr Burnett?" I asked.

His voice crackled menacingly back. "Whichever line my paper chooses. Whichever line I choose. And I reckon luring students in your care back to your pit crosses one hell of a bleedin' line."

I rose slowly and faced the portrait of Drybutter on the wall behind Amanda with my hands clasped behind my back. I considered my next words very carefully indeed. "And I presume you have multiple on-the-record sources for these scurrilous allegations, which I of course strenuously and fully deny?"

"I've got enough to print."

"I'll take that as a no."

I hoped Amanda might jump in and at least confuse him for a few seconds. Sadly, she remained — for the first time in living memory — annoyingly silent.

"Any comment for us, Spencer? On the record? Maybe you'd like to confess everything here and now and we can do a big set-piece interview. And then at the end you start bawling and get drop-kicked out of the college. You know it's gonna happen. Might as well get it over with now — it'll be simpler in the long run."

I went calmly to the desk, pushed Amanda's pot of biros to one side, and perched beside the speakerphone. "I should like to make a counter-offer, Mr Burnett."

"Bribe, is it? We'll add that to the list."

"Oh, no," I said softly. "Let me say this. You might *think* your lies about me are true. You might *believe* you have impeccable sources." I leaned in closer to the microphone. "You haven't met the Archivist."

Amanda tensed. "I counsel and suggest caution, Dr Flowers."

I imagined a brewing panic amongst the Archivist's elves, perhaps a flavour of batphone glowing red beneath a glass cloche in his lodgings. I had not, for the avoidance of doubt, mentioned this idea to him in advance.

"Archivist?" said Burnett contemptuously. "You're threatening me with a fucking librarian? What's he gonna do, stamp me and lend me out?" He wheezed in laughter.

"I'm not threatening you, Mr Burnett. I'm *offering* you. An hour, with the Archivist. An exclusive story from the archives. In return, you drop your fanciful and libellous stories about me and reinstate the publicity for the charity event."

For a moment I thought I'd left him speechless. Perhaps some asthmatic reaction.

He replied as if to a dull child. "I don't think you understand the concept of a counter-offer, son. You want me, seriously, to drop a sex scandal for an 'exclusive' about an unpaid fine from eighteen-bleedin'-ninety? You've been passing the port the wrong way, doncha-know."

I laughed, attempting an *evil villain* insouciance. "Mr Burnett, for a supposedly experienced and veteran journalist you are astonishingly naïve. You have ten minutes to perform the necessary research on St Paul's. Rest assured, sir, that we have been doing our research on you."

I hung up before he could respond, and let out a long breath. The phrase *death or glory* swam in my head briefly before I banished it and replaced it with the college motto that Conor had noticed the day before: *ex glande quercus, from acorn to oak*. I certainly felt a little growth.

I lifted my head expecting thunderous eyes, expecting Amanda to pounce across the desk and sink her fangs into my neck and have my blood repaint her purple red.

And yet she said simply: "Gin, Dr Flowers? *Gin?*"

Without waiting for my answer she rose and shuffled to the drinks cabinet at the far end of the airless room. The cabinet whistled in shock on being opened and exposed to twenty-first century air. On her return the Master bore a brace of generously filled, as-new crystal glasses and the vaguest simpering of a smile.

"I'm not sure I understand," I said, accepting the glass and its heartening contents readily. "I was convinced utterly you would disapprove."

"My disapproval is plainly and greatly zenithal. The scandal you visit upon these walls is most heinous. The allegation of malperformance in our sacred duty *in logo parenthesis* heinouser. The risk you invite upon the Archivist, heinousest of all. And yet, and yet, and still yet, the approach chosen and taken has much of admiration upon it."

"I promise no risk to the Archivist, Master. And you know that I have brought no scandal to the college. I would not and could not do so. Burnett's allegations are lies, calculated to distract from the race. Someone wishes to disrupt it, to ensure I fail and fall in disgrace."

I wondered who that could be — and answer came there purple.

The cockney one phoned Amanda back seven minutes after I hung up. It had taken only a short and rapid sweep across his network of contacts and sources — excluding Amanda, assuming she was a more recent addition to that group — to, as it were, fill in the gaps regarding St Paul's.

A double-edged weapon, of course. Burnett's time of ignorance was over, which meant his time dismissing us as a big stone box of irrelevant toffs was also at an end. The plan to unseat him would have to be utterly and irrevocably successful, or else St Paul's would be at the point of his sword and the Archivist in grave danger of terminal exposure.

I informed Burnett he could attend college that afternoon, at four o'clock precisely. Conor and I had agreed this schedule beforehand so as to ensure the maximum time for planning and

The Attack

arranging our response. We had no intention of allowing Burnett to meet the Archivist: we would substitute another in his place. I thought it best not to inform Amanda of this wrinkle, to lessen her interference. And as per the original plan we would not be supplying him with a valuable and true exclusive either: Seb and, no doubt, others under his charge in deep background not part of our little cabal, were arranging one or two suitably convincing forged documents — about Amanda, I still hoped and prayed. From that loop I was excluded for my own security.

Another reason for the four o'clock meeting: it was past the *Bugle*'s print deadline for the week's edition. Conor could and did gleefully confirm that after a small argument between the editor and his deputy — the latter wanting to persevere with the smear — the *Band on the Run* front-page story, complete with its photo of Cody and the girls cavorting in college, had gone to print. It would appear on doorsteps and in selected newsagents across the city the next morning without fail.

This was a great relief: the event planning could now proceed in earnest. My diary, heretofore containing mostly student supervisions and appointments to booze, began to fill with race-related duties. But all would come to nothing unless our deception held.

I parked myself inside the porters' lodge twenty minutes ahead of the scheduled time to ensure Burnett did not curry favour with a porter on duty via cash or other sundries and obtain advance entry. We most certainly did not want that odious man having unfettered access to the student body. In parallel I felt a nagging concern that I had heard nothing from the Archivist, the true Archivist. I had expected a tussle regarding the plan, with some unseemly knee-based pleading on my part: but I was not contacted.

On the hour, with shadows lengthening across Bottom Court,

a thin-faced man with silver slicked-back hair and a sheepskin coat of a more prosperous era nosed his way into college grounds beside the lodge. He was not as I had imagined Burnett to appear: he was decidedly scrawnier. It was evident he hadn't laughed since the dawn of the internet, and knew seven different ways to kill with bare nicotine hands. The porter scrambled to inquire his business, and then indicated towards me. Innards twisting, forcing a smile, I went to meet him.

"Mr... Burnett?" I asked.

"Wantage. Simon Wantage. Geoff's busy." He looked me up and down. Ordinarily I might have considered that a *sign*, but for this person I made a grateful exception.

"Mr Wantage. I see. And what is your role, may I ask, at the *Bugle*?"

"I'm Geoff's deputy. Who the hell are you?"

A fair question. I apologised and introduced myself.

The walk to Top Court was fraught and rather tense, and was dominated on my part by elaborate gestures and throat-clearing. I attempted to describe some of college's more impressive architectural features. Alas, he was uninterested. I was thankful no students crossed our path for impromptu interrogation.

We could not possibly allow Wantage near the true Archivist's offices, and so I had arranged for a small function room to be set aside. It had a discreet camera mounted in a corner, of course: I could do nothing about that. The device would reveal our multiple forgeries to the Archivist, who I hoped would be amused, and quite possibly also to Amanda, who I hoped would be implicated.

I showed Wantage to the room, which was bare but for a central desk of some antiquity and three similarly aged chairs: two between desk and door for myself and our fake Archivist in case a getaway at some velocity might be required, and one for Wantage across from us behind the desk. The room was lit by two rather severe spotlights, one of which seared my scalp and I suspect illuminated me like Captain Kirk at a Klingon show trial.

As a function room it was only lightly functional, but served our purposes.

I did not dare leave Wantage alone for one moment, and so I made a short phone call to set rolling the ball while the newspaperman and I failed an examination in small talk.

It was a minute of some duration, with all the warmth and relaxed nature of a political show trial on a Neptunian satellite. I learned newspapermen have a hundred words for *grunt*, and little else.

Finally I heard the door behind me swing open, and I turned to see our fake Archivist, procured by me and briefed by Seb. I had called upon the only person I could trust: Claire.

It was a great risk, to say the least. Another great risk. We dared not use Seb himself as he was too young and insufficiently pallid, and it placed rather too much temptation in the hands of the noble Baroness Fate and the Lord Sod. It was imperative that Seb stay in the shadows until the time was right. And so Claire had been drafted, or press-ganged, as our guest star and saviour. Seb had filled the gaps in her knowledge, I hoped, and we would rely on her abilities upon the local stage to spin us through.

There was, of course, the issue of gender. Claire had taken the parts of males before, though perhaps only in Shakespeare and pantomime. She assured us she could adopt the manner and tone of a fellow of St Paul's if need be, and given some of the fellows of my acquaintance I did not doubt her. Nevertheless that was a risk too far. I deliberately avoided the male pronoun on the phone with Burnett. We would not have to, as it were, man her up.

And now Claire stood before me, in a rather severe navy trouser suit, stripped of her usual soft regalia and enveloped in a college gown. Her face was wiped clean of make-up. No earrings, no finger rings, no jewellery whatsoever. The wayward hair was wrestled into an unforgiving fringe.

I barely recognised her.

"Ah, Archivist," I said, a touch of nerves hinted in my voice. "Might I introduce Mr Wantage from the newspaper? He is very eager to meet you, very eager indeed."

"Don't go overboard, Flowers," said Wantage and shook Claire's hand. Claire took the spare chair and cleared her throat meaningfully. All good so far.

"Now then, Mr Wantage, is it?" she said, her accent disguised as well as her body. She'd gone for *generic northern*, which I hoped wouldn't transmute into *comedy northern* under stress. It was in a pitch lower than the natural, but not booming pit-boss deep: it was sustainable, believable. Rather fierce, I thought.

I glanced at Wantage: he was peering closely at her. Perhaps trying to see through the disguise, perhaps trying to commit her face to memory. I worried suddenly that he might sport a hidden camera about his person, but had to admit it was a touch late for that all round.

She continued. "Spencer has requested I fish you out an exclusive for the next edition of your newspaper. I regret I am not a regular reader of the *Bugle*. I find local news all too… familiar."

Wantage said nothing. It was a decent enough start, I thought.

"It's been tricky locating summat suitable for you. I hauled these old legs up and down the stacks all morning, let me tell you."

"Really," said Wantage, apparently bored already. "What's your name? I can't call you 'Archivist.'"

I stepped in. "That is the title of the office, and that is how we traditionally refer to the officeholder. The Archivist's baptismal name is not widespread knowledge."

"But you've let me see her face."

"These are unprecedented circumstances, Mr Wantage. Do not presume that this gives you any hold over her, or over us. We are quite capable of defending ourselves." I rejoiced that this was at least partially true, though my heart was battering away at my shirt and my fingers trembled like a virgin at another's belt.

"You seem nervous. Worried."

"Merely anxiousness, anxiety. I do not regularly deal with gentlemen of the press." And I was not dealing with one then.

"Nor I," said Claire. "I fear I am neither young enough nor... pretty enough to feature in your pages."

"Listen, darlin', if you're as powerful as you make out we'll find a space," said Wantage.

"No!" I said. "Absolutely not. It is a matter of college policy."

Wantage looked at me, blinked slowly once, and turned to Claire. "Tell me about this archive, then," he said. "How big is it? When did it start?"

I held my breath.

"That is classified, Mr Wantage," said Claire. "Above your pay grade."

"Oh, is it now. You run it yourself, do you?"

"I do not think it is any concern of yours."

"A secret room full of blackmail material, held by a Cambridge college? Nah," he said sarcastically, "not of any concern to us at all."

Claire said nothing. I still hadn't breathed.

"I want to know everything," said Wantage slowly, "and I want to know now. Unless, of course," he leaned casually forward onto the desk, which emitted a frightened creak, "you're trying to bullshit me."

I breathed at last. "I can assure you," I said, wilting mildly under the *tell-me-the-plans* spotlight, "we are not making this up."

And strictly, we weren't. There was a minor case of misrepresentation and impersonation to answer, but the core was sound.

I continued: "May I remind you, the agreement with your esteemed editor was for a single exclusive of the Archivist's choice. Not unchecked access, and certainly not a biography of—" I almost said *Claire*— "of the Archivist herself. Unless you would care to return to your office clutching air, perhaps we might move to the matter in hand?"

Wantage sat back, almost slouching, and waved us on. His contempt was palpable, seeping from him and rising around us in the room. I hoped Claire could swim.

She reached into her pocket for two items: a sheet of A4 paper, folded into thirds, and a small square black-and-white photograph with a narrow white border. This was, I hoped, Seb's masterpiece of fiction. I had not yet seen what he had produced. Claire unfolded the paper onto the table, facing Wantage, and set the photograph beside it.

He leaned across and inspected them closely, without making physical contact. "Oh, right. Him. Interesting choice," he said.

Damn, I thought: not Amanda.

Still without touching anything, Wantage read through what appeared to be the transcript of a conversation of a delicate and intimate nature between a contemporaneously prominent person and his paramour. Occasionally he showed distaste or winced at its contents. The accompanying photograph allegedly showed a… *moment* from the events transcribed. From my position, attempting nonchalance, the fakes appeared very high quality.

Finally Wantage sat back and coughed, and placed his hands behind his head. "Old news," he said. "What else have you got?"

Claire looked at me.

"What do you mean?" I asked.

"And I thought you toffs were supposed to be brainboxes. Listen: it's not an exclusive if everyone knows already."

This was, to say the least, awkward. As far as I knew, we'd made up the transcript entirely and it was a splendid and vigorous libel.

"I'm afraid that is all we have for you," I said. "It is precisely what we agreed, and no more."

"Then let me see these archives and I'll find something for myself."

"That is impossible."

"It's not *impossible*. Unless, like I said, you're a bullshitter."

"Mr Wantage, you performed your due diligence. You know there is an Archivist, you know there is an archive. We cannot allow you free rein to rummage within."

"I think I've seen enough here. Archivist? Big fancy archive? Amateurs." He waved dismissively at us and went to stand.

Simultaneously, the door opened.

"Ah, is this the man of papers?" It was Amanda. My heart raced anew.

"And who are you? Princess Purple? Gonna drag me down a bleedin' rabbit hole? You certainly ain't seen a bleedin' looking glass recently, look at you."

"Mr Wantage," I said, with a trace of a tremble, "may I introduce Professor Amanda Chatteris. The Master of St Paul's."

"Indeed, Mr Wantage. *Indeed*."

"Oh, right," he said. "How'd you bleedin' do. You come here thinking you can sell me this shit an' all, have you?"

"I shit you not, Mr Wantage. I attend in assistance of Dr Flowers and our esteemed Archivist. When, I wonder, does he reveal himself? And which lady is this?"

My face became the very definition of a picture. A Dali, to be precise. My right eye surely jumped my nose, and my mouth was busy sliding off the end of my chin.

Wantage laughed. "Like I said: amateurs." He stood.

I rose in a panic and grabbed the forged items. "You're not going to print this?"

"You know we're not going to print that. And you know what we *are* going to print. Enjoy the last few days in your job. No need to show me out of this godforsaken pit, I'll find my own way."

He slammed out, taking all the air with him, and I sagged, winded, into my chair. Claire's head dropped.

"Was it something I said?" said Amanda.

twelve
The Replan

I messaged Spencer on Gaydar when I got home on Thursday evening. I hadn't heard a word from him. I had no idea whether the super-secret fake Archivist and Seb's wonder document had done the trick, and Simon had been suckered right in, or not. Either Spencer was out celebrating, drowning himself in gin, or he was in commiserating, drowning himself in gin. All systems go, or computer says no?

Seb reached me first and gave me the bad news over the phone, as retrieved from a pretty miserable Claire in the debrief. Apparently, after Simon had run off snickering, the Master swept out in a puff of confusion and Spencer gave the forgery a good honest seeing-to and tinkered with the feng shui of the place a little. Then he'd clattered away to hide in his office and await the apocalypse.

"Should I go over there, do you think?" I asked Seb. "Give him a cuddle and a cup of warm milk and tell him it's all gonna be alright, somehow, as the lava starts flowing through the letterbox?"

"Inadvisable. I suspect he would not be too coherent." He sighed. "I assume the *Bugle* will train its sights on him and St Paul's — you will no doubt discover tomorrow. We need to subvert this for next week's edition."

I shook my head sadly. "I hate to say it but are you sure you want to keep on with this? Our little conniving hasn't exactly gone well so far."

"It was a miscalculation. Poor research. Speed-libel is not my area of expertise, I admit. I take full responsibility of course."

"That's all fine but it doesn't do Spencer a gram of good. This is his life, his career, we're talking about. I freely admit I might have thought he was an arsehole before but he's doing some good there, I've seen it."

"But how can we walk away now? If we do nothing, if we let it go, then your editor, your paper, will crucify him."

"I might be able to talk Geoff away from the edge."

"You do not really believe that, I think. You know what he is like. We both do."

He was right. Geoff might have had an air pump trained up his arse for the last two decades but the old killer instinct was still there. Once his fangs were fixed on a story he wouldn't let go no matter how much you shook. I'd seen it a few months after I joined, when some local sports guy — in the soccerballs or the cuddleballs or whichever it was — drove his cockmobile a trifling thirty over the thirty limit and tried to celeb his way out of a ticket. Word got to Geoff by the usual channels and he was bang, bang, bang, a two-year-old with a hammer until he whacked him out of the team. Big headline, *DISGRACED*, by-line Geoff Burnett, naturally, even though most of the legwork was by Manish.

Spencer didn't call me until much, much later in the evening, full of the doom and the gloom. The sky was falling, a big chasm was opening up beneath him, a dark storm was brewing, he was running low on gin, and other natural disasters. He said he'd felt like — my words — that twat in *Titanic*, all *top-o-the-world*, then next minute he's having a cold bath and watching his toes drop off. Needless to say he was spannered to within an inch.

He told me it was a *nine point nine recurring*, and I asked what that meant, and he said something about scales and, I think the word was, asymptotes. The cogs in my maths brain locked up at school when Mrs Foster told me x could mean either multiplication or a top-secret number that might not exist, so I just agreed and hoped I sounded convincing. Apparently Claire would understand, but he couldn't face telling her. I said "OK" a lot and made sympathetic noises like my grammy made to me when I came home from school with my ego or my nose bent out of shape.

I promised him it would feel better in the morning, which I knew it wouldn't, and that we'd sort something out, which I was hazy on at best. On the plus side — I told him, before realising it now made *me* the twat — the charity race story with the photo of the booby girls was sitting there pride of place on page one. Headline: *Lady Ma-Donor*. One of Manish's suggestions, the git.

A bright and breezy Friday morning came, all set for a lynching.

I tried to ghost my way stealthily in to work, fifteen minutes after I was supposed to have begun my usual routine of cocking up the templates for the next edition and then rebuilding everything before anyone else noticed. But Geoff had sprung a trap. An unannounced editorial conference, unprecedented on a Friday to my knowledge — the usual Fridays were kind of like bring-games-into-school days, nothing serious, no actual acts of journalism committed, and lunch on the playing field.

I knew what the conference would be about, of course. I said three Hail Simons in penance and let Geoff have my editorial doughnut.

"Oh, right, on a diet are you ginge?" he said. "Trying not to lose your hourglass figure?" He made the universal sign for a curvy lady.

"Trying not to look like you, boss." I made the universal sign for a lardy-arse in response and gave him a big fat grin as I wheeled my chair over to the group. Give and take, give and take.

"OK, who died?"

"Your mate," said Simon.

My blood froze. "What?"

"Oh, relax. Not yet. Next Friday, maybe. Once we've finished with him. Dead, or as good as."

Manish raised a curious hand. "Um, who are we talking about?"

"Conor's *chum* at St Paul's. Spencer Flowers. Gave us the right run-around yesterday, got himself a nice, friendly lead for his charity bollocks as a result — with ginge's generous assistance. Next week, we'll have him."

Geoff added, "I doubt the prat realises it'll be ten times worse for him now. He tried to palm us off with some celebrity crap or other, reckoning it was all hush-hush doncha-know. Open bleedin' secret, weren'it." He made a cackle-wheeze-cough noise and his face reddened.

I tried my best to act nonchalant as my heart rate thudded back down through the stratosphere. "So, that sex pest piece. That's the lead next week?"

"Early doors, ginge. I reckon we can have a bit of fun with St Paul's. Looks as though there might be two or three stories to choose from. Candy from a baby."

"What are the other stories?" asked Manish.

"You got St Paul's itself — dodgy reputation, bit too queer for its own good. And this race — who's actually gonna benefit? Bound to be something going on there. Bit of a bung, a backhander, thank you very much? Then there's this 'Archivist' fella. Not the fake bird Psych saw, the real one we've heard about. Who is he? Snooping on students? Is this how the college gets funded, by blackmailing people?"

I took notes like a good boy. In all honesty the questions weren't that unreasonable. It couldn't hurt to dig a little, just in case.

"Do we get straight on it?" I asked. "Who's doing what?"

"Keen, all of a sudden, ain't you?"

"Big story, Geoff. My first exposé. I'd be happy to look into the race, since I'm pretty clued up on that already."

He held up his chubby hands. "Hold your horses, son. No good you fart-arsing around town on a chase right now. You've got to clean the toilet before you take a dump, as my old mother used to say."

I nodded as if I had the faintest clue.

"I reckon you should go after Flowers. You're both, you know— *that way*. He can trust you. You can commiserate over a bleedin' Babycham."

"Nobody has drunk Babycham in a hundred years, Geoff, not since you were a wee slip of a lad."

"Well, whatever you lot drink then. Go and hunt him down and get drunk together. He's paying."

Simon cut in. "Geoff, he can't do both Flowers *and* the race. He's right, he should concentrate on the race. Twiglet can do Flowers. He's prettier anyway. Closer to jailbait."

"You know I am still here, guys," I said. "I could do both."

Geoff weighed it up. "OK, Psych, point taken. Twiglet, you're on Flowers. Ginge, the race — once you've done your chores. Simon and I will sort out the college between us and see if we can't make head or tail of this Archivist bloke."

That plan lasted about five minutes. I'd barely started breaking the templates when Simon crouched beside me, knees cracking, and whispered nicotine nothings in my ear. "I think you and I are going to stick together on this one, Mr Geraghty."

"What do you mean?" I said quietly.

"I mean, I want to keep my eyes on you. Make sure you remain objective."

"There's no such thing as objective, it's—"

"I'm not sure I can trust you, you see. And I think you know why."

"You can trust me. I'm a *Bugle* boy through and through. All for one and all that. Was that the ninja turtles? Anyway. I'm your man."

He patted my shoulder. "I hope so," he said, and grunted to his feet and back to his desk.

Manish immediately shone a hypothetical bright light on my face and began an interrogation. I replied using the medium of shrug, until he realised he wasn't getting anywhere and changed tack.

"This Flowers man," he said. "Who is he? Where do I start?"

I threw him a few bones, a couple of dollops of info — objective, trustworthy, ninja, Simon-friendly nuggets. Technically I might have missed out the middle third of *the truth, the whole truth, and nothing but the truth*.

"So you reckon I should, you know, go down the gay bar and chat him up?" He made the frown-smile of a child watching a cat vomit.

"You might not be his type, Twiglet. He might prefer a Twix or a Bounty."

"Sod off, I'm everybody's type. I've had so much interest from men it's not true."

"Have you ever actually been to a gay bar?"

"There's a place back home—"

"I'll ask again. Have you ever, actually, walked through the door into a gay bar?"

Two, one, zero. "No, but—"

"Right. I think I ought to come along and help you out a little. I'm a pretty decent chaperone, I won't try it on or anything, and I won't desert you if someone gives me the eye. Not unless, you know, he's *really* hot."

He thought quickly. "OK. Yeah. Cool."

I left it until the early afternoon, when the post-lunch lazy times were kicking in and nobody was paying me much attention, before I slid out my phone and texted Seb one word: *call.* Although it was my own phone, and I paid my own bill, I didn't want *Bugle* airspace invaded by any incriminating radio waves if I could help it. For all I knew Simon had had a portable 3G cell inserted in the space where he'd never had a heart, and he'd fart out transcriptions every night before bed.

Seb called a few minutes later and I bundled myself out of the room. I told Manish it was a man about a man, you know, and made what my grammy would call a *suspicious gesticulation.* It's the ideal way to kick one of those insecure macho types off your tail.

I made small talk about weather and cocks until I was downstairs and outside on the street with a 360-view and a red plastic beanie marked *paranoid* on my head. I told him I had to keep it brief or Simon would be sniffing after me, and rattled off the outcome of the editorial meeting. I waited for a few words of considered reason, some Greatsholme insight to guide us, but all I got back was "Right", which might have been considered and might have been reasonable but it wasn't particularly insightful.

So I let him know I'd volunteered to hold Manish's hand down at Bar Humbug that night to stop him being dragged away to see a wonderful wizard and a wicked witch and a couple of other W words, and he said "Right" again.

And at this point I thought he was either not listening too closely or he was giving me directions somewhere, so I asked him whether he'd been paying any attention at all, and I felt two firm taps on my shoulder from behind.

I've never been much for ballet, apart from the men in tights, but right then I could have *pas*'d *de* fucking *deux* for Ireland. I jumped and spun round, thrusting out my crystal jaw ready to be splintered into a thousand pieces by Simon's baseball bat.

And it was Seb.

Which was almost worse.

"What the hell are you doing here?" I said into the phone, hearing it echo from his a fraction later.

"I'm here to see Burnett," he said into his, ditto. Both voices were firm, tight, holding back. "Would you like to show me in?"

"I'm afraid Mr Burnett's busy right now. I think he's eviscerating a small child. Can I take a message?"

"In here, is it?" He hung up and pointed into the dreary, fifties-era building behind me. Eyes darting, jaw tensed, decision made.

"Listen, you can't go up there, Seb," I said.

"You were right. Last night. We have been remarkably foolish." He started to pull open a door. "We really should not drag St Paul's into this, and we especially should not risk Spencer's career. This is not his war."

I followed him through the door, past the faux-marble reception and its faux-marble receptionist. "It's too late for that," I said in a kind of stage whisper, trying not to echo. "They're not going to agree to another deal."

"Who said anything about a deal? Up here?" Two flights to climb, two flights to stop him. "I'm going to threaten him." Matter-of-factly, breathing more heavily.

"Seb, don't do this." He started climbing the steps.

"I will simply say: drop the stories about Spencer and St Paul's, or I will go public about what you did to my family."

I chased and ranted, with a tight tinny echo. "Listen to me, that won't work. Trust me. You know what they'll do? Print the stories anyway, and add a bonus one about you trying to blackmail and besmirch the good name of a free press, and how they're shocked, *shocked* to the very core. They'll get to dictate the story about you just like they dictated the story about your dad twenty years ago."

I grabbed his arm, and he stopped. First floor: some little

shitty software start-up, all glass and chrome and skateboards and hipster twats pretending they're gonna change the world with their beards and their cat videos.

I continued, more softly. "Let's just… talk to Spencer, at least. See what he wants to do in the cold light of day. You never know, he might want a career change. It's not long to Christmas, John Lewis will need a Santa." I tried a smile and received a flicker of eye contact.

He relaxed, his jaw slackening, his blazing eyes cooling. Reluctantly I let his arm go. It was the most emotional, passionate, I'd seen him, even more so than the night we met. Not the cold, calculating Seb he normally showed to the world. It was good to see, in a bad sort of way.

He nodded, slowly, almost sadly.

"Good," I said. "You know I'm right. It's one of those annoying things about me that you like."

He turned and started downstairs again, and the calculator was back. "I shall contact Spencer. Let's all meet up this evening."

"Do I not get a hug? I'd like a hug." I held out my arms.

"I bet you would." He kept walking. I was sure I could see the glimmer of a smile.

thirteen
The Lie

I awoke at a distressingly late hour on Friday morning with the Adam and Steve of all heads. I was sprawled in my college room, approximately on the sofa. I had either been viciously mugged or had fallen into a dead sleep on the two-metre journey from my desk, scattering various items to the four winds as I descended. I eventually located my mobile phone nestling up to an unread copy of Gibbon's *Decline and Fall*, and grunted at the brash, unsubtle ingenuity of smartphones.

The device glared the time at me through the orange bus-depot gloom and I swore inventively. I knew a student was due within half an hour for an earnest discussion about a subject of no importance, and although I was an adept at failing to prepare this was bordering on magisterial. I was proud I had never yet bailed entirely from a supervision — on two occasions I had excused myself briefly and swiftly as I felt a tsunami rising — and had no intention of cancelling this one. The show, as it were, must go on.

I cleaned up the room as best I could with the timpani accompaniment belting out an old favourite in my frontal lobe. I managed a half-hearted wash in the miniature bathroom along the wonky hall and was grateful that the morning's stubble was camouflaged by the beard. At the arrival of the student, precisely on time, I was at least half-present and correct and hoping terribly that the emergency instant coffee would enable me — and the poor boy — to survive the hour. The lad was vocally furnished neither with a hypnotic monotone nor a piercing squawk, which was a source of much solace. For an hour, musings upon the upcoming *Bugle* disaster were temporarily banished. I almost enjoyed myself.

At the student's departure my thoughts returned immediately to sleep and the abandonment of the day. Perhaps I could forge some kind of maternal letter excusing me from whichever games were planned. It couldn't, I observed with the day's nth grunt, be any less discoverable a fake than the transcript provided to Wantage by Seb. Though, brutally, our failures there were multiple. Circular finger-pointing would help us little.

A knock at the door interrupted my attempt to shut my eyes. It was, I was startled to learn, the Archivist. I let out a short moan, which was at least a change from a grunt, as I saw from his expression how the conversation was likely to proceed.

"Dr Flowers, I should like a word, if it is convenient."

I ushered him in to the chair recently warmed by the student.

"I suppose you have heard of yesterday's events," I said glumly.

"Heard, and saw." He was efficiently brusque. "I was off shift, of course, asleep, and despite in hindsight the obvious urgency I was alerted by an elf only as I arrived for duty last evening. Otherwise I would have come sooner. Preferably a day sooner, before the nonsense occurred. If only I had known of this!" He struggled to contain a whirlwind of anger.

"I thought you might find it acceptable or even tolerably amusing under the circumstances. Needs did must, if that's a phrase."

He huffed and fidgeted, and his hair shuddered. "Good god man, protocol, *protocol*. I wish you had come to me first. We have *contingencies* for precisely this scenario. And you instead bumble along and present a false Archivist! With a concocted story well known to be true! And allow the Master to bluster forth and bring the house of cards tumbling down!"

"Protocol, contingencies. How was I to know?" My defensive shields were raising. *All hands on deck. Red alert.*

He puffed out his cheeks and calmed a little, then glanced up at the camera watching over my room. "Now there is a question, Dr Flowers. A question indeed. Come with me. Swiftly."

He jumped up and went to the door, his gown billowing. I followed meekly behind clinging grimly to the struggle bus. There was no speaking as we walked at speed in procession across New Court into Bottom, students scattering before us, and directly to his secure underground facility.

"I apologise if I have done wrong," I attempted after the external doors were locked. "And I suppose you would now normally be in bed after your shift."

"That is of no consequence at the moment. Come through."

He led me to one of the other, heavily secured doors I had seen on my previous visit, and paused to allow an instrument to identify his retinal pattern. A green light shone above the door, which clicked open easily despite being of some implausible thickness. He beckoned me through after him, like a parent to a child on the first day of school.

It was an anteroom of some kind, of a generous size: warm, softly lit, with the college's familiar wood panelling. The carpet was, I suspected, the most luxurious within a large radius. The wall along my left held a number of portraits, the right-most being the familiar face of the man before me. I realised with a throb these were all the Archivists of college history, faces I had never seen, burdened with truths I could never know. The opposite wall held a large pinboard near-overwhelmed by photographs: black and white, colour, small, large, all neatly annotated either by hand or by typewriter or by, I surmised, laser printer. A third wall included two further unmarked doors to destinations unknown.

There were also four large purple-leather chesterfield armchairs, empty until the Archivist took one and indicated I should take another.

"I have never seen this room before," I said, unable to hide the wonder in my voice. I had a curious, lopsided feeling, as if I had stepped out of my flat in town and found myself in Times Square in New York. "Those photographs—"

"Try not to look too closely. *Viewer discretion advised*, is I believe the phrase. An old tradition, not unlike maternity wards in which photographs of newborns reassure new admissions about to pop that the staff do, in fact, know how to deliver a baby. It is a record of our success, you might say."

"That's... a lot of success," was all I could manage.

"A large fraction. Some information is still too sensitive even for this room." He rattled off the next sentence at well-rehearsed speed. "Incidentally, please be assured that in this room we are not being seen or heard or recorded in any way by anyone or anything, within or without." He coughed. "Now to business. Dr—"

"Wait. Why am I suddenly granted access to all this?"

He sighed. "Because, Dr Flowers, if I might be savagely blunt, you have recklessly and needlessly endangered the college by potentially exposing us to unfettered outside scrutiny. And, in particular," he hesitated and looked around as if forgetting where he was, "because the Master didn't stop you."

"Of course not. The woman has a vendetta against me."

"You must admit you have not done yourself very many favours. Remember, there is little that escapes the elves and me. There is a file of some thickness."

I hung my head in agreement, though a gremlin hidden on my shoulder giggled and let off a celebratory party popper.

"But you are correct. She knows the protocol. She knows there are contingencies. And yet she only half-heartedly counselled you on your blundering counter-strike against the newspaper. Worse still, she intervened personally. And all while I slept. This is worrying, Dr Flowers, I make no bones about it."

"Why did an elf not wake you?" I asked.

He grimaced. It was a sore point. "A confluence of unfortunate coincidences. A shift was swapped, an alarm failed, and an inexperienced elf was given a little too many spaces to cover. I am unhappy, to say the least. Elf-herding can be similar to cat-herding, you understand. I must make allowances. And I cannot personally attend twenty-four hours a day."

I nodded in sympathy. "I am sure you do your best. It must be especially difficult and confusing to monitor Amanda. Dear god, how fed up you must be of Lulu."

He allowed himself a rather forlorn laugh and we sat in silence for a second.

"But what's done is done, and who's done is recorded," he said, perking up somewhat. "And we do not have time to introspect. We must act. Hence I have decided to bring you some way into our confidence."

He leaned forward and I did so too. It seemed appropriate, although the room did slightly spin a little too extravagantly for my tastes.

"You are aware, I am sure, of our national counterparts," he continued. "MI5 and MI6. The Security Service, and the Secret Intelligence Service. The former with responsibility for domestic threats, the latter for foreign threats." He smiled, the thrill of revelation sparkling in his eyes. "A similar distinction applies at St Paul's."

My eyebrows lifted. "You mean, there are two groups — two Archivists?"

He shook his head. "There can be only one Archivist. That is enshrined. But within my team there are distinct responsibilities, and — without going into too much depth, for operational security reasons you understand — these include intra-collegiate and extra-collegiate activities. It is now time to deploy some operatives in the field. Now, if you'll follow me through one more door." He made to rise.

"Before that: what do we do about Amanda?" I asked.

"First things first, Dr Flowers." He stood and went to one of the inner doors, which slid open gracefully and silently as he approached. Beyond I saw darkness, and the tell-tale glow of banks of screens.

He was taking me to the beating heart of his enterprise, the monitoring stations, where all was seen and noted and classified and stored on behalf of the grateful future.

I followed him in. The room was stifling and poorly fragrant and vibrating with the constant hum of computer and disk. There were two large grids of screens, showing in total perhaps fifty scenes across college: several views peering out across the three courts, and many more within rooms. Four of the Archivist's elves sat in meditation before the screens, drinking in the detail, bathed in a silvery-blue light — with one floating elf acting, I presumed, as shift leader and toiletry reserve. I recognised one or two. One pair of eyes flickered over and double-took as he realised who I was.

This was my first visit to the Hub, as I learned the elves called it. In truth I had expected more screens, more elves, and my face betrayed me.

The Archivist saw and clapped me on the shoulder. "Automation, Dr Flowers. We cannot physically watch over every room and listen to every microphone. We concentrate — in theory — on the more important narratives. For the rest? Well, we have made great strides over the years in fine-tuning various sensor technologies. Noise activation, heat activation, flesh tone detection, miniaturisation, all deployed to great effect. Not to mention data compression, and automated voice recognition and transcription. We have the world's largest corpus of pillow talk, you know, all indexed and fully searchable. Fascinating trends. This year the word is 'babe', incidentally. What, you thought we would scribble things down on paper?"

"I confess it is more passive than I had anticipated. I suppose I had expected something more akin to a wartime listening station."

At this he roared. "Perhaps decades ago. We benefit from our reciprocal arrangements, of course, and many Old Paulines have provided us with a steady trickle of technology. But," he said with no little pride, "there have been one or two PhDs awarded to elves past, on the basis of work pioneered in these rooms. The literature glosses over the precise origins, naturally."

The Archivist led me on through one final door. Unless I had hopelessly lost my bearings my mental map had me now way under Bottom Court's central lawn. This was a much quieter, less intense and thankfully fresher room. It appeared almost a workshop, with long benches and equipment and the ubiquitous laptops, and a lone elf wielding a soldering iron. And there stood a conference table, around which sat familiar but unexpected faces.

The Archivist gave me a warm smile, as did they all. "You know everyone, of course, but let me furnish you with a few details they may have inexplicably kept from you." He gestured to each around the table. "Helen: bursar, but also social engineer. Dennis: Praelector with a sideline in what I shall loosely call identity management. Arthur, porter by day, hacker by night. And a new recruit, who will be revitalising our costume department: Jonathan, whom you may also know as Cody. While we have been talking, they have been familiarising themselves with the present situation."

He directed me to a seat and took one himself.

"Good Lord," I said. "I am rather overcome. Hungover to buttery, but nevertheless."

"Welcome, my dear, my dear," said Dennis. He was positively beaming.

"Colleagues in Truth," said the Archivist, and I realised the formalities had begun. "We face, I perceive, two dangers. One immediate, one unpredictable. The *Bugle* and the Master. Either or both might result in the end of our work here, and the end of our college — at least as we currently know and love it." Around the table heads nodded gravely. "Dr Flowers has unwittingly brought the former upon us, due in no small part to the latter. The former is, I suggest, more urgent."

Arthur, who always called everyone darling, spoke throatily beneath his hairpiece. "But Amanda's at the back of all this, darling. Take her off the board and the problem goes away."

"I'm sorry, Arthur, I don't agree," said Helen. "Long term, you're right of course. Short term, no. We must focus upon the newspaper."

Dennis added: "Long term we're all dead, all dead. Some of us not so long." He chuckled. "Helen is correct."

Jonathan added quietly, "Newspaper first." He even blushed shyly.

I had no idea whether this was intended as some form of vote, or whether indeed this was even what one might term a governing council with the Archivist as its supreme authority, but it appeared so. I kept my mouth firmly clamped, believing I was considered an unofficial and rather wide-eyed observer, a fly hovering by the Cabinet table.

"And what say you, Spencer?" To my knowledge the Archivist had never before addressed me with such informality, using my first name.

I stuttered as though suddenly favoured by one I desired. "I— I say the *Bugle* is the highest priority. Not that my view—"

"Spencer, around this table all have a say, no matter how or why they attend. We realise there is no black, there is no white—"

"All is grey, above, below and beyond," said the group.

"...and beyond," added Dennis.

I'd heard the phrase before, with Dennis, in the Archivist's office now several doors away, and began to understand.

"As Archivist rest assured I have the final responsibility and the final decision."

I chose not to voice my immediate response: that his decision was very much monochromatic and no tint of grey. I was in any case near erotically grateful for his help.

In the next hour or two, my pounding head began gently to settle and elves brought distinctly non-elven water and sustenance — mere college buffet fare: sad white doughy squares of unidentifiable sandwichesque content, bowls of off-brand ready salted and cheese and onion potato-effect crisp substitutes, and some grass and pebbles and cloth masquerading as a salad. The Archivist and we his knights hoovered up the crisps and as much cuboidal uncertainty as we could stomach, leaving the salad to its fate as some variety of altarpiece, and tiptoed toward a plan.

We took it as read that the *Bugle* would attack me personally, and my various *interests*, and no doubt make unsourced, whispered allegations about the charity race I had barely had time to concern myself with.

The paper would most assuredly also try to crack open the shell of the college: "It's raining albumen," as Dennis put it. "Hallelujah, hallelujah." It was thus likely to attempt to unmask the Archivist and reveal the *shock horror truth* of the archive — without revealing any of the actual shock horror truth it contained, since that would leak slowly and lucratively into the grateful hands of Fleet Street.

Naturally, I told them about Conor, and about Seb and his

family history, and how this monstrosity had all come about simply because I believed I could help right an old wrong. And this led to the germ of an idea: to be precise, the flowering of an existing one.

It was decided that to counter the truths, the near-truths and the speculation, we would revisit Seb and Conor's concept and broaden it and tweak it. There would be no great libel sold to the paper about Amanda, or a famous name with deep pockets: but there were other options. It would be a lie great enough to switch the points and reroute the *Bugle*'s investigation, and yet demonstrably and obviously false to ensure the overdue demise of their journalistic careers. It was Seb and Conor's idea revisited, on a grander scale.

But what would the lie be?

Once we had agreed all we could without the active involvement of Conor and Seb, the Archivist and his team began to prepare. One of the elves, a tired-eyed statistician awaiting the end of a shift so he could prepare for an evening recalculating his averages, escorted me from the Archivist's domain into the light and the air.

It was the afternoon, I discovered, though it seemed a different day, a different world. Despair still pricked at my heart but now I also felt hope. And guilt too, of course, and I had little doubt that emotion would stay with me a while. The tussles in my head showed no sign of concluding, albeit no longer alcohol-derived. *Ah well*, I thought: *fac fortia et patere, do brave deeds and endure*. Or as I'd heard it many years before: *once you've kissed a boy, you fear nothing*. Less succinct but more actionable, I think.

It was, I suppose, for the likes of the statistical elf and his friends that I hadn't immediately packed up my belongings in a tottering pile and headed for a hermit's life in the Lakes, or perhaps cut out the tediums of middle age and swan-dived under one of the never-ending streams of sightseeing buses that stalked the city. I still had those options open to me if this latest plan failed, as despite the hope I knew it very well could.

Today's newspaper is tomorrow's fish paper. Today's disgraced academic is tomorrow's case study, dissertation, cautionary tale, comedian's punchline, and reality show contestant.

It sometimes seemed that the only people permitted to make more than one mistake in life were journalists, and the people who — directly or indirectly — paid them.

The temptation to succumb to the booze was strong and violent, but I had a deal of work ahead. Yet not true, proper work, the work I was paid to do. Although I had a further supervision scheduled for later that afternoon, I had first to descend once again to the dread monster, the purple-eyed Gorgon, and her talismanic biros.

It was, I thought as I knocked on her door, a week since she had summoned me here to thrash and berate me and curse me with her committee. I entered with a steely heart and frisky bowels.

"Dr Flowers," she said, looking up from some redlined document. "I had been meaning, a chat, to organise." It was coherent, if excessively teutonic in grammatical tone.

"I felt I should report back to you regarding the newspaper *contretemps* you witnessed yesterday afternoon," I countered with a little French and a littler smile, taking the unoffered chair. I did not include *cheerfulness* in my current emotional *milieu* but on the whole it seemed wise not to slit my throat there and then.

"Ah. Yes." Her calmness was unnerving.

"I am sorry to say it did not entirely go according to plan, as you might have detected."

"So quite."

"I do not— know how you located us in that room," I said, generating a rather pleasing double negative with the pause, "but that is no matter. I had no intention to risk the Archivist

The Lie

in person. The information was all faked, forged, concocted. An attempt to deceive Mr Wantage and his newspaper, which was unsuccessful."

"Please allow me therefore and hereto understand your point." The biro began to flex and whip between her purple-tipped fingers.

I looked to my feet. "It was an utter failure. I can scarcely imagine worse. Entirely my fault, and mine alone. Consequently, after many hours of careful deliberation, I would like to offer you my immediate resignation." I lifted my head and met her mildly steaming spectacles.

The biro stopped. "Immediate, Dr Flowers? *Immediate?*"

"Immediate, Professor Chatteris. *Immediate.*"

"I see."

"I do, of course, wish you every success. Especially with your endeavours next week and beyond."

She removed her spectacles and wiped them absently on her purple blouse. "Your crypticism favours you not. I am permanently endeavouring. Please increase your specificity to a more acceptable dosage."

"Well, naturally, the race organisation. I am sure you can identify another SPAIN committee member to crown as chair. The upcoming newspaper exposé you will undoubtedly take pains to focus *yourself* upon, I am sure."

The biro ticking began, splat splat splat on the blotter, battering and bloodying an abstract kitten drawn upon it. I kept her gaze. I even ventured a smile. She remained in control, mirroring the smile as best she could approximate, her blinking frequency increasing hesitantly and lumpily. Were I very lucky she might froth from the mouth and slip slowly under her massive desk into a pool of her own distended grammar.

"Let me be absolutely at no risk of unclarity, Dr Flowers," she said after some dozen seconds of perverted cogitation. "In whole and in part, in sickness and in health, I do reject, deny and disclaim your resignation."

"You… I'm sorry?" I affected confusion, because I could. I knew the Archivist would be watching.

"I desire your persistence, Dr Flowers. Unhand me your resignation."

Despite my various shortcomings I have few regrets in life. Occasionally one seeks or is sought by a gentleman who proves uninterested or uninteresting, or one chooses a dark path hiding a thief, and one regrets it when the inevitable emptiness occurs — but only for a short while. I do though most sincerely regret not taking with me into this meeting my own red biro, to tap upon the chair arm while I pretended to consider her request.

I upturned my mouth and nodded thoughtfully, offering a frown and a head-tilt and all but adopting the pose of Rodin's *Thinker*. A long ten seconds later: "I shall mull it over."

Later that afternoon I heard from Seb, and we three conspirators, one for all, *et cetera*, agreed to assemble around a cosy Humbug table to synchronise metaphorical watches. Here I learned of the *Bugle*'s plans for the next week's edition in detail, and they of the Archivist's ideas. It was apparent that our fates were messily intertwined and that our only hope for success was to join with the Archivist and trust to his dark arts. And yes, we made all the wand jokes.

After merely one unhealthily soft drink, and to the protestations of Eddie who was I suspect more concerned about the evening's bar takings than with me, I abandoned my two friends to return to college: I had preparations to make.

fourteen
The Innocent

"Here we are again, then," I said to Seb after Spencer had toddled off. "Just the two of us. Bonding over a common enemy. Whispering sweet romantic conspiracies. Planning the downfall of an evil regime over cocktails and footsie. Your face fair lights up when you talk about the forty-nine different cuts you want to slice Geoff into, it's so cute."

We were sitting around a small circular table dotting the "i" of Humbug's long chrome bar and pressing against a plate window. The music was still low, still back catalogue. It wasn't busy yet: it'd be another hour or two before sales officially opened at the meat market. Quiff was in his vodka zone at the opposite end of the bar, of course, as honorary bar mascot. Eddie and his crew made themselves useful disinfecting tables from daytime kiddy juices but left the two of us alone.

Perhaps they thought it was a date. Perhaps it was. Two french martinis with extra fruit, after all.

"I want to apologise for earlier," said Seb.

"There's no need, I—"

"No, please," he interrupted with a hand on mine, left only for a second and then yanked away as if burnt. "I have tried so hard not to let my heart take over. It is vital that I focus on the task in hand and not let my anger win. Anger makes poor decisions."

"Don't get all Yoda on my arse, Seb, it was only natural.

Spencer got turned over, the rug got pulled, and you wanted to do something about it. Your fists would just bounce off Geoff's gut, though, you know? He hires himself out as a bouncy castle on bank holidays. He's not allowed in zoos in case someone thinks he's an escaped elephant."

Seb looked down at his drink, a sharp puddle of red in a shallow glass cone, and smiled softly.

"Believe me, there are more insults where that came from," I said.

"I do not doubt it." He took a sip. A wailing nineties ballad came over the sound system, at least until Eddie could lunge for the *next track* button.

"So don't beat yourself up about it," I said, gently batting a fist onto his arm. "Hey, it was good to see a bit of passion. A bit of fire in your eyes. You know what that tells me? You're not doing this for fun. You're not gonna do this hammy cackle after it's all over and shoot off on a monorail to your submarine hidden in Jesus Lock. You're doing this—"

"Because I want revenge." He was still looking down.

"Because you want the truth to come out. Which happens to coincide with a little public career-ending humiliation for Fat Boy and Slim. And nobody's gonna lose much sleep over that, are they?"

"I suppose."

I downed what was left of my martini. I could drink those all night, which was far too dangerous a prospect to consider right then, with Manish due before too long. A clear head was required. Well, clearish. Seb and I had to work out how to deal with him, or at least how to make sure he didn't screw everything up for us. But that could wait for a few more minutes.

"*I suppose* sounds like an agreement to me. Do you want to buy me another?" I waggled my empty glass. "You know how easy it makes me. Well, you don't *know*, I keep telling you, and you keep taking no notice."

He finally looked up, and across to the bar. He caught Eddie's eye and signalled for two more of the same. "You are so relentlessly cheerful and optimistic."

"The words you're looking for are *horny* and *desperate*. And also *thirsty* and *sober*. Cheers."

"Is that what drives you? Testosterone and alcohol? Is that why you are helping me?"

It wasn't an accusation as such, more a jokey aside. But it stung a little. Probably because there was a decent slab of truth in it somewhere. A salty frosting on the cocktail glass.

"I'd be lying if I sat here and told you I'd be doing this even if you were a one-eyed, toothless, haddock-faced, teetotal old biddy with halitosis," I said. "But mainly because if you were we'd probably never have got any further than hello and goodbye. Once I'd dragged you back here and wrung the story out of you, you got me hooked. Even though my career's hanging on the line here with me, and there are a couple of rough old sharks on my tail. I'm not sure that analogy totally works, but it'll do. You know what I mean."

Seb finished his martini just as Eddie brought across the replacements, with a flourish and fluttering eyes and a cheesy grin, and left with delicate pats on our shoulders as if in encouragement.

I made a start on the new drink. "I'm helping you because you need help, and it's the right thing to do, and I like you. I don't have little hearts for irises or chubby little angels with bows and arrows floating around my head, if that's what you're worried about. At least, I don't think so. I don't, do I? Jeez, how embarrassing would that be?"

He studied my eyes and scanned above my head. "Nothing I can see," he said, and smiled.

I looked away.

"Of course," I said, "if either of us has the hots for the other, it's you for me. I know that much for sure."

"Is that so?" he said. "How do you make that out?"

Something modern and trancey-dancey came on the sound system, and Eddie turned the volume up a couple of notches. The evening was beginning its protracted, steady build-up. Before long a few of the regular faces would start to arrive, shirts tight against gym-slim or chip-fat bodies, faces eager for booze and boys. The bar would pack out, and conversations would become loud and raucous and spill out into the alleyways.

"Simple," I said, taking another mouthful of martini. "You stalked me for god knows how long to see if I could be trusted, and you didn't run away screaming. I take that as a sign."

He laughed and shook his head, but it wasn't a denial.

Ah, the wide-eyed innocence of a straight boy in a gay bar for the first time. It's a sight to behold. One of the seven wonders of the modern world, I'd say, up there with internet pornography and internet pornography.

I was glad I was there before Manish arrived — I didn't want anyone to pounce on the poor unsuspecting kid and put him in a cock-lock. I caught sight of him through the window beside the table, walking along the alleyway attempting casual manliness. He was strutting like a rookie cop disguised as a seventies pimp.

Straight over the threshold, hit by the heat and light and noise of the Friday night crowd, his journalistic aloofness evaporated. I went to meet him and cheekily stuck my hand into the small of his back to lead him to Eddie at the bar.

"You're popular today, dear," Eddie said.

"Work colleague," I replied. "Go easy on him, it's his first time."

"Aww," he said to Manish, stroking his face sympathetically. "My advice, darling? Plenty of lube."

The Innocent

Manish laughed like an escapee. "No, I'm not gay, it's—"

"The number of times I've heard that one, dear. What are you boys drinking?"

I stayed on the martinis, and Manish ordered the manliest beer he could find. Eddie threw in an umbrella for good measure. I took him back to my table: it was a prime slot to view the comings and goings of the usuals and the unusuals, and I could highlight a few of the characters without looking like a tour guide. Quiff, of course, still remained clamped in his usual spot with a queue of vodkas waiting patiently. I carefully failed to mention the person chatting casually to him: Seb.

The two of us had closely choreographed the evening. Half an hour or so for Manish's nerves to settle and for the drink to kick in. Then I'd tell him Spencer wouldn't be in the bar that night, despite what I'd promised at the office earlier, and Seb would walk over with a tray of the finest mojitos and a big smile and an official invitation to join the extended conspiracy.

If we could get Manish onside we'd have a much better chance of *controlling the narrative* as Seb had put it, since it looked like I'd be lashed to Simon for the duration. Manish was supposed to be writing a standard hatchet job on Spencer: unearth a few vicious, snarling exes with axes or one-nighters, add a couple of accurate but context-free quotes from the poor man himself, sprinkle with unsubstantiated innuendo and gossip from unattributed "friends", serve with a highly selective personal history, and drizzle with fresh spite. Best served cold. If we could bring Manish into the fold, then even if the Archivist's grand plan didn't come off, whatever it was, we could fill the piece with plausible nonsense that would never stick. We could give him an unlikely history as a womaniser and get his home town or his middle name wrong, and hope that Geoff and Simon would be too preoccupied tossing each other off to do anything other than trust Manish's big, brown, imploring, innocent eyes. With any luck they'd give the piece no more than a cursory glance, a sniff up and down, before taking his name off it — which they were guaranteed to do.

If they did check it, of course, our heads would be mounted on pikes outside the office for generations to come as a warning to others.

When the mojito moment arrived, Manish's eyes popped. He couldn't spit out the questions quickly enough, raising his hand and jiggling like a five-year-old needing a piss. I told him that with my superior journalistic experience I'd asked those questions a full week ago, and he told me to sod off, as was the ritual.

Seb explained everything patiently, including all the embarrassing details of the week and the slightest hint of a plan to come — keeping the few details we knew firmly to our attractive chests — and we pretty much begged him to join us, or at least not to blab everything to the barrow boys.

And then Seb had to run off: he had other crucially important business to attend to.

After Seb left us I saw Manish relax a little. He came out of journalist mode and began to speak more freely, a mate in a bar rather than on a job.

"Right, ginge," he said. I knew what was coming. "It kind of makes sense with Seb, all honourable and shit, all that justice stuff. I'm not too sure about this Flowers guy and the toffs, but OK, I'll take your word. But — you're mad, you know that? Because if it goes wrong, you're out of a job. And if it goes right, you're out of a job."

"This is true," I replied with a curt nod.

"You want revenge on Geoff and Simon for old lies told in an old paper by telling new lies in a new paper. And those old lies weren't even anything to do with you."

"This is also true. You are very perceptive, my young apprentice."

"So, you're doing it for love, are you? Seb got you under his thumb?" He crushed his thumb onto the chrome.

"Bollocks," I said. "I'm not saying I wouldn't. He's a good-looking fella. Loaded too, not that that makes a difference."

"Which it does."

"Which it does," I nodded. "Getting a smile out of him's like picking food out of your teeth with your tongue. You work away at it, niggle, niggle, and eventually it comes loose and you relax and rest your tongue for a few seconds, and then you feel another bit of food and it all starts again."

"You could just use your toothbrush." Manish mimed a brushing action, mockingly.

"Where's the fun in that? And that doesn't even make sense. What does it even mean?"

"I dunno. Maybe you could tickle him or something."

"Tickle him? He's not *eight*. I'm just saying, he can be hard work, but he seems worth it and I still would. But I'm doing this because it's right, not because I want his babies. Not entirely because I want his babies."

He held up his hands, almost pleading with me. "But isn't it all madness? Total ginger Irish madness? When you're out of work, either because you've won or because you've lost, what are you going to do? Nobody's gonna touch you. You won't get another job in the papers. And if I sign up to this, I won't either."

"Well, I've thought about that a little," I said, leaning in. "If no other paper would employ me, I'd just have to start my own. After all, if it all works out, that's the end of the *Bugle*, so there'd be a decent, handy gap in the market. I'm sure Seb would throw in a couple of quid, you know, as thanks. He could be the media mogul and you could be my deputy. Now how's that for an enticing offer in a gay bar?"

fifteen
The Secret

My offer to the Master was of course designed in conjunction with the Archivist and his team to attempt to quiet the delightful old lady's efforts to unseat me: a light psychological tinkering to impress upon her that, should I voluntarily self-defenestrate, she herself would be required to juggle the flaming clubs in my stead. I knew she would rather bury herself in her college coffin in her purple shroud of Lulu, resurrecting purely to burble nonsense and receive all the plaudits and bouquets should by some miracle the college ultimately triumph.

Despite the kerfuffle with Amanda and the *Bugle* struggling for brain-space I could not ignore the charity event — it would go ahead whether the next edition of the paper savaged me and St Paul's or not. I had assigned a college administrative officer to handle inquiries from press and public and to process applications from prospective competitors. She was gratifyingly eager and dreadfully efficient. She indicated to me that, at close of play on Friday — the day the *Bugle* announced the race with such drag-based fanfare — there had been much traffic into and out of her systems, and firm registrations for the race were in the high tens.

With the event only a week away it was time to begin actively promoting and publicising it. A small, trusted team had been charged with an idea and a selection of large denomination notes supplied by Seb, and were nearing readiness. Early on Friday evening, upon word, sent by old-fashioned and yet rather exciting walkie-talkie, I dashed from my college room to the front gate on St Andrew's Street. Here I met Seb — straight from Humbug and in good cheer — and team member Bryce, a lanky man-child from Exeter who had gleefully informed me how his grandparents had heard dimly of *The Beatles*, thus causing my avoidance of mirrors for half a day.

Bryce led us across the road, threading our way through bus queues and into the deserted, cavernous interior of Cambridge's Grand Arcade capitalistic emporium. Then via a Staff Only doorway we climbed to a set of management offices overlooking St Paul's and the front gate. From these windows we saw the beginnings of the usual Friday crowds, gathering and pawing their way haphazardly between drinking establishments.

St Paul's was impressive: I had never seen it from this angle except in photographs. Three graceful Georgian storeys of creamy Portland stone, full of deep and multiple symmetries and mathematically quite tingling. At least, that was Bottom Court. To the left in the direction of Christ's College was New Court: its own facade was prim Victorian brick, discouraging the eye, careful to reveal not even a delicate ankle of mortar lest the public become wildly unstable with such muscular emotions as *like* or *disinterest*. Of New Court, we cared little.

Bryce and another student made last-minute tinkerings with their equipment, whispering and pointing at a laptop screen I could not see.

"I am looking forward to this," said Seb to me. "You must be excited."

I gave him an anxious look. "The week has gone frightfully poorly so far. I dare not become excited. I shall be glad to get through the evening with my head still on my shoulders."

"Well, I am excited."

This was not, I have to say, immediately apparent from his demeanour. Seb had a Vulcan expression, a Spock-like regard telling nothing and everything. The universe is empty space, at first approximation, and empty space is a quantum fizz, a broil of nothingness grazing the meniscus of reality. Seb was remarkably similar.

He attempted to reassure me. "This will set the tide turning back in your favour, Spencer, I am sure of it. Tell me, is this equipment all from college or newly bought?"

Bryce answered, face lifting briefly from the laptop screen. "New, sir. Thanks to our mystery donor." It was unclear from his smile whether Bryce suspected Seb to be the money supply or merely a gentleman friend of mine, as it were, tagging along.

"Ah, excellent. Are we nearly ready?" asked Seb.

Bryce pressed a series of keys and dabbed expertly at the touchpad, and the light on his face shifted in tone. A momentary frown disappeared. "We are now."

A crackle on the walkie-talkie and a static-enhanced voice confirmed the St John's half of the team was also set fair and awaiting the up-thumb. They were similarly ensconced in a room opposite that college's front gate.

I glanced at Seb for encouragement and took a breath. "Well then," I said, thrusting out a hand. "Engage." One rarely has the opportunity to issue an order as Jean-Luc Picard. It would have been such a shame to waste it.

The instruction was relayed over the airwaves to St John's, and both teams pressed their respective buttons. Seb and I watched as the lights illuminating Bottom Court's facade dimmed to darkness and the newly purchased projector beside us shone a new image, large and bright upon the stone. Faces and voices on the street below turned and exclaimed, with scatterings of applause.

"Fantastic," said Seb. "Perfect."

I concurred, still not daring happiness.

The Secret

The tentacles of news slipped quickly across college, and a stream of students began to pop through the gate and across the road to see with their own eyes. We received radio word that a similar, though less drunken, result was achieved at St John's. Within moments an image appeared on the internet — our main target. More followed, of St John's and St Paul's, seen from multiple angles on the street below. Through the window I saw camera flashes firing, and faces looking up toward us, seeking the source.

I began to believe this might actually work.

The projected image showed, thanks to the blessed and holy Photoshop, the words "Band on the Run" and a web address framing a famous image of the four Beatles in their pomp, each re-dressed as saints beneath halos: St Paul, St John, St George, St Ringo. The latter two were overlaid with large question marks, indicating those colleges as having not yet been allocated.

"That should go viral," said Seb.

I nodded. "We are about to test a new adage: *when in a hole, dig faster*. I might perhaps adopt its Latin formulation as my family motto."

He laughed. "It does, literally, shine a spotlight even brighter upon the college, does it not?"

"This, at least, was as the Master required." I braved a smile. "We have students on standby to revert any malicious changes on Wikipedia and alert us if any... *relevant* information is unfortunately published elsewhere. Thankfully for this project I do not dig alone."

"Even so, I hope you are prepared for the stress, Spencer."

"And you too. Your time is almost here."

"It is strange. At the moment I do not feel any stress at all — in fact, I cannot wait. This is the end for me. If all goes according to plan it will lift a massive weight from my shoulders. I am very much looking forward to meeting your— your *colleagues*."

"Interesting times, Seb. Interesting times."

After a damp night of fitful sleep in a proper bed I arrived at college early — outrageously early for a Saturday. I nodded greetings to the duty porter — strange fellow, suspected heterosexual — and made my way directly to the Archivist's bunker.

I resided somewhat in the administrative limbo of this world, neither outsider nor elf nor special operations, and as such required particular handling. I passed efficiently through the initial security checks only to be delayed in the plush anteroom with its wall of photographic infamy, at which I lingered only briefly, learning much, until the Archivist himself arrived and limbered up wearily. The poor man had inverted his shifts for the duration to concentrate upon our wretched predicament.

"How goes the jet lag, Archivist?" I asked by way of very small talk indeed.

He grimaced. "I have coffee somewhere. Everywhere. One copes. The first casualty of war is sleep."

I nodded and inspected the carpet in a gallant attempt to obscure the onrushing guilty scarlet. Last night's successful promotion of the charity race could hardly even begin to pick away at the tangled knot I had proudly tied. Aged thirty-five, and still presenting my snotty nose for matronly assistance.

"I apologise, again," I said.

"Dr Flowers, please." His stretches were perfunctory, and I thought of little practical use. "I am sure that lessons will be learned, but let's please first ensure we still have a college before we set up a commission of inquiry. I do not blame. I merely observe, record, report and preserve. I leave the pointing of fingers to more sensitive souls. And that dreadful Chatteris woman. Now, let us go through or we shall miss the action."

He led me through to the Hub and its many screens, most showing unchanging views as college rose slowly from its slumber. A fellow walking over the grass of New Court leaving a rod-straight trail in the dew and cutting a tangent against the arc of stone surrounding the fountain. A strange miscoloured view, no doubt infra-red, of a silent and occupied student room. A suited, disheveled, bleary night warrior setting forth on the stumble of shame, gazing into his phone perhaps in an effort to ascertain his location. It would likely be another hour before the stretching and the scratching began in earnest.

Overnight in the Hub a new, small monitoring station had been wheeled into position and connected to what the Archivist called the Grid. This station comprised just four screens, three of which were black. The other showed a jumping, disorienting, fish-eye view of a street I did not immediately recognise. Curved along the right edge of the fish-eye was the elongated face and body of Helen. The camera was embedded in a button on Arthur's jacket. They were headed toward the offices of the *Bugle*.

I stood behind the screens with the Archivist. An elf, the fresher Jay I had seen here a few times now, sat adjusting sound and vision via mouse and laptop in consultation with another.

We heard the voice of Helen announce breezily: "And here we are!" It was to us as well as Arthur.

The view darkened and adjusted as the two agents entered a building and the camera's light rebalanced automatically. We saw some kind of marble-effect security desk, imperially dominated by a middle-aged uniform with cap askew and it seemed a fleck of pastry clinging to his lower lip.

"What have we got here, then?" said the uniform. "Not like you lot to be up and about on a Saturday."

"Unfinished job from yesterday," said Helen, her voice now Home Counties Newcastle. "Someone's bonus on the line."

The uniform emitted an I-know-that-type grunt. "Where do you need?"

"The *Bugle*, darling," said Arthur. His inability to avoid the endearment often sped up these interactions, I was informed. "Report of someone being able to open a window."

"Can't have that," said the uniform, reaching for a piece of paper or a clipboard, it was unclear. "Go on up. Second floor."

"We'll need you to let us in," said northerly Helen.

"It's already open, love. Someone else's bonus on the line, probably."

"Alright, cheers, darling." Arthur's voice revealed no trace of worry. Although this was not the most desirable scenario, I was sure it had been anticipated and planned for. I glanced in concern toward the concentrated face of the Archivist.

We saw the two walk to a lift, in deference to Arthur's disintegrating hip, and made out their reflections, doubly distorted in the scratched polish of the lift door. They both wore the outfits of a maintenance crew, as observed and duplicated — or obtained — at short notice by Jonathan. Both carried bags of some kind.

A *ting*, and the doors slid open. Helen and Arthur were the only travellers. The Archivist warned me the signal would likely cut out as they ascended, and it did, and my heart beat faster regardless. This was hardly as threatening as a loss of signal during a spacecraft's atmospheric re-entry, I thought, and yet its predictability seemed to make it equally as dramatic and tense.

The signal crackled back to life as the lift doors opened. In front were a set of double doors, above which was fixed the newspaper's logo. The two passed confidently through into a new room and the stronger light washed out the view for a second. It resolved into a rather pedestrian office, not at all how I had imagined, and recognisably the *Bugle*'s only by a pile of copies at a desk to one side. And at another desk, turning towards us — towards Arthur and Helen — sat a stick-thin young gentleman, of perhaps Indian or Pakistani heritage.

"Can I help you guys?" he said — ah, it was Brummie heritage,

I realised. I was thankful he wasn't about to see immediately through Helen's impersonation.

The two explained the reason they were there, and the young man seemed content to leave them alone. They went straight to a corner window and worked smoothly and silently, pausing occasionally to make an unsuspicious noise or stage-whispered exclamation. Helen climbed upon the table beside the window, we saw, and then Arthur turned away, perhaps to identify whether our Birmingham friend was paying attention. He was unseen behind a monitor.

Arthur lowered himself slowly and noisily to his knees, The room shook and tilted and then we saw only dull, worn, grey squares of what used to be carpet, flitting and rotating as he moved about apparently on his hands and knees. I prayed we would not see his hairpiece flop into vision.

Then I caught a glimpse of a flat black box with flickering lights and spaghetti wiring, which I recognised as network-related. With a swift move Arthur located one particular wire, unplugged it, and then reinserted it via an additional, unobtrusive device he could camouflage amongst the techno-jungle detritus.

We heard a muffled, quiet noise of inquiry in the room. Arthur replied, "Sorry, darling, I must have kicked something. Is it OK now?" It seemed so.

A second screen on the monitoring station in the Hub lit with lines of data. The elves whispered and indicated, fingers silhouetted against the slowly scrolling figures and words.

And then a third screen came to life, full with Helen's distorted face. She withdrew from the newly enabled camera and climbed off the table. This screen showed the entire office, apparently from one corner. Arthur was clambering slowly, assisted by chair and table, to his feet. I marvelled at the technology.

"An invisible fly on the wall," I said to the Archivist.

"And a spy on the network," he said. "Know your enemy, Dr

Flowers. Tell me: have you read *The Art of War*?"

"I have not, I am afraid. Though I do frequent gay bars. I expect there is some overlap."

Once our two infiltrators had tidied up, covered their tracks and gently scarpered we kept a nervous eye on the Brummie for signs of suspicion. I knew that on the previous evening Conor had tried to, as it were, sign the gentleman up, but he had as yet affirmed no decision. It was prudent to proceed with utmost caution.

The Archivist said his elves would keep watch and report. He had adjusted the elf rota to ensure existing coverage was unaffected, and boasted of the procedural changes he had introduced to ensure no repeat of the week's shortcomings.

I left him and his elves to their shifts. I had other business: welcoming Seb once more into college and escorting him to what I publicly called his *orientation* meeting. He would spend the day locked in a room with various of the Archivist's special operations team, being initiated into his temporary new role.

I had been worried that Amanda, with her camera access, would discover the truth about Seb and alert the newspaper. The Archivist said this would not be a problem: there would be a cover story involving a piece of performance art. The truth would be known only to highly trusted parties, personally vetted by the Archivist.

Seb anticipated his day in training with gusto.

"Do you know what it is, Spencer?" he asked me. "Is it something I will enjoy?"

"In good time," I said, sounding suddenly like the Archivist. I did not want to speak of it in public view. "You will be fine."

I checked in regularly with his progress as I dealt with the many race matters that began to pile up and tried to avoid the paint-stripping rays of the purple eye. I knew Amanda would be hankering for the response to my supposed mulling regarding my position. She would have to hanker on. Every half-day's hanker, I estimated, added about a finger of gin to my jolliness. By the end of the week, with a following wind, I hoped I would be utterly hankered.

sixteen
The Hack

"OK, let's have some sort of order," said Geoff, chewing on a lump of curried chicken I could still see far too much of. It was our usual Monday editorial meeting over glorious fragrant Thai food. "It's a big week, boys. You kids could make your names with this one if you keep your noses brown."

I nodded eagerly, playing the part like a pro. Simon was Simon, struggling with some reluctant bean sprouts and wishing we could be in a greasy spoon. Manish met nobody's eye.

Geoff pointed his fork at me. "I know it's early, but what have you got so far?"

"I've spent the morning being blinded by websites that look like shite," I said, which was true, and shovelled in a pepper-hot pineapple and some rice.

Geoff refused to make a website for the *Bugle*. He claimed it would stop people buying the print edition, but we all knew it was because he didn't want to shell out the pennies for one, and he didn't understand the whole internet fad anyway.

A toxic concoction of liquids escaped his mouth. "Is that what you call research, ginge?"

"I was trying to find out what people are saying about the race. It's sort of like interviewing, but without the exercise. I mean, if you *want* me to wear out my shoe leather all afternoon I'll do it. It's a decent enough day, I could top up my tan." I was working up a decent sweat from the curry, and the endorphins were kicking the hell in.

Simon cut in. "I found a possible lead, in some godawful student *chat room*." He spat the words as if they were *vice den* or *crack house* or *teen-ager*. To me *chat room* sounded as ancient as *wireless* before it became all modern again. A glance from Manish, a barely perceptible smirk, showed he thought the same. But then, hey, people still said *horse power* even though nobody had ridden a horse in, like, sixty years.

"What was in this *chat room*?" I asked, making cutlery air quotes. "Hippies on beanbags with the marry-joo-ahna?"

"It was about how these poor old toffs were having such a poor old time in this shit-hole of a city — I'll give 'em that — because there weren't enough stick-up-the-arse restaurants to take mater and pater to. And then one fella, no proper name, just some string of letters and numbers, started up about foreigners. The usual gubbins, too many, all the jobs, go home — no offence Twiglet."

Manish put his hand up. "I'm British."

"Whatever. And then he says, there's a foreign student at St Paul's. Big deal, someone says, place is full of 'em, and then he says he's 'unregistered.'"

"Hello," said Geoff, mouth full again. I think he only spoke with his mouth full. "Does that mean illegal? Or is it one of those la-de-da college words?"

"Dunno. I'm gonna look into it." He hacked away at his bean sprouts like he was forking a hay bale, except he never picked anything up.

"Yeah. Promising," said Geoff. "That'd be a story, illegal immigration funnelled through the college. Back-handers for the left-footers, that sort of thing."

"Or maybe trafficking?" said Manish, plate already empty. "Bound to be a top headline for that. Something about red lights, maybe. You want me to start thinking?"

"Keep your hair on, Twiglet. Flowers piece first."

"I was thinking *Spencer De-Flowers* for that one."

I laughed, despite myself. I hoped it didn't mean Manish wasn't going to support us. "Have you found anything out?" I asked pointedly, spearing a piece of chicken.

"Nothing since Friday night," he replied equally pointedly.

"What happened Friday night?" said Geoff.

Manish hesitated and I held my breath, which was a bad idea given the mouthful I had.

"Ginge just filled me in, that's all," he said finally.

"Did he now?" Geoff laughed. "Filled you in up the wrong 'un, did he? Told you you should never go to those places. Was it the Rohypnol again, ginge?"

I chewed and swallowed quickly. "For the record, there was no Rohypnol and none of *that* kind of filling in. It was a perfectly respectable knowledge transfer over a beer or two. I *may* have innocently brushed against his knee a couple of times. But there was no mad fumble down an alley. I'm not that kind of girl."

"I bet you're not. So, possible illegals, nothing yet on Flowers, and ginge has been surfing the bleedin' internet. Well, I've—"

"Actually, I did find something about the race," I said, putting down my cutlery. "Might be worth a bit of digging."

"Go on then, tell the class." Geoff spread his hands grandly and sarcastically. Simon had progressed to lifting his plate to his face. Soon he'd be like a horse with a feed bag, dead-eyed and thinking of fags.

"What's interesting," I said, "is it wasn't something that Sp— that Flowers mentioned when we spoke last week for the puff piece with all the boobs. I've discovered the race has a sponsor, funding all the publicity, the equipment, everything."

"Oh yeah? Who?"

"I don't know."

"That's no bloody good. Find out."

"That's it. Nobody knows. Except Flowers, apparently."

Manish gave me a crafty look, the git, and I wished he hadn't. "How do you know that?" he asked.

"Know what?"

"That only Flowers knows. He might have told someone."

I thought quickly. "Well, that's what people are saying."

"What people?" said Simon, nose up from the bean sprouts, glaring at me.

"The people... on the website I looked at. One of the ones that made me go blind. Not a porn one. I don't look at porn, of course. Not at work anyway. OK, I have, once or twice, but only accidentally. I clicked when I should have run away. What can I say, he had a decent smile on him. And that wasn't all he had, either." That was better: I tried to drag the subject elsewhere. Jeez, if only there was a squirrel I could point at. Everybody loves looking at squirrels.

"Alright," said Geoff, "enough. Illegal immigrants, secret donor. Query trafficking, query laundering. Very bleedin' queery indeed. Plenty to get your teeth into. Bit like the good old days, ain't it Psych?"

"Next time I'm having chicken and chips," he replied, clattering the half-empty plate onto the table. "You get anywhere with this Archivist?"

Geoff made a face, curling his lip. "Trail's gone cold. I've put the word out, made a few more enquiries. The ones who were going 'yeah, yeah' last week and singing like a canary are now saying they heard about him from each other. Like a bleedin' echo chamber. There's something in it, though, I'm sure. Everybody's keeping zipped up tighter than a kipper's arse. No offence, ginge."

"On behalf of all kippers, none taken."

"Right," he said, slapping his hand on the table. "Who wants another beer?"

* * *

Just because I made fun of the old man's crazy words like *chat room* and *free education* Simon made me stand over him back in the office while he cracked his fingers and attempted some kind of advanced hacking jiu jitsu. He'd been on a course, apparently, but I suspected that actually meant someone with kind eyes had taught him which way round to hold a mouse and that the little x in the corner made the program go bye-byes.

"I didn't realise you were a hacker," I said to him. "What have you broken into? The Pentagon? Number 10 Downing Street? Weight Watchers?"

"You scoff, kid. It's easier than you think." He opened up a new browser window using approximately the slowest means possible. It would almost have been quicker to build my own computer from rock and sand. I already wanted to tear the mouse from his yellow stick fingers and wheel his chair into the lift shaft.

"What are we hacking today?" I said. "I'll make notes."

"No notes, you pillock. That's evidence."

Of course every page he loaded hopped across the network potentially leaving an audit trail at about forty-nine points along the way as well as at the website he was visiting and also by any spooks who might've been watching, but no, I had to put my pen down.

He typed in the web address for St Paul's College, including the http prefix which he got wrong twice, and I tried to imagine what life must have been like for him back in the early part of the twentieth century.

When he finally hit the Go button the front page popped up quickly enough. It wasn't too bad, as these things go: decent looking, full of links to the usual galleries and fluff and maps. We skimmed through the information for prospective students, including arty photos of the prettiest undergraduates smiling in a library, which I was almost certain had never happened in the history of mankind. We both recoiled at what looked like an artist's impression of some enormous purple gargoyle with deflated Marge Simpson hair and fifties glasses being surprised in a brothel. Inexplicably it was captioned "Amanda Chatteris, Master" and I was convinced it must have been a student prank for rag week, but Simon said he'd met her and the picture showed her on a good day.

Finally after much slow-motion clicking Simon located the link he was after: the St Paul's staff intranet. Internal college web pages, not supposed to be accessible by Johnny Public, and especially not by Psycho Journalist.

He clicked the link, and a new page appeared. It had the usual logo and shite, and a big box asking for username and password.

"Oh dear," I said like I was talking to a two-year-old. "Never mind, you had a decent go. One house point for trying."

"You think you know everything, don't you, ginge," he said.

He typed in the username *admin* and a password that showed up as blobs — I couldn't tell what he was typing. He clicked the big OK button, and it rejected him with a large red error message.

"It's calling you an invalid," I said. "I'd get onto the authorities about that, it's discrimination. I mean, you're old, but you're not infirm. I guess you might be incontinent. Does that count as invalidity?"

He ignored me and tried again, typing whatever he was typing more carefully this time. And on clicking OK, it let him in.

I was genuinely gobsmacked. Not speechless, obviously, but definitely gobsmacked.

"Would you look at that," I said. "What the hell password was that?"

His aged mouse trundled over the screen like Stephenson's Rocket off the boil and he picked out a different browser window lurking behind the first. It showed a thread on some Cambridge gossip forum somewhere, apparently more open to the public than its users thought it was. Here someone had blithely pasted the username and password for the St Paul's intranet and gone on their happy way.

I was about to say how much of a fantastic stroke of luck that was. But I knew it wasn't. I reckoned I knew what was going on here: Seb had told me the Archivist had taken unspecified "countermeasures". This was information planted specifically for us to find. It was some kind of honeytrap. Were we supposed to be bees? Bears? I wasn't a bear. More like a kind of ginger otter. But we were definitely being led somewhere.

"Clever," I said finally. "Looks like I underestimated you."

It was just about the least likely phrase I had ever uttered and it made Manish's ears prick right up. He wheeled his chair over to see what we were doing.

What the St Paul's staff intranet lacked in design, it made up for in… no. It lacked in design and it lacked in everything else. There wasn't a lot to see there. Just a few links to internal policy documents and student and staff mugshots and the like. We had a browse around. Curiously, in amongst the photos of students there was the drag star Cody as well as her undressed alter ego Jonathan. Maybe she was more of a permanent fixture in his life than I'd thought. We also discovered a photo of Spencer with more hair and less beard, and that gargoyle again, and other miserable but less frightening specimens.

Manish peered closely as they scrolled slowly by. "Oh, right, I see," he said, and looked at me. "Interesting."

A few links down some kind of rat hole we found a page with big bold blue letters: *Foreign Guests*. "Aha," said Simon, and clicked it.

The browser popped up another login page, taunting us. Inviting us.

"Try that password from before," I said.

He did. It rejected him. He tried again, just in case. Another rejection.

"Another level of security," said Simon. "Annoying. And suspicious. Why would they hide a page on foreign guests from their staff? Don't staff need to know that kind of thing?"

"Personal details, something like that?" said Manish. "Cleaners don't need to know your bank account number."

That was entirely plausible, so I ridiculed it. "They're not going to put that stuff online. This is Cambridge, they're not that sophisticated. It'll be on six-by-four index cards in a big dusty filing cabinet guarded by a griffin. And in any case—"

"Why doesn't it say *students*?" asked Simon. "Why foreign *guests* and not foreign *students*?"

"Good question." I resolved not to praise him too much, it was getting out of hand.

"Visiting speakers?" said Manish. "Or business people staying in the college during holidays when no students are about — you know, conferences. Or parents popping over to check little Raoul's allowance hasn't been pissed up the wall."

"Maybe," said Simon.

"Try some other password," I said. "You can't give up now."

"Ginge, think about it. I can't sit here typing any old rubbish into it, it'll set off an alarm."

I thought he'd been watching too many crappy films. "So you're gonna walk away? The master hacker, defeated by a bunch of stuck-up pansies?"

"No. I'll keep digging. But I'm not doing it with you two breathing on me. Playtime's over, kids."

Twiglet and I were banished back to our desks. I began to worry that I'd been too obvious, too eager to make him push on and find whatever it was we were supposed to find. Or too much of a suck-up.

Manish leaned over: I expected him to confirm one or the other. "Ginge," he whispered. "This college lot. Are you sure they're on the right side?"

I glared at him to keep it down. "What do you mean?"

"Only... those photos, the staff ones. Old guy, bad toupee. Did you see that one?"

"Yeah? He's a porter, I saw him at the college the other day. Smells of talc and peaches."

Manish nodded. "Funny. I saw him in here on Saturday morning. And before you say it, no, I don't think all white guys look alike. You couldn't forget that wig if you tried."

"He was in here?" I was genuinely surprised. "Doing what? Measuring up for curtains?"

I had a quick look around. Simon was still learning how to double-click. Geoff was staring at his laptop screen and rubbing his chin, sending ripples around his face.

"I don't know," said Manish. "He was dressed as maintenance. With some woman. I thought at the time she was the too-posh-to-push type, know what I mean? She was probably one of them too."

"A lesbian?"

"At the college, in those mugshots. But yeah, probably. They were messing around by the window. She was up on the table at one point, and he was on his knees. And— yes! And the network blinked off for a couple of seconds. The internet disappeared."

"Cross my heart, Twiglet, I had no idea," I said. "Maybe they just... moonlight?"

"Moonlight my chuddies. You know what's going on, don't you? We're being tapped by them because we're investigating them. Doesn't that make you feel uneasy?"

It did, and I nodded slowly. It made me very uneasy. But I knew why they were doing it, assuming they were actually doing it. It made perfect sense from their point of view at the top of their pink ivory tower.

"Forget your race and your sex scandal," said Manish. "College hacks newspaper? There's your story right there. I could go to

Geoff right now—"

"Don't!" I hissed and pleaded. "Don't even think it. Please. BFFs for ever, I promise. Remember, this is about justice for Seb and his family."

"Yeah, and the rest."

"It is! Fundamentally. Just— please don't say anything. Why the hell were you in here on a Saturday morning anyway?"

He shrugged and shook his head. "Why do you think? Checking out Seb's story. Like you did."

"Oh, jeez," I said. "We're fucked. Royally and doubly."

"What? How?"

"Simon knew, he found out I'd been sniffing around the story, and he warned me off. If he spots that you've been looking too…"

seventeen
The Surveillance

In her chair in the Bandolinum conference room in Top Court Amanda glowered and sulked, a wrinkled child-beast about to receive a spanking for smearing herself top to toe in purple make-up. Beside her sat Helen, bolt upright in a pale green trouser-suit. And beside me around the corner of the table was Dennis, bolt asleep in his usual suit and gown. It was the second SPAIN committee meeting. This time I, as chair, had been graciously allowed to chair it. The Master still awaited my fake decision over my fake resignation and, I suspected, was reluctant to overly irritate.

I was delivering a status report. "I am exceedingly pleased to announce that the saintly Beatles images projected upon front Bottom and St John's were a great success in all the places that matter — and also *outside* Cambridge. The enabled communication pathways begin positively to glow and hum with activity." I referred to my notes. "At my last check an hour or so ago prior to the mush designated as lunch, we were closing on five hundred registrations for the race. Registration closes on Friday: four weekdays of further publicity — agreeable publicity — should hike the total significantly."

"Splendid, splendid," said Dennis, though I was unconvinced he was not nattering in his sleep.

"Dr Flowers," squeaked the Bursar, "I am a little concerned —

and I can hardly believe I am saying this — at the sheer amount of money that might literally flow into college on Saturday afternoon. It must be secured and dealt with in an efficient manner. Do we have a process? Some form of handling procedure that I might examine?"

It was a fair point. "We shall of course merely be counting the money rather than banking it," I said. "I should imagine a group of feisty young undergraduates and some harassed auditors would suffice."

Amanda harrumphed, and slouched fractionally further. "I would suggest incapacity," she grumbled.

"I think perhaps I rather agree with the Master," said Helen, failing to conceal her surprise. "How long does it take to count a bucket of coins? Do we know? Is there a website?"

Dennis perked up. "Is there not some device we could hire, hire?"

I had been rather preoccupied and I must confess I had not given much consideration to these critical matters. I begged forgiveness and wondered whether Helen might perhaps volunteer to investigate further. She agreed. I hoped this would not mean a late-night raid on a local bank or 24-7 video surveillance of a car park ticket machine.

In this fresh week I was seeing St Paul's in fresh eyes. Of course I had been aware of the Archivist and his netherworld, but in one's general day-to-night activities they tended to fade away, obscured and obfuscated by the ever-present bureaucratic niceties and personal jollities or lack thereof of college life. As we sat uncomfortably around that conference table listening to the hooting and beeping of the buses and of Amanda it was easy to forget that the room held one, two or more cameras watching over us, cold dark silicon eyes and ears at the Archivist's call and beck. Our utterances would be transmitted and interpreted and retained in some underground electronic guise for— how long? I pitied the elf responsible for backups.

Other matters in the meeting were dealt with more competently. I had continued to mentally massage the local police, and promised them a decision in two days, on Wednesday, regarding the two substitute colleges. I would deliver them a firm, immutable race route, which would also go to our anonymous donor — still unnamed, of course — for sourcing and installation of barriers where deemed necessary for crowd kettling purposes. There would be a form of dais by the front gate to college, upon which speeches and coronations would take place. I had dispensed with one early notion of a large screen to display a running count of the total raised, in case Amanda claimed it hungrily as a mechanism for the dissemination of exotic Powerpoint presentations to the massed runners.

There being no other AOB business, or at least none to discuss in Amanda's particular company, the meeting closed and scheduled to reconvene two days later for a further update and for college selection. Dennis and Helen hurried off at their respective paces, perhaps to further whichever tasks the Archivist had given them.

I felt the meeting had passed exceptionally reasonably. It was not a feeling I usually associated with meetings, especially those I chaired, and especially those attended by Amanda. I tried not to strut or preen, as I was well aware of the Master's ability to leech away any feeling of satisfaction or pride: some called it the *tumble in the jumble*.

But she had been quiet, by her usual decibellic standards. When we were alone, as I gathered my papers, she leaned forward and stared blankly down at the table, her arms stretched out before her, her nails dotting out two purple arcs across the wooden surface. The words came slowly. "Have you reached a verdict upon which you are all agreed upon?"

"I beg your pardon, Amanda?" Upon which *we were all* agreed?

The Surveillance

Was this a reference to the Archivist and his team? Had she more access to his data than I knew?

"Regarding your proposed vacancy. Am I to recruit, or to not recruit? That is the question." Her voice was low, soft, almost vulnerable.

Perhaps a mere verbal tic, then: a running away of the mouth, a cascade of word association football. I hoped the Archivist's systems were sufficiently hardened to prevent unauthorised ingress. Perhaps she was extrapolating: reaching mentally as well as physically. I wondered whether she knew, if not the detail, then that *something* was afoot over which she had no control.

"Master," I said plainly and quietly, papers in hand. "I have no desire to leave St Paul's. Despite the hardships and troubles, I believe we work for a common good, for the students, as our founder wished it. I may from time to time inadvertently topple from the wagon into a flowerbed, not necessarily unaccompanied, but these are mere unfortunate lapses."

"Lapses, Dr Flowers? *Lapses?* I assure you they are geraniums." Even this had no bite, no spat venom.

She was in a curious mood, one I had never seen. It unsettled me, like the mechanical clanking as you are hauled to a localised maximum of a roller coaster knowing but not knowing what is to follow. Had the fight entirely left her?

Her reign as Master had always been turbulent and, as it were, event-filled. There were protests at her appointment, from a certain subset of the Old Paulines — all gentlemen, naturally — who declared her genetically unsuitable. I had supported her then. I was less in favour when two fellows whose friendship had grown beyond friendship broke up apocalyptically, and she proclaimed that we must thenceforth no longer mix pleasure with business. That struck me as too unnecessarily strict a rule, too black and white, and I said so vigorously. In retrospect it was perhaps not so odd that I soon found myself in the regular company of our then-and-now-69-year-old Praelector, Dennis. Perhaps he had been grooming me.

I stood to leave, and Amanda did so too.

"May we walk?" she asked.

She was silent as we descended the staircase together, her clog-like shoes thumping on the worn stone like a mason's blunt mallet. Through a tall glass door into the fresh air of Top Court she became invigorated somewhat, more animated. She took my arm, a most unnerving experience: cracked old purple-tipped fingers slithering past my inner elbow, locking me to her. I had, I noted disturbingly, left my pen-knife in my flat and would be unable to slice off my own arm should the situation make that necessary.

"How are *things*?" she asked in attempted friendliness as we began to walk anticlockwise around the court. I could think of no worse — or, indeed, unlikely — question to emerge from her lips. Its openendedness and breadth rendered any answer either uninformatively brief or liable to continue via a mix of subordinate clauses, subparagraphs and weeping until we were both desiccated corpses lying, entwined forever, in the ditch we had carved around the lawn of Top Court with our endlessly circling feet.

"Well, you know," I said, opting for the former variant of answer.

"Might there be anything with which I can help you with?"

I could think of many things, none of them pleasant.

She continued: "Perhaps in respect of our— friends at the *Bugle*?"

I laughed. "If you could arrange for them to drop this week's stories, that would be simply magnificent."

"Is not that, as it were, in hand?"

"We are having a good stab, Master. A thrust here, a slice there, the occasional pirouette."

A hesitation. More quietly: "We, Dr Flowers? *We?*"

"In the royal sense. I am—"

"I have the eyes, Spencer."

I had slipped, and she knew it.

Perhaps this was the source of her apparent malaise, I thought. She still retained her limited access to the Archivist's systems to view cameras around college: a simple monitoring, a broad overview, with none of the Archivist's whistles and bells. She had undoubtedly seen me visiting him. I hoped she had not seen Seb, or at least not connected him to the growing conspiracy.

"The Archivist and his team are assisting in their usual capacity," I said, saying nothing.

"In regard of which?"

"In regard of… it is perhaps best I say no more. For pl—"

"In regard of which, Dr Flowers?" Her voice hardened. Her grip tightened.

"I should not say. There are aspects—"

"Aspects? Which aspects?" The gentle stroll changed up to a march.

I began to worry. "You know better than I how the Archivist works, Master. Please— would you mind awfully excusing yourself from my limb?"

Her elbow stiffened closer to her body, pinning me. I smiled and wrenched as pleasantly as I could given our location, in full view of chunks of college. An undergraduate dawdled a few paces ahead, another across the court. There would be faces within glancing distance of windows. She parried my wrench with an inverse wriggle and an unladylike jiggle.

"This is requiring of utmost discussion, Dr Flowers." Her volume rose with her temper. "Please, tell me your actions. This I do here command a response."

I stopped, whether she wanted to or not. She tried to pull me along. I resisted. "I am not a child, Amanda."

"Then why so do you act? I ask of you one item."
"Why?"
"I need to know."
"Why?"
"I am the Master. Of further 'why' there is no need, let me say simply. My request demands an immediacy of response."
"I refuse to tell you."
"Why?" It was her turn.
"You do not need to know."
"Why?"

All my instincts clamoured for me to say *because you are a part of all this*, but I resisted. In that brief moment of thought, I heard something: a quiet, strange, familiar warbling on the air.

Uh-meh-meh-onna-OW-puh-yuh-air-onna-OW.

What was it? Where was it coming from?

She heard it too, and scrambled in her jacket pocket with her free arm.

OW-um-on-aah-OW.

"Oh," she said, confused.

OW-um-on-aah-OW.

"Is that you? It's coming from— Is that— Is that Lulu?"

"Nothing. No matter. The singer, having sung, moves on." She fumbled with something, and it went silent.

"Show me that," I said firmly. "What is it? What are you doing?"

"Inconsequential."

Proprieties be damned, I thought, and broke free with a most impolite wrench that left her staggering. I grabbed her shoulders and spun her to face me, looking angrily into her eyes. Then I plunged my hand outrageously into her pocket.

I pulled out an ancient recording device with a miniature tape within: a dictating machine from the stone age.

"Were you recording me?" I demanded.

The Surveillance

"No, I—"

"Let us see, shall we?" I inspected the device quickly. "Well. Assuming I can make it rewind. Ah."

I hefted the appropriate buttons. Very shortly I heard the latter part of our conversation, ending at her imperial command to tell me my actions — when I presumed the jolt of my stopping had disrupted its function and inflicted an ancient, younger Lulu upon us.

I thought rapidly. I could only assume she had intended to take whatever I had revealed to the *Bugle* as incriminating evidence. But to what end? To sacrifice me to save the college? The newspaper could not be allowed to hear what I had said, of course. That much was easy to achieve. Less trivial: how to deal with Little Miss Scattershot herself.

I took her arm and contrived a smile. "Come with me," I said, with a degree of force and two degrees of butch.

The Archivist was waiting for us underground at his outer door. He was mid-shift and his hair showed signs of biscuits — perhaps he had been napping. He told us his elves had quickly alerted him to the unsightly fracas.

He took us through hurriedly to the plain room in which Dennis and I had met him a week before: the room with no secrets proudly on display, no plush carpet. A worried elf brought sufficient chairs and met nobody's gaze before scurrying away.

The Archivist paced to and fro silently, his hair bobbing like a conductor's arm. I indicated to the Master to sit, and thankfully she acquiesced mutely. I was too enraged to join her, bouncing on my toes and boggling repeatedly at the obsolescent recording device I held before my face.

"We cannot allow—" I began, pushing it towards the Archivist.

He wafted me to silence. "Professor Sauvage will be here

shortly," he said. "Nothing can begin until he is here. And until he is here, neither of us can leave."

"Deniability," I said, and he nodded. "But are we not currently monitored, recorded?"

"Yes, of course," he said, his stride unwavering. "But everything can be falsified given sufficient inclination. One trail of evidence is necessary, but not always sufficient." He stopped, and glared witheringly at me. "I thought by now you might have learned that lesson, Dr Flowers."

I looked to the floor, desperate for a hole into which to cast myself.

It was four or five excruciating minutes before Dennis was shown in. He was pale and out of breath, and I fussed him quickly into a chair.

"Dear jeebus, at my age, at my age," he said, mopping his face with a light blue handkerchief from his left rear trouser pocket.

The elf returned once more with water, pounced upon eagerly by Dennis, and then left us in peace: perhaps to watch whatever was to happen next on the screens in the Hub, or perhaps to wind up the organ of gossip and transmit updates by jungle drum to the far corners.

My stomach began to cartwheel. I felt the fart of history upon me.

The Archivist brought Dennis — and everyone watching — up to speed. There had been a gross and unprecedented betrayal of trust, he said, and glanced at me before looking more fiercely upon the drawn, purple, mouldering face of Amanda. He explained how the college was in the midst of a great crisis, how its very future was in doubt, and that we must all work together to ensure its continuation. *The Pink and the Grey* had lasted two centuries, he cried, and while breath remained in his body he would make it last another two. It was a stirring, passionate political manifesto sprinkled with flashing knives and vaguely homoerotic imagery and had undoubtedly been circulating around his head for the previous several years.

The Archivist was relishing this chance to finally say his piece, and he laid into Amanda with some abandon.

"And so we have no alternative," he said finally. "We must, for the enduring good of the Holy and Glorious College of St Paul, for all that is right and true, for the pre—"

"Might I mitigate?" said Amanda quietly but firmly, her warble cutting through the Archivist's waffle.

His ranting red face halted, arm aloft in splendid oratory, spittle frozen mid-arc.

Dennis had recovered sufficiently and regained what remained of his colour. "It would only be fair, Archivist," he said.

The Archivist's arm dropped and reluctantly waved her to speak. He retreated to lean against a wall, his hair splaying out behind him.

"I thank. I speak trepidatally in fear of made-up minds. Yet speak I must, and heard be I must." She rose slowly as to confront the Archivist. "I am aware of my dispopularity, amongst the here and the there. It is impossible so to dispute. I have the screens, as does the Archivist. Yet these screens he may record and database without punity. I may, as it were, not. A simple action of dictaphone and the heft is upon me and all a-blister. How dare I! Betrayal! Such nuclear wording!"

"She rather has a point," I said. "Well, a fuzzy blob. The Archivist keeps records. Why cannot she?"

"It is my job!" said the Archivist. "Enshrined in our rules: a separation of concerns. I act purely in the future interests of our college."

"Do I not?" said the Master. "Do I work against such interests?"

"I do not claim that, Master. The fact remains that you have not explained your reason for this recording."

"Master," I said, "you wanted information about my dealings with the Archivist. Regarding the *Bugle* business."

"This did I," Amanda said, nodding. "Of this am I not entitled? Is it... *secret* from me?"

I looked away.

"I see," she continued. "Then perhaps I was right to record." She sat once more, her point I thought well and truly made, and not a biro in the vicinity.

"But to what end!" cried the Archivist. "Why would you think to do so? Is there a third party pressuring you? Have you begun your memoirs?"

"In my future interest, Archivist," she said with some intensity. "*My future interest.*"

The Archivist could only huff uselessly at that. He went to the Praelector and muttered darkly to him. Dennis nodded and replied, and his face paled again. I could not hear what was said.

"These are pressing times," the Archivist began finally, "and I hope it is plain that we must all work together to ensure the continuation of St Paul's. Any conflicts between us work against that goal. The Master has made some valid points, I willingly concede. But now is not the time for this debate. The external forces upon us are too great, too immediate, to allow for the niceties of a constitutional subcommittee. That is for a better time, when the crisis is resolved and we may attend properly and respectfully to all matters arising. For now, under present circumstances, Professor Sauvage and I are agreed that we must declare, in common parlance, a temporary state of emergency."

I felt a ripple of events wash over me and begin to expand.

"You coup me?" the Master said, unbelieving. "Throw me over?"

"We do not, Master. We are placing you under temporary Lodge Arrest. Study leave, you might say, and we shall. Until this crisis is averted. You shall have no contact with the outside world."

"We do not do this lightly, Amanda," said Dennis.

"For the duration of the emergency Professor Sauvage, as Vice Master, shall take on the Master's duties to the best of his abilities."

"Bar Lulu, Lulu," he said, unwisely attempting a joke.

Amanda began electric verbal exchanges of some vigour that led only to a rapid exit in the company of some trusted and toned elves and in the direction of her apartments, grandly called the Master's Lodge, on the St Andrew's Street side of Bottom Court. Here, I was told, she would be watched closely by cameras and eyes, and would not be allowed phones or computers. She would be isolated, for the good of the college.

It seemed to me a drastic step and I felt almost sorry for her. Dennis murmured in duplicated agreement, but believed we had no real choice. "She is a loose cannon, a loose cannon, my dear Spencer. We are already holed well below the waterline."

"Indeed, Dennis, indeed," I replied. "We flounder, sails askew, wheel spinning, at a dangerous list, low on rations, high on scurvy, pirates on our tail, sandbanks tickling our keel, and guided only by a faulty moral compass."

He laughed grimly and grabbed my arm. I helped him to his feet.

"You must excuse me, young man," he said, leaning in with a conspiratorial twinkle. "I believe it is time for me to walk the plank."

I watched him leave, hoping his words were neither prediction nor euphemism.

At around six that evening, with college still fizzing at the day's events, I received a text from Conor. He was coming to see me on a matter of urgency.

My nerves were by then a boxed, plastic-wrapped thousand-piece jigsaw under the sofa bed and I had rather begun to top up my levels of adrenalin from the gin bottle as I relayed the news — in only the most circumspect of terms — to Claire on the phone.

I attempted to bat Conor away at least until the morning's grey blast. He persisted, abusing exclamation marks like a twelve-year-old, and ultimately I gave way: I never could resist a ginger.

I met him at the front gate with, I hoped, a sober air.

"Jeez, pie-eyed already, Spencer?" he said before even a *hello*.

"It has been a day of some stress, which I hope fervently shall not be added to." I laid a hand on the curl of his shoulder and let it drift marginally south. "Gin? The bar will be—"

"No, please, no booze. I need your help. The Archivist's help. I know youse lot have been in the office."

I failed to fake surprise. In my enhanced form I could merely affect a cartoonish goggle that I imagine should have been accompanied by a throaty klaxon sound effect from an animated cartoon.

"We have a situation," he said. "A shitty situation. A shituation. Can I see the Archivist?"

I brought him through briskly into the poorly illuminated Bottom Court where passers by might not hear the A-word.

"I suspect he might not be in the appropriate mind for a meeting," I said, and related the tale of the day with the strongest counsel regarding its sensitive nature.

He absorbed the news showing no surprise or shock. I supposed that once you'd attended a meeting of the Women's Institute you were incapable of such emotions.

"My turn," he said. "Manish saw your camp old porter at the *Bugle* office, pretending to be a maintenance man. We reckon he was adding some network doohickey, are we right?"

I nodded reluctantly and began to explain. He held up a hand to stop me.

"Now," he continued, "Manish was in the office that morning to set the Googles on our mutual friend. To find out whether he was all he cracked up to be. And when *I* did that, Geoff's deputy Simon found out somehow or other and I damn near got a fist up me. If Simon sees that Manish has done the same thing…" He trailed off.

"I understand," I said. "I am sure the Archivist can assist in some fashion."

I took him the few metres to the Archivist's ground floor entrance on the east range of Bottom Court. This was A Staircase: that is, the staircase labelled A, rather than merely a capitalised indefinite. Through the doors we descended the stone steps, slightly bowed through use, toward the restricted area, the all-seeing basement of knowledge.

Not half-way, yet already more than a few degrees warmer, we were met by an elf. It was Jay, the fresher I had seen frequently in the Hub in the last week.

"Mr Beardsley," I said. "Going up for some air?"

"Still on shift, sir. I am here to turn you both away, I'm afraid. I'm sorry, but—"

"We must see the Archivist urgently."

The lad's gaze never raised above the nipple. "The Archivist says all is in hand, sir."

"This concerns the *Bugle* affair," I said, not wishing to say any more.

"Yes, he said all is in hand," Jay repeated in an apologetic tone. His arms were outstretched, barring further descent.

"Runs a tight little ship, does your Archivist," said Conor. "Do I have to beg on my hands and knees? I can be good at that."

Jay chanced a smile. "I'll bear that in mind, sir. It's unnecessary in this case."

"Am I given that the Archivist was, as it were, tuned in to our conversation a moment ago?" I said.

"I can tell you nothing else, Dr Flowers. It is all in hand."

"That's three hands it's in," said Conor. "Is it me, am I unclean? Do I smell of journalist? Do I need to be scrubbed down with antiseptic before I'm allowed in? The red doesn't come off, you know."

"All I can do is repeat the message, sir. Four hands now." The boy blushed shyly, perhaps unsure whether he was allowed to joke with us.

"I believe we are wasting our precious, Conor. The Archivist is a busy man. He will set his elves upon the problem. A swift drink and then you can be on your way."

I led Conor back outside so the four-handed elf might return to his duties.

"Is it like that all the time?" Conor asked as we stood beside the lawn under orange light-polluted clouds. "Do you get halfway through a sentence and some poor undergrad runs up with the rest of it on a bit of parchment? Jeez, I hope you boys don't have a quiz night here. He must win every week. Question one: *what is*— and he'll shout out *pomegranate* and everyone will tut and moan."

"It is not quite as awful as that," I replied, a foot straightening the edge of grass. "In normal times, such as these most definitively are not, we go about our business with hardly a thought as to what occurs below ground. On occasion one might spot the blinking of a red eye in a public or private corner, a gentle prod to the cerebellum. I dare say it does not alter behaviour greatly. I scarcely believe there can be anything the Archivist has not already seen, in some variant or another, in some multiplication, and you must admit that some gentlemen even find the concept... attractive. On the whole we feel the value outweighs the cost. Technically, of course, it's a great achievement and something the college is terribly proud of, in private that is."

Conor was thoughtful and about to respond when the

Archivist's double doors burst open and the same blond elf appeared once more.

"He has another message," said Jay, marginally breathless. "He doesn't enjoy quizzes or pomegranates."

Conor accepted the offer of a drink.

eighteen
The Research

With the hot blood of a chase pounding through his veins Geoff insisted on a Tuesday morning quick meeting around his desk. Not surprisingly I kept my mouth shut about the insignificant matter of the Master of St Paul's being locked up. Neither did I mention the camera that was sitting up in the far corner watching every tea break, or the mysterious device plugged into our network that I now knew secretly copied everything that went through it straight back to a bunch of geeks at the college.

Spencer had been on a full-on drunken blab the night before in the college bar. I'd had to drag him away from the students into a quiet corner in case they were taking notes. Of course, he'd thought I'd had other reasons for a little privacy, and I was forced to let him down gently. OK, not so gently.

It had been painful to watch. I'd told him he really ought to knock off the gin and dry out for a while, at least until everything that was going to happen, whatever it was, had happened. And he'd gone all maudlin, and switched on the woe-is-me fairy lights, and I'd kept wishing that the cute barman would wander over telling me to leave Spencer there for the cleaners to mop up in the morning while we had a drink by ourselves somewhere nice and cosy and preferably not with a camera looking at us. But it hadn't been my night.

"The more I think about this," said Geoff, chewing on a pen

The Research

since all the doughnuts had already gone, "the more I'm buying the immigrant angle. No wonder St Paul's keeps a low profile. Don't do anything too interesting, keep your heads down, here's a few hundred grand and an Azerbaijani to put up for a few weeks until the coast is clear."

"Why do the race thing, then, and come to us for publicity?" asked Manish.

"It's a cover, ain't it," said Geoff as if it were the most obvious thing in the world. "What you do is, you get everyone looking at a bunch of poofs running around Cambridge while you sneak coachloads of Muslims in the back door."

"It's not just St Paul's students taking part," I said. "They're getting people from other colleges, and people who aren't students at all."

"Careful, ginge, it sounds like you've been doing some research. I wouldn't want you to overdo it, pull a muscle." He glanced across at Simon to get a smile of approval at the gag.

"Special occasion, boss," I said. "Don't get used to it."

"I won't. I'm spiking that story anyway."

"What? Why?"

I tensed, waiting for him or Simon to cackle and rub their hands and reveal they knew everything about everything and were going to help me to accidentally fall down the stairs if I would just come this way...

"Cos it's a distraction from the real story," said Geoff. "I'm not gonna print a bloody great splash on illegal immigrants and have to make space for your shitty little piece on some tenners disappearing from bleedin' charity buckets. I want you to start hunting down the routes in and out. How do they do it: come in on a student visa and then jump into the back of a bus? Very handy, next to the bus station. No coincidence."

"Geoff," I said, trying not to laugh, "They didn't build the college next to the bus station. I'm pretty sure it was the other way around."

"Well, how long has the bus station been there? Fucking Chaucer might have come here for a day trip on the back of a bleedin' donkey for all I know. Find out."

I wrote "fucking Chaucer's bleeding donkey" in my notebook for future generations to decipher, next to the growing collection of snowman-like spheres with steam rising from them that were my artist's impressions of the editor.

"But before you do that, I need to borrow your pink passport."

"My whatnow?" I tilted my head like a confused puppy.

"This place you go to. Bar Humbug. Crappy name for a bar if you ask me."

"Are you on the turn, boss? I tell you, there's someone out there for everyone, even someone of your— of your calibre."

"I'm not on the bleedin' turn. Psych found a reference to it, didn't you?"

Simon turned up the snark. "Some *forum* — is that better, ginge, happy with that word, are you, *forum?* — some forum, some bitter young queen going all handbags. Said the Archivist was always propping up the bar at Humbug, had given him the brush-off there."

This was a plant, surely, I thought. Unless it was real actual honest journalism, in which case the Archivist could have been any one of a dozen bar-proppers I could recognise even if I couldn't put a name to. I hoped St Paul's weren't trying to push the spotlight onto Quiff or someone. And then I realised that for all I knew Quiff *was* the Archivist. Maybe the whole secret squirrel thing could be run from there when Quiff fancied a drink. Maybe Quiff downed a special vodka and all the tables flipped over to the peep show.

All I could do was go along with whatever it was. I knew someone at the college was watching. I tried desperately not to peek at the camera and give it a little thumbs up.

"OK," I said, "so what's the plan?"

"Me and you," said Geoff. "We go down and give it the once over."

"You need me for that? It's not that big. And I've given it the once over more times than I care to remember."

"Well, you needn't think I'm going to that place by myself."

I laughed. "Fine. Conor Geraghty, ace reporter, chaperone to the straights. First Manish and now you. Of course, you can't go dressed like that."

"Like what?" He spread his arms and looked down. Pale blue shirt and a gut hanging over his slacks. I'd seen far worse, but it was worth the wind-up.

"Like that! We'll have to butch you up a bit."

"Geoff," said Simon, cutting in. "Far be it from me to interrupt all this flirting, but if we're done, can I borrow you for a moment?"

"You're just stealing him from me now, so you can have your wicked way with him on the fire escape. And I thought it was me you liked." I turned to Manish, who was enjoying this. "Men! They're all bastards. You mark my words, Twiglet."

"Enough," said Geoff. "Clear off back to your desks."

The two Londoners disappeared into a secret huddle out of sight, and I tried not to climb the walls in panic. *All in hand*, said the Archivist, or his shy blond representative on Earth with all the hands, and I had to trust him. Surely with their network gizmo it should've been the work of seconds to insert a seek-and-destroy virus that hopped between the computers taking an axe to the log files? But then most of my knowledge about this sort of thing came from TV shows and films where the password was always guessed on the second try and everything looked and sounded like a fairground ride, and when it went wrong the computers exploded as if they had a tank full of petrol.

I thought maybe I should mosey on over to Simon's computer and at least try to look for something. I'd just got as far as telling myself not to be such a cocking idiot when they bounced back into the room, laughing and joking, and entirely failed to kill me. I took this as a good sign.

Geoff can barely walk ten metres without stopping for a rest and a cake, so he drove us across town, creeping in a few minutes ahead of the usual lunchtime traffic. It felt like getting in a teacher's car at school, with the other kids looking and pointing and you turning crimson and reassuring them that you're not related and that no services were about to be rendered, for cash or grades or otherwise.

"So who runs this Humbug place?" he asked as we drove.

"A guy called Eddie," I said. The fewer words I allowed myself to say, I thought, the better. I clamped my mouth shut. It's like talking to royalty: only speak when spoken to. "He's decent enough." *Shut up.*

"Fancy him, do you? Or have you had him already?"

"No, and no," I said, slowly.

"Not ticked him off your list?"

"I don't have a list. Nobody has a list."

He laughed. "Not so mouthy, are you, ginge, without Twiglet to flash your teeth at."

"I see where you're going with that, Geoff, and you're wrong."

"You'd be all over him given six pints and a head start. Go on, admit it."

I couldn't tell whether this was the usual office wind-up or something else, goading me into revealing more than I ought, something he could use against me.

"Sounds like your fantasy, Geoff, not mine."

"Fuck off," he said, with the extended syllables of denial, and let it go.

The Research

We turned left into a road slicing between some shops and a pub, and approached a bridge.

"How many gay guys do you actually know?" I asked. "I'm guessing, now correct me if I'm wrong, that you don't have that many gay friends."

"The wife knows one. Lifeguard where she goes swimming. She reckons he'd only save the men."

"Yeah, that's right, cos it's a well-known fact that straight boy lifeguards only save women."

I caught a quick glimpse to the left of some rowers out on the river, and another crew outside their boathouse with their boat over their heads.

"This chip you've got on your shoulder," said Geoff. "You always had it?"

"Why, are you hungry? They do nuts at the bar." I wasn't in the mood to tell him my life story.

"Seriously. Lose the attitude."

We drove through the trees past Midsummer Common. I remembered my chat with Seb beside the bridge I could just see in the distance, and his story, and what Geoff had done to his family.

"I think it's a very healthy attitude," I said. "You can't be a journalist without a cynical soul and a thick skin."

"And you can't be a journalist without making a mistake every now and then."

We turned right at a roundabout. Was this trip a pretext for a *chat* about looking into his past? Would we claim the last space on the car park roof before a tussle to the death? The story ending with a ginger smear on the ground, or a crushed marrow, or both?

"What do you think about the immigration story, ginge? Right or wrong?"

I took a deep breath. "It looks like a story," I said. It certainly did: that was the plan. Baiting the race-baiters. Giving them a shovel and an X on the dirt and hinting at gold.

"You'd put your by-line on it?"

If I did you'd take it right off again, I thought.

We slowed for some traffic lights. A coach came roaring past.

"More immigrants," he said, laughing, and I did too.

I answered his question. "I— well, if it holds up I'd put my by-line on it. Might be—" *Don't say made up, don't say made up.* "Might be a misunderstanding. Might be all above board. Might have to spike it, go back to the story about the missing tenners or the car impaled on the traffic bollard."

"Yeah. Easy, ain't it, this newspaper business." He laughed again, but I didn't laugh this time.

We queued, and looped up inside the multi-storey to the roof, and we didn't tussle, and neither of us ended up a little worse for wear on the pavement. We took the lift down and toddled at tourist pace towards Humbug.

I was glad that Geoff didn't mention the Cambridge Union as we passed by. I hoped he'd forgotten all about the mysterious man with his mysterious tip and his mysterious non-pissing-over-the-balcony.

The surreality of being in a car and on foot with Geoff paled into nothing compared to his appearance in a gay bar. He stood just inside the entrance, arms crossed, piggy eyes narrowed towards doggy, sniffing in the place.

Humbug was in its daytime mode so the aroma was mostly martinis, coffees and nappies. There was a small collection of those off to our left. The long bar was freshly polished. Behind it, Eddie frowned at some mechanical part in his hand that by all accounts should still have been attached to the coffee machine. Quiff sat, as anticipated, in Quiff's usual chair, wearing Quiff's usual hat. To Quiff's usual left, just one of the high tables in the bar was occupied: by Seb. My heart leapt out of my chest and ran screaming from the building.

It wasn't Seb's typical fashion selection. He'd normally wear something from the current decade, at least. This was older, greyer, half a size too small. Dark grey shoes. No socks. As we walked in he didn't look up, and he didn't look round. He simply stared out of the window and held a coffee cup by his mouth with both hands.

Normally of course I'd have rushed up, said hello, and offered him some witty banter and my body, not necessarily in that order. But with the fashion police about to arrest him for crimes against humanity and with Geoff at my side, not a chance. This was a St Paul's operation, no doubt about that. At least one of the CCTV cameras was surely patched straight through to the Archivist, who right now was probably sitting in an enormous leather armchair stroking a fluffy white undergraduate. *Unless it was Quiff.*

"You're buying," I said to Geoff and walked to the bar. "Have you broken that machine, Eddie? I'll need a strong one. This is my boss, Geoff." I smirked as Eddie looked over. "He's all yours."

Eddie scanned Geoff up and down. "Should I go and order in all the pies?"

"I'll have an expresso," said Geoff.

"What was that, darling? An expresso? I think we might be all out of expressos. They went very very quickly." He laughed. "I could do you an espresso though. An *esss-presss-o.*"

"Whatever," said Geoff, not altogether feeling the humour. "And whatever ginge wants, and a gag for yourself."

"A gag?" Eddie stage-whispered to me behind a hand: "Forward, your boss, isn't he?"

I was beginning to enjoy this little adventure out of the office.

"Who's this fella?" Geoff asked me, indicating Quiff. "Is he here all the time?"

"*He* can speak, you know," said Quiff. "I don't believe I've had the, uh…?"

I smiled to Quiff. "I think he's asking you, do you come here often?"

Geoff stuck out a hand towards him. "The name's Geoff Burnett. I'm the editor of the *Bugle*."

Quiff shook daintily and then wiped his hand unconsciously on his purple chinos. He didn't give his name, I noticed, and I wasn't going to volunteer it.

"I've said before, I'm not talking about my operation again," he said. "Not with you, and not with any newspaper."

At that last word I heard a clatter behind me: Seb's coffee cup rattled in its saucer. I looked round, as did Geoff. Seb sat studying the shop opposite carefully as if nothing had happened. I began to see what might be going on here.

Geoff turned back to Quiff. "I'm not interested in your bleedin' operation, mate. Unless it went wrong. Did it go wrong?"

"They all say that, love, until they find out."

"Listen. I want to know what's going on." The words had the menace of something that usually comes just after "This is the police" and just before the door flies off its hinges.

"You'll have to enlighten me, dear." Quiff straightened his furry hat. "I gave up the crystal ball several years ago. There was no future in it."

"I'm talking about—"

"Espresso for sir," said Eddie, pushing a small cup Geoff's way. "Be careful, with your hands you're like the Incredible Hulk. Except, you know," that stage whisper again, "in retirement. And a black one for you, Conor dear, wasn't it? Fussy much?" He stroked his right eyebrow with a little finger.

Geoff was getting impatient. "When you queers have *finished* playing fucking mother."

"I think you'll find the fucking mothers are over that side

of the room, dear." He pointed to the gaggle with babies in the corner. "And enough of the queers, if you don't mind, or I'll have you barred from every pub in town." Said with a charming smile, as always.

"Enough," said Geoff, as if these people worked for him.

I swear the smile on my face was about a mile wide.

He continued: "This is about St Paul's, and that Flowers geezer."

Seb's coffee cup rattled again.

"Flowers geezer?" said Eddie. "You mean a florist? We do get a couple of florists in here. Strange boys. Two pansies short of an arrangement, you might say. I think it's the pollen. Right up the nose." He rubbed a finger across his nose and sniffed hard.

"Shut the fuck up, Doreen, or whatever your name is," said Geoff. "St Paul's College. Spencer Flowers. Illegal immigration. Tell me everything you know."

Seb's coffee cup rattled for a third time and he climbed down noisily from the stool. He called out "I— I must—" in a strong Chinese accent, pointing outside, and moved hurriedly towards the door.

This got Geoff's attention. "Hey! Wait!" he cried. "Do you know anything about St Paul's? Stop for a couple of seconds."

Seb attempted to hide his face: and Geoff was sold.

"Come back! Conor — after him."

Seb was outside and running. I followed, knowing that I mustn't catch him, at least not anywhere Geoff could see. Seb did the right thing, skidding off to the side at the end of the alley and up towards the market. Even on a Tuesday lunchtime it'd be full of stalls and full of people, easy to hide in. Before I lost sight of Humbug I checked back: Geoff was puffing along in pursuit. I could hardly call it *hot* pursuit. More like a hot pursuit you've forgotten about and only come back to five minutes later. The kind of pursuit that's not even hot enough to dunk a biscuit in.

Seb was way too fast for me, crashing along between a couple of bikes and a couple of baby buggies, looking like he'd taken a wrong turn in the Communist Party hundred metre sprint. Decent pair of legs on the guy. Not that I'd noticed before, mind. I saw him stop by the market and spin round and wave to make sure I could see him, and then dip into the stalls somewhere between the forty-nine varieties of soap and the Cambridge-branded tea towels that were almost identical to the Oxford-branded tea towels and the London-branded tea towels.

When I finally caught up with him he was standing by a pile of sculptures made out of scrap metal, testing a finger against a buffed edge.

"Fancy dress is it?" I panted, hands on knees. "Almost got a glimpse of ankle there. Careful, you might set me off."

"I found that quite invigorating," he said, not out of breath in the slightest, the git. "It should pique Burnett's interest, at least."

"What happens now? Do I wrestle you to the ground and accidentally kiss you?" I stood up straight and blew hard. "Jeez, I need the gym."

"Now you go back and tell him you lost me."

"Right. I should've guessed it'd be my fault."

Seb smiled. "I shall speak to you later."

He skipped off, zig-zagging between the rows of stalls and dodging tourists fanning out banknotes in funny colours in exchange for shapeless wooden items.

I walked back towards Geoff shaking my head. He'd barely reached half-way to the market. "Lost him in the stalls, boss," I said. "Great deals on seventies vinyl, though. Something tells me you're a man with a needle."

We returned to Humbug but Quiff had gone, spooked by Geoff, and Eddie was distraught that his most reliable income stream had suddenly dried up. If Quiff had any sense, I thought, he'd do his liver a favour and stay away for the rest of the week.

The Research

* * *

We returned to the office with Geoff firing on however many battered cylinders he still had remaining. "Developments, boys, developments. Round the table, please."

He recounted the tale of Eddie and Quiff and the enigmatic Chinese man. Mysteriously, it turned out that my memory was mistaken and in fact *we both* gave chase. We were apparently two New York cops crossing busy streets and hurdling cars, and avoiding old ladies with shopping baskets on wheels and tiny yapping dogs. Naturally it was still *ginge* who *lost the chinky*, as he so delicately put it.

"Right, Twiglet," said Geoff. "How's your Flowers piece? Anything juicier than you had this morning?"

Manish shook his head.

"OK. Spiked. We need to focus on hunting down this Chinese fella. Get on to that. Bound to be reports. Stood out like a bollock in a bikini, didn't he ginge?"

"You want me to investigate Chinese people in Cambridge?" Manish asked. "It's Cambridge! The place is full of tourists! Chinese people, Japanese people, Korean people. Every day there's a new tour."

"They don't run off when you mention St Paul's."

"I bet some of them do. I bet some of them run towards it, too."

"I don't care," said Geoff, showing Manish the hand. "Can't you get Faceplace or whatever it's called to list everyone in Cambridge? I thought it could do that sort of shit. Or some *app* or something? Knobsquare? If not, go out on the streets. Find him. He's key to this."

"What do you want me to do?" I asked. "After all, I know what he looks like. You want me to doorstep the college? He's bound to go in or out at some point."

I was thinking how I could pop by Spencer's and see what kind of a state he was in, and maybe have a relaxed couple of hours with the illegal immigrant and a plate of illegal digestives.

"Good idea, ginge. But not today, they'll be expecting that. He'll have warned them, assuming he can speak English. And the college toffs know what you look like, they'll be sniffing out for you."

So I got to lay out the classifieds, and Manish had the onerous task of spending the afternoon on Facebook and Twitter, and inventing increasingly outrageous search terms to throw at Google.

"Hey, Twiglet," I said quietly about an hour later when Geoff and Simon were nattering away about something. "Your Spencer story. Did you find out anything you haven't told the boss? Something I might, you know, need to worry about?"

"He likes gin," Manish replied, scrolling down another set of search results.

I grinned. "I know that much. He likes a *lot* of gin."

"There's not much out there about his life before Cambridge. I guess he went to a shit school, doesn't want to talk about it. It's all just research papers and men, pretty much. Not many friends outside college, hasn't spent long in the real world. I could possibly spin a piece about him getting his PhD by knobbing around, call it Cocktor Flowers or something, but that's about it. He's pretty clean. Dirty, but clean."

I nodded. It was about what I'd expected. A long row of notches on his bedpost, no long-term relationships, no secret wife, and no slaves locked in a basement — at least as far as anyone could tell. About as close to angelic as I'd been expecting.

The afternoon was deadly dull, the time passing slower than a caravan on a motorway. Laying out the classifieds was Geoff's equivalent of giving you lines. *I must not lose the bleedin' chinky fella, I must not lose the bleedin' chinky fella, For Sale, 04 Peugeot, good condition, crack in windscreen, one lady owner, Contact*

The Research

Saucy Susan for intimate massage, no pooves. Did these people not have the internet? Most of my brain was otherwise engaged watching Manish's screen.

I saw the tweet at the same time he did. In amongst a huge scrolling list of tweets that mentioned St Paul's — mostly all about the charity race, with a thousand different but identical photos of the four Beatles projected onto the college — was one that said: "Thoughts of Chairman Wang: Have saki? Will travel".

"Aha!" said Manish. "This looks promising."

The bio of the person who'd sent the tweet said he was an undergraduate at St Paul's. The face was unfamiliar, and its left half was mostly obscured by a great slice of black hair that acted like an eye patch.

We looked at the guy's other tweets. Mostly the usual student woes about early morning lectures — as early as ten o'clock! — and the exorbitant price of their subsidised beer. Oh, and would anyone like a ticket for the May Ball at a hundred and fifty? But over the last few days there'd been some grumbling about *our honoured guest* and the odd gag about his name.

"Do you have a Twitter account?" I asked. "I bet you do. I bet it's called Twiglet. Does it say you work for a newspaper?"

He did have a Twitter account. It wasn't called Twiglet though. We tweaked the bio to make it more student-like — subtract job, add essay crisis, change to profile photo with a pool cue in hand — and deleted a couple of tweets that made him look vaguely professional and grown up. I was sure it didn't matter that much, but at least I learned how much he hated Birmingham City football club, and that was my Christmas present to him sorted.

Trail covered, we sent a message to the one-eyed tweeter: "Whose Chairman Wang?" I was particularly pleased at the use of *whose* instead of *who's* — a touch of authentic student there, I thought. We hung around hitting refresh on the page waiting for a response, since we could tell he was online from the timestamps on the newest tweets. By the look of it he was currently having an angels-on-a-pinhead discussion with a beard at Trinity about the influence of Baroque madrigals on the works of Kylie Minogue, and by the time they'd written about four words in each tweet they'd run out of the 140 characters they were allowed. Despite my pushing, Twiglet refused to send them both a tweet telling them to get a room.

We finally received our reply after a couple of minutes of constant reloading. One-eye tweeted to Manish: "Annoying guy, passing through college lol x".

"Ask the guy's name," I said. "And add an x. I think you've pulled."

Manish tweeted: "That his name? Chairman Wang? x"

A reply came back straight away this time: "No lol it's Wang Ming. Nice cue! ;-) lol x"

"Yeah, Twiglet, you've pulled. Jeez, I've got to get myself one of those cues. Right, now ask what room he's in."

"Which one, the tweeter or this Wang Ming?"

"Why, are you interested in Captain Nerdseye there? Go for it. A whole new world'll open up for you. With all the lols he looks like he spends most of his time in fits of laughter anyway, which is what you're used to when you're naked."

"Sod off."

Manish tweeted back: "Where can I find Wang Ming? x ;-) lol"

"Jeez, don't overdo the emotishite, it's not sign language you're writing."

Another quick response: "Who are you?"

"He's stopped laughing and kissing," I said. "I think you're dumped already. And we're rumbled."

We didn't reply to that tweet. And shortly the other tweets blinked out as one-eye deleted them to cover his tracks. It didn't matter: we had the name we wanted, which was not coincidentally the name they wanted us to have. Dance for your puppetmasters, boys.

We took the name to Geoff, after first figuring out how we were going to explain Twitter to him without having to describe the entire genesis of the internet yet again, and also why I was in a double-act with Manish rather than helping Diana, 45, look for "companionship" in Chesterton High Street while her husband was "away". Being the sophisticated multi-cultural that he was, his first reaction to the name Wang Ming was to say it sounded like a Chinese takeaway, so I said that Geoff Burnett sounded like a racist arsehole, which I have to admit didn't go down *amazingly* well.

nineteen
The Deception

I found Seb in the cacophonous dining hall enjoying, if one could call it that, a college salad. He was becoming a rather familiar figure around the three courts these nervous days, hardly the anonymous donor of blessed memory. He wore his cunning disguise as Mr Wang, our honoured temporary guest, and the unsubtle fragrances he emitted, courtesy of a chemist in the purview of the Archivist, helped ensure him a satisfying exclusion zone. Although most of the college were aware of the situation we battled, they were not aware of the reality of Mr Wang, of the person beneath the disguise. The continuing reminder of his presence assisted greatly in realism.

The noise of the hall obscured our conversation from ears both present and absent.

"Mr Wang, how delightful," I said as I eased myself down opposite him on the old, much-buttocked long bench, scanning for splinters. I selected the least cloudy of a cowering clutch of glasses and poured myself some water. I was most certainly not eating.

More confidentially, I said: "I understand yesterday's excitement with the gentlemen of the press produced the desired effect."

"It did. They now have my name. And also, so I am told, the network tap is working very well indeed. They are discovering many exciting things about me." He seemed almost proud.

"All bad, I hope and expect," I said. I took a sip of water, hoping it had not been piped here directly from the Cam.

"It is an ingenious device, that tap. The ability to modify data *on the wire*, as Arthur put it, is proving extremely helpful. And it was an inspired choice of cover name. There was a real Wang Ming, you know, many years ago." He forked something limp and dripping into his uneager mouth.

"The Archivist is nothing if not thorough. I wonder," I waggled a finger in a circle in the direction of his mouth, "was that some variety of leaf?"

"I am not entirely sure." He chewed and cogitated. "It has a texture rather like potato. Any taste it once had has been bred quite successfully out of it. Would you like to try?"

"I shall pass, thank you. I prefer my food readily identifiable. I have a SPAIN meeting to attend shortly, hence the reason for my dropping in upon you, and I'd rather not have a college lunch escaping in its many varieties from either end."

Seb grimaced. "It will I suppose add depth to my character, assuming my character is not dead and buried. How may I help?"

"The race, Seb. More particularly and delicately, the buckets. I have moderate concerns I hope you shall allay. We have processed over a thousand registrations. Can you possibly lay your generous hands upon such a number of containers?"

"You have my word. I will bring in five thousand just in case. Where do they need to go? Do you think this used to be a tomato?"

I peered at the item his knife prodded tentatively, like a bomb-disposal robot at a discarded sports bag.

"Or a sweet pepper," I said. "Or possibly a kidney. The Master — Amanda, that is — was insisting that we distribute the buckets evenly between the rooms of volunteers, to avoid upsetting the serenity of college and its historic vistas. This morning I inquired nervously of Dennis whether he might overturn that ruling. He responded, and I quote, *feng shui Chatteris bollocks bollocks*, and said we could pile them up on New Court lawn around the fountain."

Seb grinned and nodded his approval, then resumed the hunt for any remaining food on his plate. "How is the dear old man doing? Enjoying the power?"

I considered carefully before answering: the unblinking eyes still gazed upon us, and Dennis could tune in if he desired and practise his lip reading. "I do believe it's taken fifteen years off his age," I said, smiling. "He dislikes the Admin dungeon, of course, and felt no more than a child perched behind Amanda's monstrous desk, so he performs his duties above ground where there are windows and life. It is, as it were, a quite literal breath of fresh air. I do strongly caution you not to eat that."

Seb glanced at me and I shook my head. He shrugged and unforked the item, designed to resemble a pickled onion and yet, I knew from gastroenteritic experience, lacking any of the features traditionally associated with such a food.

"What is it? Or was it?" he asked.

"I suspect strongly it was excreted by a genetically engineered alien-vegetable podule, steaming and shivering, in the darkest recesses of the kitchen where none dare roam unaccompanied. Though I might have seen a former celebrity being forced to gnaw upon it on a reality television show, after it had been recently liberated from an animal, possibly a marsupial. Either way, please consider it an onion for illustrative and decorative purposes only."

He laid his knife and fork on the plate in surrender. "At least I now understand how everyone at this college is so skinny."

"A popular theory is that the kitchen interprets *five a day* to mean pure chemical elements rather than fruit and vegetables. Today's special is, I think, shredded tantalum with a mercury sauce. We probably have a geiger counter somewhere if you have concerns."

"How big do these buckets need to be?" he asked.

I indicated a diameter and height using my hands. "A standard adult size. Of sufficient volume to satisfy a common or garden builder in his labours. We are not making sandcastles, for the avoidance of doubt. Imagine how much you will be vomiting later, and allow for that."

There were of course only three of us present at the SPAIN meeting: myself, Helen and Dennis. The oppression and latent volcanism of the previous meetings were thankfully absent, and the discussion was punctuated by laughter in a scandalous break from tradition. Dennis, in particular, impressed by remaining almost entirely awake.

The meeting felt rather decaffeinated, in point of fact. Unquestionably better for us and no less flavoured, although lacking a certain bite, a kick, to keep us on our toes. It would take a while to overcome the lady's absence. Occasionally there would be a memory, a bitter flashback, a toxic flood. I resolved to leave any and all biros in my bag until required.

The main order of business per the agenda that I allowed Helen to produce and circulate, and thus assuring my presence on her Christmas card list for the foreseeable, concerned the system for counting the donations we hoped would arrive by bucket post-race. Helen had procured two machines and enlisted via means undisclosed the assistance of a number of bank tellers who would be less overwhelmed than student volunteers by the presence of such a density of Her Majesties rendered unto metal and paper. She had also detailed a process — a production line, almost — for the handling of the buckets as they arrived at the finish. It fit precisely our requirements, and she flushed with success and our congratulation.

Then to what was the more nerve-wracking moment, and a moment of some significance for the event and for the college. We all sat properly upright, and Dennis notched up the sensor on his hearing aid.

It was time to select which two colleges of the university would become designated as the honorary St Ringo's and St George's.

The plan of record in my original proposal had stated a random selection from the available pool of thirty — St Paul's and St John's already being spoken for, of course, from the full pack of thirty-two.

Dennis, however, brought forward a last-minute amendment as I placed crinkled names into a porter's threadbare bowler upon an unfolded map of the city.

"Dear jeebus, not Girton, not Girton," he said. "Not Girton." An unexpected additional repetition suggested strong feelings indeed.

I sympathised. Girton College has many attractions, not one of which is its distance from the city centre — near four kilometres. There would be slim charity pickings along the bland old Roman road to The North, with spectators overwhelmed by the corpses pushed to the side as competitors expired to and fro. Girton is the Outer Hebrides of Cambridge. Beyond, desolation.

"In opposite vein, Dennis, perhaps we might also excise Christ's and Emmanuel," I said — both colleges immediately adjacent to St Paul's, one on each side.

"And by the same token, Trinity?" suggested Helen, tapping on the map, that college being the neighbour of St John's.

I sensed an outpouring of short-held doubts. "I agree. We should ensure a full-bodied quadrilateral rather than a beheaded triangle or worse, a thick line," I said, invoking various religious blessings upon the Ordnance Survey.

Motion carried without a formal vote or, helpfully, any record other than the Archivist's. I removed the offending four colleges from the bowler. As the senior in role, age and true age, Dennis was granted the honour of withdrawing the first name. Helen took the second.

I tossed a coin and said: "For first name: obverse Ringo, reverse George."

The coin came up Ringo. "Dennis?"

The Acting Master flattened his piece of paper on the table. "Murray Edwards. Murray Edwards? I'm sorry, my lad, I think you have a rogue, a rogue. I shall pick again."

I explained that Murray Edwards College was the new name of the college he knew as New Hall. All these news had passed him by.

"Even so. It is too far out." He waved a hand in objection. "Virtually Huntingdon."

I sighed. "By implication then, Dennis, we must rule out Fitzwilliam too, as that is farther."

He nodded.

"How about Churchill?" asked Helen. "Would that be too far?"

"Too far, too far."

"I think perhaps we might then have to exclude the similarly distant Lucy Cavendish and St Edmund's." She prodded at the map. These were not much closer than Murray Edwards. Dennis nodded vigorously. I was barely convinced he had heard of Lucy Cavendish.

This was turning into a decimation. Hundreds of students cast charitably adrift.

"How about, say, Robinson?" I asked.

"Robinson?" Dennis scoffed. "Acceptable distance, but the brick, my lad, the brick!"

Down at last came my foot. "Dennis, we cannot omit a college on the grounds of architectural disfavour. Where then is the randomness?" I tipped the bowler out upon the map and scattered the colleges amongst the colleges.

"The answer is trivial," said Dennis. "Each of us creates a list in priority order of colleges meeting our subjective criteria, and we work through the lists together, together, until we agree."

"Or perhaps, to assuage Spencer's concerns," said Helen, "we could select randomly from the intersection of the three lists? I'm sure I could convince my spreadsheet to assist. There are functions, I'm sure."

"We should though weight the randomness, my dear, by acceptability."

"Surely, though, Dennis, each of us might assign different levels of acceptability."

"We could weight those too."

"How would those weights be decided?"

"Perhaps by the tossing of a coin? A number of coins, as there are three of us, three of us. I forget how the mathematics expands. Should we call in Dursley? He supervises matters such as these."

"Would Dursley then have a vote?"

"On what? The selection of colleges? Or the assignment of weights? Or both, or both?"

"Perhaps the three of us could vote on that. Goodness, this is getting rather complex. I should be taking notes."

I had by now sunk in my seat until my eyes were level with the table, focusing upon the rough balls of paper strewn like boulders across the two-dimensional city. I resolved to continue my descent until I sobbed great tears of despair curled around Dennis's feet and recited the committee's lament in nineteen sections and forty-five subsections, as amended by voice vote of the Lamentation subcommittee and accepted by an appropriate quorum of the Appropriate Quorum subcommittee.

Before that depth was reached the room became quiet, save for the ticking of a bomb in my head. It was apparently my turn to wring the process's neck.

I sat back upright and dared not risk a sip of water lest I set the glass flying.

"Here is what we are going to do," I said, my jaw clamped, my eyes iron. "I shall brook no argument. All the colleges not yet declared unsuitable will return to the bowler. Dennis will pick one at random. Should any of us find it unacceptable, Dennis will pick again. When we have two acceptable colleges, I will become soundly and severely incapacitated by gin."

This was, I am glad to report, a solution on which we were all agreed.

The selection proceeded as follows. St Catharine's: rejected as "already a saint". Wolfson: rejected as "too far to the west". Hughes Hall: rejected as "too far to the east". Homerton: rejected as "practically London". Downing: accepted, as St Ringo's, to ironic cheers. Darwin: rejected as "inconsistent with the tenets of creationism as espoused by many of those who also believe in saints, and also too small, too small". Peterhouse: rejected "for an unspecified feud". Pembroke: rejected "for a specified feud". Corpus Christi: accepted, as St George's.

Thus, finally, our selection was done. Our fair calloused hands had chosen Downing to be our saintly drummer and Corpus Christi to be the other one, and the band was complete. As the *Corvus corone* flew, if you squinted sufficiently, the route inscribed a true rhombus about two kilometres around. When we plotted the most desirable pathways on the map, it was just under half a kilometre further: and passing through prime tourist trails with plenty of befuddled visitors to shake legs-up over the collection buckets.

I cracked a broad smile, closed the meeting, informed the police and Seb and the two successful colleges, dictated a press release leaving out all but the briefest detail, and returned to my room to spend half an hour tipping my gin down the sink.

* * *

The three empty gin bottles stared at me accusingly. They had barely settled into my college room, huddled like nesting penguins in a cold corner, and now they flocked with the recycling.

"It's only temporary," I reassured them, brushing lightly with a finger. "Consider it a vacation. A rest is as good as a change, and fine words don't butter the parson's nose, or thereabouts."

I allowed that to sink in for a moment. Quite where it was sinking, I was unsure.

It had been entirely on the spur that I had declined the seductive advances of the bottle. I had long been a loyal friend to both Dorothy and Gordon, each bringing orthogonal and occasionally simultaneous pleasures, and yet one — for the avoidance of doubt, the gin — emptied the wallet and furred the mind, and sometimes blew the fuse. This week, this week of all weeks, I needed wallet, mind and fuse intact. It was not to be a permanent shift to teetotality, of that I was convinced — except why then did I not simply place a towel over the bottles and send them budgerigarring to sleep?

A bus outside wheezed and beeped as it presented its rear to the terminus. It coughed and spat out a furball of children: by the mix of voices, tumbling over the cliff of pubescence. I hoped they knew how to swim. In all my years I had yet mastered only a few strokes.

I was roused from my morbid reverie by an unconfident knock at my door. I'd had no supervisions planned for that time and was expecting no crisis-ridden weeper for at least a further two weeks according to the timetable. I called for the gentleman to enter — I knew the gender from the softness of the knock.

It was Werner, one of our German undergraduates and unofficial deputy to Jonathan of *Cream of the Crop Top*. He said that Jonathan had been called away from a rehearsal by a messenger of the Archivist, and wondered if I knew why. I did not — this was one loop I was evidently excluded from. When

Werner told me the messenger had mentioned the name Burnett, I assured him I would investigate without delay.

We hurried under flat ivory skies across New and Bottom. I affected calm and confidence, primarily for Werner's reassurance but secondarily to give the Archivist fair warning that I was attending and unlikely to bring with me panic, or brimstone and fire and all manner of crazy paving. I left Werner fretting at the ground floor entrance with a smiling promise of future tea and macaroons, then entered and descended.

An elf waiting at the boundary of the outer sanctum showed me quickly through to the Hub, which buzzed above the warm hum of the disks. Since I had last visited yet another monitoring station had grown from the electricity and network ports peppering the floor. This was a tree trunk of half a dozen screens, with eight elf-leaf eyes seated around and the Archivist worshipping before it.

"May I ask—" I began as I stepped into the room.

An irritated wave from the Archivist silenced me, then summoned me.

I orientated myself with the locations surveilled by the screens. Three showed high fish-eye overviews of the three courts, distended diamonds with no pathways unobserved. One screen was dark, showing only unidentifiable, grey-black static blobs. One focused on St Andrew's Street by the front gate, and particularly on the spheroidal shape draped in an ill-fitting jacket I knew to be Geoff Burnett. The view on the final screen shook and bounced, another fish-eye lens, evidently embedded in clothing. I had little trouble gauging who the clothes were currently wrapped around.

The sound from this camera had been patched to the speakers. I could hear the ballsy percussion of heel on paving stone I knew to be Jonathan, in character as Cody. She muttered under her breath that she was turning onto St Andrew's Street — from Christ's Lane, which runs beside the college — and we saw, as the camera's aperture adjusted to the change in brightness, the steadily growing beachball of the editor occupying the pavement.

"He has been here for an hour," said the Archivist to me in a low voice. "He has not tried to enter college, nor even to look through the gate. But every person who passes through, in or out, student or otherwise, he attempts to engage."

"What does he say to them?" I asked.

The Archivist looked severely at me. "He says: 'Tell me about the Archivist.'"

"Has anyone—"

"Of course not!" he snapped in a hoarse whisper that grew louder. "Most people — *most* people — know better than to drop my name into casual conversation. *Oh, you should come and meet the Archivist, Editor, he'll give you an exclusive.*" His mocking sarcasm rang through the room, and the elves gripped their workstations more tightly.

I clenched and attempted: "What is Cody—"

"Enough questions, Dr Flowers. Watch."

Cody was approaching Burnett, heel frequency decreasing. From her embedded camera, Planet Burnett — a gas giant, I surmised — grew until his bulk filled the screen. He faced away from Starship Cody: we saw folds and rivulets in the jacket, like a satellite photo of a low-circulation desert.

The gate camera looking down on the scene showed Cody in her mighty, blonde, taxi-rattling pomp.

She coughed. "Roll on by, honey," she said, her voice as smooth and soft as her legs and her accent direct from Alabama's little-regarded county of Essex.

Geoff spun slowly around, orbital period uncertain. "You what love?"

"I said, roll on by. These heels don't walk in nobody's gutter. That's strike one." A finger in the air, then she flicked her long hair behind her shoulder.

The Deception

He looked down, of course, to her heels, then slowly up her endless legs, and skipping to a point — well, two points — in the vicinity of her plunging lime green neckline.

"Rihanna and Loretta," she said.

"Sorry darlin'?"

"Rihanna's on the right, Loretta's on the left. Cody's the one up here doing the talking, if you're lost on the journey. And you're *still* blocking my way, honey." On the other screen we saw her pose, hands on hips, weight on one leg, eyes of ice and thunder. Then she made a V with her fingers. "That's strike two. Three strikes and you feel my hand, you hear?" The fingers came together in slapping configuration.

"Where are you trying to get to, love?" he asked, briefly making eye contact.

"College. Supervision. I'm studying—" She looked him up and down. "—Geography. And something tells me you're pointing north."

The monitoring elves laughed, despite the tension in the room. The Archivist hushed them.

"St Paul's?" said Geoff. "You an undergrad?"

"Under graduate, under undergraduate, under lots of things, you know what I'm saying?"

"Tell me about the Archivist."

I held my breath.

Cody looked down and then quickly away to the left, to the white stone wall of the college. Her pose shrank a fraction: her arms loosened, her shoulders drooped almost imperceptibly. "The who now?"

"Have you spoken to him? Who is he?"

She hesitated, seemingly unsure what if anything to reveal, and shook her head in tiny-sassy movements.

The editor continued. "Let me take you for a coffee and we can talk about him."

The Archivist jumped in alarm. He gestured to a group of watching elves and told them to make ready to scramble.

"I shouldn't talk to strange men, you know honey," said Cody, fluttering innocent eyelashes and lowering her voice.

"I'm not strange," said Geoff slowly. "I work for a newspaper. And I can write you a cheque, love, here and now, if you tell us about this Archivist fella."

Cody was silent again, weighing up the offer.

"How... big is it?" she asked finally.

We saw Geoff's round eyes widen as she swam closer to the bait. "Let's discuss that over coffee. I know a—"

"No," Cody interrupted. "I don't like to drink in cafés. Loretta and Rihanna, they get too much of the attention, know what I'm saying?"

"A bar then?"

"What's your name, roly-poly newspaper man?"

"Burnett. Geoff Burnett. I'm the editor of the *Bugle*."

He rose to his full height and attempted to suck in his chest by twenty years or so.

"Cafés, bars, all the same, Geoff Burnett. I have coffee in my room, and I'm always on the boil. Would the boogie-woogie *Bugle* boy like to come on over for a little... revision?"

She flashed him a flirting smile: head minutely down, the barest tip of her tongue.

"I can't—" His voice cracked and he coughed. "I can't go into college, love. They wouldn't let me through the gate."

She turned on her heels and looked back teasingly towards him.

"Follow me," she said. "You'll have to squeeze yourself in the back way, honey."

We watched him waddle after her, a sheen of damp already upon his forehead. The rear entrance to St Paul's was dedicated to deliveries and maintenance, and not for daily use by the student population. Vehicles approached cautiously through the jungle of the bus terminal and waved the appropriate device or signal to cause the wide gate to unlock and swing open and beckon them through. The gate led to a small unloading bay cut into the north-easternmost corner of New Court, where it merged with Top as seamlessly as Arthur's poor hairpiece.

The glamorous Cody and her heels, pursued by Geoff, took the Christ's Lane path around to the back gate. The Archivist and his elves switched cameras to view their progress. Cody always kept two or three lengthy paces ahead of the editor, glancing back to chivvy him along like a recalcitrant child.

I learned that the back gate had been configured to accept what must have been a recently manufactured college ID card in the name of Cody. The rough oak gates were the nineteenth century originals, still flecked with dull remnants of the grey and pink college colours that once adorned them splendidly. A smaller human-sized doorway was embedded within them: we saw Cody press her ID card against the reader fixed there. A light flashed, and the door clicked unlocked.

She pushed through, and Geoff forced himself through the narrow doorway after her. We saw a brief infrared shot cutting through the darkness of the loading bay: curious and unfamiliar greys, with shining cat-eyes. Then we followed them on the New Court overview screen along the rectangular path surrounding the lawn and across to — not Jonathan's room, I was sure.

The Archivist had anticipated my question. "We have configured an unused room on Q Staircase. Arthur is quite the dab hand at boy band posters, you know. Very *a la mode*."

A question formed but melted away as I watched the screens. The cameras jerked in all directions keeping them in vision into Q, up one flight of stairs, along a listing corridor — all corridors along that side of New were distinctly off the level — to room five. All the while, Geoff remained a pace or two behind Cody, a fat shadow on her tail.

Cody's ID card unlocked the door. The screen on the monitoring station that had heretofore remained dark glowed a brilliant white as she flicked on the lights, then faded to resolve the duller colours of the room.

A new microphone was mixed up. The voices sounded thinner, more metallic.

"Make yourself at home, *Bugle* boy," said Cody, still with the sultry faux-American tones. "Excuse my laundry, won't you. I believe you'll find the little wooden chair is made for a more delicate frame than yours, and the springs on the armchair tend to… dig in to unsightly places. The bed, however, is just right."

She tousled a strand of blonde and teased the end into her mouth. "Goldilocks right."

Geoff rested his weight on the side of the single bed, which rather groaned in panic. From our camera, tucked discreetly into the corner above a drab college wardrobe, we saw him scan the room with his dodgy journalist eyes: desk, chair, wardrobe, kettle, mess. Standard-issue untidiness. Multi-coloured posters of the year's manufactured closet-case musical grouping stuck to the wall alongside a well-tended and mildly pornographic calendar, all dutifully breaking college rules of some kind or another. Low scattered piles of books, spines intact. A teddy bear, missing an eye, on a single pink pillow.

"Nice place you got here, love," said Geoff.

Cody fussed around with the coffee.

Part of my brain prodded an awareness into me. "Archivist," I said quietly, "If Burnett had been doorstepping college for just an hour, how has all this—"

"It is my job to prepare. I do my job very well. Cody's photo was in the forged intranet seen by the newspaper. Her ID card was prepared. The room was prepared. We anticipated these tactics."

This silenced me for a second. "What else have you—"

"Pay attention."

Cody's coffee was instant. She joined Geoff on the bed, sitting along the end, across a corner from him — within groping distance but with sufficient time to dodge should he pounce.

"How's your coffee, Mr Burnett?" she asked.

"Piss-awful, love, but I ain't complaining. I haven't been in a student room like this for bleedin' years."

"Is it just how you remember, honey? Knickers and boy bands?" She giggled.

"Fuck off. I didn't have no bleedin' teddy, neither."

"If he bothers you, *Bugle* boy, I'll have him face the wall. He only has—" A glance at Geoff. "—one good eye."

"How did he lose the other one?"

Cody put her coffee mug on the floor. "First night of term. All the girls in here, a little whiskey, a little frisky, and it just—popped out. I think he saw a little more than he bargained for." She licked her lips. "You know what I'm saying?"

"The girls?"

"The girls. And the boys. I ain't so fussy. I like... all shapes and sizes. What do *you* like, baby?"

Geoff's adam's apple quivered. "The wife..."

Cody inched toward him, her voice lowering. "The wife is for life. But Christmas is coming. And Cody, here, well, she wraps a present *real* good."

"I don't think—"

"You don't like me, baby?" She shrank back. "Am I too... inexperienced for you?"

"I like you, I like you. I just—"

"Then what's the problem?" She gave him a look. "Nobody will know," she whispered to him, to me, to the Archivist, to a room of rapt elves, and to a frantically spinning disk. "Nobody will find out."

Geoff's eyes darted left and right, his brain evidently

overloading.

I began to worry: was Cody prepared to persist with this approach? Was there not a chance—

"Archivist," I said. "You must reveal the plan to me. This is a tactic not without risk."

"I know what I am doing," he said evenly.

"In the next room, you have a team?"

The Archivist merely indicated the screen, and smiled.

Geoff had begun, slowly and uncertainly, to lean towards Cody.

She licked her lips. "Yeah, baby," she said.

His lips puckered and quivered as he approached her. A hand began a hesitant journey toward her leg. His bulk rotated upon the duvet to present his front oval to her.

She brought a soft finger quickly to his lips: "Dance for me, honey."

"What? I— Fuck that." He pulled back.

"Dance. I like to see your moves before I see your moves, know what I'm saying?"

"I don't dance, love. I haven't danced in fifteen fuckin' years." This was a softer voice, a gentler Geoff, with a chuckling finish. He was remembering those earlier days. His face smoothed for a moment, its lines fading.

"You like to dance, *Bugle* boy?"

"Used to. Made a great Prince Charming in my day. A right dandy bleedin' highwayman. *Adam and the Ants*, ever heard of 'em? Ancient history to you, I bet."

"Show me, honey. Show me. I like to see history comin' alive."

He laughed and shook his head slowly. "I couldn't."

"Do it," she said, almost a whisper, a hand on his arm. "Do it for me?"

The Hub crackled with electric tension. We had all unconsciously leaned a few degrees toward the screen as their conversation became more personal, more intimate. We willed him to his feet. Thieves might have been making off with the college silverware, nobody paid the slightest attention to any of the other screens.

"There were these moves," said Geoff. "You make a cross with the arms. Even had Diana bleedin' Dors in the video." Still on the bed, he balled his fists and raised his arms into an X shape level with his head.

"How did the song go, baby?"

He cleared his throat and began an embarrassed mumble: "Prince Char*ming*," emphasis on the *ming*, "Prince Char*ming*, ridicule is nothing to be scared of. Something like that, weren't it."

"Sing it, baby. Dance it. For me." Her voice was even lower, barely detectable by the microphones.

Hesitantly, Geoff rose to his feet and turned to face her. An elf quickly switched cameras so we could see his face. He shook his arms as if loosening up, and a small smirk came on his face, as if he couldn't quite believe what he was about to do. Neither could we.

"It was... here we go, like this," he said. And then quietly but clearly, a warble: "Prince Char*ming*," he sang, one arm raised above his head almost in salute. "Prince Char*ming*." The other arm joined with the first to form an X. "Ridicule is nothing to be scared of." Both arms down, and now into a strutting pose.

I gave the Archivist a confused smile. Is this what we had been waiting for? His eyes did not waver from the screens.

Cody was laughing and clapping, excited feminine claps with hands close to her chest as in prayer. "Another!" she said.

He obliged, at first reluctantly and then less so. For the subsequent five minutes he introduced us to excerpts from a medley of what I remembered as eighties hits, gaining in confidence and becoming more vocal and more outlandish in his dance moves. Cody responded with ever greater enthusiasm. She flicked back her hair repeatedly in non-verbal encouragement. Her body language communicated precisely what we knew he wanted.

Finally he returned to the bed, in anticipation of his reward. He breathed out heavily. "I'm all warmed up now," he said. "Was that good, love?"

"Delicious, honey," Cody replied. "One more, for me?"

"No more."

"Strip for me, honey. Dance off your clothes and shake your booty for me."

"I'm not a bleedin' stripper. Your go now. Come here, give us a kiss."

"Strippin' before kissin' in my house, baby. Show me the goods or my lips are sealed, know what I'm saying?"

"Enough," he said, and his mood darkened, and my heart skipped a beat. "Give us a kiss and stop all this American shit."

Cody hesitated. I thought I saw her mask begin to slip. "No kissing, honey. Time for you to go."

"You've had me dancing like a prick and I get nothing?"

"You've had my coffee and my company, and I don't like your tone, so you can please now leave." Her voice was firm but I detected a hint of fear. I became unsettled. The Archivist, though, watched on impassively, eyes narrowed.

"I'm worried," I said. The Archivist ignored me.

Geoff spoke again, more angrily. "One kiss. Fucking students, pissing you around. I'll have this college, bitch."

Cody stood and pointed to the door, still in character. "Leave now."

Geoff got off the bed and moved towards her: short, slow steps. "I'll take this college down. You think this is a fucking game, don't you. *Dance for me.* I've been dealing with fuckers like you for twenty years, and believe me—"

The Deception

I grabbed the Archivist's arm: "Do something!"

"—Believe me, I know what I'm doing."

Cody backed away from him. "I'm not afraid of you," she said, her character unravelling, her voice deepening.

That was enough. I bolted, almost slipping on the dark tiles of the Hub. I ran out into the anteroom, through the secure door into the corridor and out to the stairwell, and rushed up to the ground floor and the threatening grey outside. Straight across the lawn and through the arch to New Court, students pressing against the stone at my shout to allow me by, then sprinting along the path to Q Staircase. I hustled past the few people milling outside. Crashing through the doors and up the steps and along to room five, in less than a minute, I was banging on Cody's door, shouting her name. I didn't wait. I threw myself at it violently, once, twice. On the third hit it splintered open and I clattered through, red and puffing and dander well up.

Geoff was on the bed, face smushed into the pillow, with an arm wrenched high behind his back. Cody kneeled upon him. Her wig was half askew and authentic Jonathan peeked out from underneath.

He saw me and grinned, somewhat flushed. "Strike three," he said.

twenty
The Fallout

Knowledge is power. With great power comes great responsibility, or so said a man in spandex climbing up a wall a decent few years ago, and my great responsibility was to avoid revealing to Geoff — when he arrived late and subdued to the office on Thursday morning with his wrist wrapped in bandages — that I'd been told *all about* what had happened at the college and had, literally, rolled on the floor laughing. Were it possible to laugh your arse off, I'd have done that too.

I'd woken up specially early to prepare a page of wrist-sprain jokes. It was going to be one of those unforgettable days, like your first kiss, or your last kiss, or the time the posh girl at school farted during class and for some reason it was the funniest thing *ever*.

I'd struggled not to let Manish in on the secret — we'd have both been giggling in the corner like a couple of old maids. And Simon was either pulling the straightest of faces — although he was hardly a smiler at the best of times — or he was just as in the dark as I wasn't.

The previous afternoon, Geoff had never come back to work after his "stakeout", as he'd called it. According to Spencer he'd barely recovered from the shock of being beaten up by a beautiful, petite boy in a mini-skirt and a wig when he realised that the only way Spencer could have known what was going on and crashed his way in to save Cody's honour was if the pair of them were being watched. Jeez, I'd have paid money to see the fat man rolling around begging. *My wife'll kill me* and *I wasn't going to hurt her-him-her* and *I'll drop the story* and everything. And all *that* would've been on camera too.

Of course, he now knew *for sure* there was an Archivist, but — like everyone else who knows *for sure* — he thought it was a subject best left well alone.

Oh, those college toffs and their funny ways. Plenty of arseholes, sure, and plenty of bollocks too.

The morning meeting around Geoff's desk couldn't come quickly enough, which is not a sentence I found myself thinking often. I couldn't wait to find out how he'd try to spin this one. I bet Spencer and the Archivist and their mates were crowding round a screen thinking the same thing.

"Right," he said after we'd wheeled ourselves over and settled down with a biscuit. "What else have we got?"

"What else?" asked Simon. "How do you mean?"

"I'm spiking the St Paul's stuff. It doesn't hold up." He made a chopping motion in the air with the wrong hand, and winced.

"Have you hurt your wrist there boss?" I said.

"What do you mean, it doesn't hold up?" said Simon. "What doesn't hold up?"

"I didn't get nowhere with the… with the stakeout, did I. Waste of time. Can't afford to spend any more on it, we've got a paper to get out. It's dead. No more questions. What else have we got?"

"What about the immigration story?" asked Manish. "I've got—"

"Fuck the immigration story. It's all dead, I'm telling you."

"Jeez, that wrist must really be hurting you," I said. "Have you been trying the press-ups again?"

"But I found something new yesterday afternoon," said Manish. "You never came back, I could have told you about it."

I kept going. "Or have you perhaps been sitting on your hand to make it feel like someone else? Not something a man in your condition ought to be doing."

"I don't give a shit about new evidence." Geoff waved dismissively at Manish and the wrist complained again, making him growl. "Shit, shit."

"Wait a minute. This is a big story," said Simon. "And we haven't got anything else. You've spiked the Flowers story, you've spiked the race story. Have you been got at?"

I held my breath.

"Of course I haven't been bleedin' got at, you pillock." He raised his voice at Simon: not common at all. "If we can't make the stories stick, we can't print 'em. Christ."

You've changed your tune all of a sudden, I thought. Twenty years late for Seb and his family.

"Simon," I said, unable to resist, "you think maybe they've been… twisting his arm?"

"Gawd knows," he replied. "But if we can't print the immigration story we're going to have to make something up."

"Hey, I've got a great idea," I said. "We could do an exposé on criminal injury compensation. 'We interviewed Mr G. Burnett, fifty-five, who'd sprained his wrist in an unexplained and mysterious accident and tried to claim—'"

"Yeah, alright, leave it out," said Simon. "We've heard that joke now, change the record. Twiglet, what did you find out?"

"Psych," said Geoff, "Forget it, I'm telling you. It's spiked. Rehash a punt wars story. Churn some PR. Plenty of easy pickings out there."

Simon gave him a long hard look, then turned to Manish. "Twiglet?"

I sensed a disturbance in the force. A static charge building between the two men, balloon-Geoff rubbing up against wall-Simon. All I could hear was the beating of my own heart.

Manish hesitated, then did as he was told. He spoke to both men, eyes flicking evenly between them. "I've been hunting for that name, Wang Ming. It's a pretty common name, I think, Wang — that's the surname. I got a bit sidetracked with someone high up in the Communist Party, but it turns out he died years ago, so it's either not him or a much bigger story. But then I found this."

He slipped a sheet of paper from his notebook and passed it across the desk into a space almost exactly half-way between Geoff and Simon. Nicely done, I thought. It lay there untouched, both men leaning over and staring at it, avoiding each other's gaze. If they got close enough I thought a spark might flash between them.

Manish continued. "There's an intelligence officer with that name — or there was, it's unclear — in the Chinese Ministry of State Security. The secret police. That's the only known photo."

The paper the editor and his deputy were looking at showed a blurred, almost smeared photo that was *obviously* Seb. And Manish had met Seb. I caught his eyes, and he caught mine in return: he knew, and he knew I knew he knew.

"Is that the fella you saw?" Simon asked Geoff and me.

Geoff nodded, saying nothing.

I said, "I mostly only saw him from the rear, vanishing over the horizon. If you had an arse shot I could have given you a definite. But, yeah, I think so."

"Is he known to be in this country?" asked Simon.

"Everybody's denying all knowledge of the guy," said Manish, which I'm sure was true as he didn't actually exist. "But that picture came from a reliable source."

"Which source?"

Dr Spencer Flowers and friends, St Paul's College, Cambridge.

"A reliable one," he repeated.

There was a moment of silence, during which I tried

desperately not to do the smug face or the smug dance. I couldn't say anything: they had to shovel themselves down into this hole all by themselves.

"We have to print it," said Simon. "It's either a defection, or the college is importing spies on student visas. Either way, it's a story. We have to. Spies, Cambridge, queers — not like it's unheard of. Maybe — maybe — all that from the fifties never stopped. Maybe this is the biggest story of our careers."

Simon's eyes started to fill with dollar signs. I bet he was thinking of Watergate, of movie adaptations, of the pair of them played by Brad Pitt and Danny DeVito. More like Laurel and Hardy, long into retirement.

Geoff sat for a fair while, spinning back and forth in his chair, blinking rapidly and rubbing his bad wrist. His thoughts were plain as day to me: head down, or head up? Be intimidated out of printing and save his own arse, or print and hope the story and the college explodes before it brings him down? I knew, somewhere deep inside the Churchillian rolls of flesh that jellied before me, there was a spark that couldn't be stamped out. The cold, mechanical, beating heart of the journalist. The desire for, if not the truth, then the story.

"I'm too old for this shit," he said. "Fuck it. Print it."

I breathed out in relief as quietly as I could. I imagined a room full of people in St Paul's jumping about six feet in the air.

A few hours later came the weedy shout across the office from Simon that I had been expecting. "Twiglet, you done with that story? Send it across and I'll give it the once-over."

That was code for: "I'm about to make a few trivial changes and rewrite the intro and put my name at the top." And for once, Manish couldn't wait to be rid of it. He polished a few pars and topped it with some rubbish for Simon to replace and then washed his hands of the whole thing.

"I've got a headline for you," he said, almost as an afterthought. "*The Spy Who Bummed Me*. Can we use that?"

"No," Simon replied. "What else have you got?"

"*The Porn Identity*."

"No."

"*Con-spy-racy*. You know, like conspiracy but with spy in red. And you get *con* and *racy* for free."

"Hmm." That was about as close to a *Yes* as we were going to get.

The headline worked for me. A decent trigger word to draw in the punters with a nice scary commie red. All it needed was a shitty pun and we were sorted.

"Oh, and a subhead: *Student? St Paul the other one.*"

That got a groan from Geoff, which made it a dead cert. Either that or he'd tried to flex his wrist again.

We wrapped up the rest of the paper in a flurry of activity, having devoted far too much time to spiked stories.

Curiously, all of the photos in that edition seemed to magically take up twice as much space as in a typical issue, and all the headlines and subheads grew a couple of points. We all became beard-scratchers about the importance of white space — especially in stories without enough copy.

There was one sad accident. The never-popular, award-losing *Cat of the Week* feature somehow managed to double its allocation of mangy old pussies as several dozen unfortunate slips of the mouse and the keyboard caused a bunch of cats from several weeks ago to find themselves stars for a second time. We knew there'd be letters about that, because the people who write letters are generally the people who write letters about that.

I managed to squeeze a full page out of the week's ancient photo of Cambridge, a very popular space-filler, on the grounds that it included two boatered toffs leaning up against the St Paul's college front gate paying absolutely and suspiciously no attention to a passer-by in a huge hooped dress and a flowery hat. Manish dared me to Photoshop in a small Chinese boy. It wouldn't have been the first time. I didn't, though: the letters, again.

The time went in a flash, buzzing and darting and fussing with an energy I hadn't experienced before at the *Bugle*.

Simon did almost all of the last-minute editing of the paper. Normally he and Geoff would share it, swearing back and forth at each other. This time Geoff sat back a little, nursing his injury and perhaps placing some plausibly deniable distance from his old friend should St Paul's happen to inquire as to *what the hell*.

And then it was finished, and sent to print, and Manish and I gave each other the what-have-we-done face.

And Simon gathered us round, having apparently promoted himself. He said Manish and I had performed pretty decently under trying circumstances in the last week, and was sorry the other pieces lacerating St Paul's had been sent to story heaven, the great holy spike where all shall be subbed and found to have ended a sentence with a preposition or some other toss nobody gives a shit about. About which nobody gives a shit. Whatever.

And then he fired us.

Gross misconduct, he said, as Geoff looked on with arms crossed and face ambiguous. Unethical behaviour, his finger wagged. Use of newspaper facilities for personal research with a view to freelance activities incompatible with our contracts. Section blah, subsection bollocks, paragraph shite (b), and about forty-nine other breached clauses. He showed us a printout of the GH Instruments searches we'd both done: all dutifully logged by the firewall, he said. None of it wiped by the Archivist's little helpers, he didn't say. Obviously a conspiracy between us, or a con-spy-racy, he said, complimenting Manish on the choice of headline.

Under the circumstances, he told us with a thin smile, we would not be held to our notice periods and would instead be clearing our desks there and then. He would graciously donate a couple of bin bags. If we wanted to argue, he said, he would happily call security and we could be escorted out by their big dogs with freshly painted holes in our arses.

I took it on the chin. Manish took it somewhere in the stomach, by the look of him. But we both knew that as soon as the paper hit the streets the next day and the full truth emerged then we'd have been ejected into the gutter in any case, along with the two of them. If anything, we were hauling our arses out of Dodge before whatever people got themselves out of Dodge for happened. I admit it did feel a little like jumping out of a diving, pinwheeling plane without a parachute, though.

I thought about unleashing a volley of insults as I left the office for the final time. The truth is, I'd used them all up already. There was nothing left to say. As the door closed behind me I simply called out: "Good luck."

twenty-one
The Speech

Two front-page stories about St Paul's in two weeks: college profile duly risen, and Amanda's challenge accepted and gloriously, soundly defeated. In a certain fashion. Two piddling trifles desired a slight finesse, that was all: an authoritative refutation of the spy allegations that would be sufficiently nutcracking to close the newspaper and deliver large doses of ignominy to Burnett and Wantage, and the logistics of a couple of thousand runners with charity buckets.

I learned the critical management technique of delegating in several directions simultaneously.

I stayed dry.

In the fragrant suburbs of the Admin dungeon the college switchboard sizzled and sparked with outrage, poutrage, uninformed media, and lawyers on the tout. The delicate administration staff, bless their dedicated college socks, overheated in short shifts and recited mantras to all callers from a script prepared by the Archivist: flat denials, *sans* detail; a universal unavailability for media of all denominations; and a reminder of great business regarding the *Band on the Run* event at which they would of course be treasured guests, along with their wallets.

It was the day before the race. The day before all would be resolved, one way or another. The part of me desiring to pack

The Speech

up and run had been boxed into a corner by the endless *things* that overflowed my mind. I was reduced to a liaison machine: the vertical kind, for the avoidance of doubt. And gradually the jigsaw formed.

I might still fail, crushed beneath a purple thumb or a media stampede or both. I might yet succumb to the fast-acting poisons of the college lasagne. *Unus maltorum*: *one of many*, nothing special. I would still try.

New Court began to echo with the crump and pop of nested buckets on grass. They arrived by lorry, by back gate and by chain gang, groups of eager student volunteers sacrificing their Friday afternoon naps for a trace of physical exercise. The multiple snakes of bucket-conveyors rippled along the gossip and news in the traditional fashion: that is to say, with mutations toward the vulgar. I encouraged instead a rousing work song, which transmuted rapidly into an impromptu performance of *HMS Pinafore*. I had not seen such a buzz around the college since the last Gaga.

Dennis came to inspect progress in a brief respite from tongue-lashings by harassed University officials unhappy with the day's headlines. The poor man was not used to such limelight either within or without college, as his face rather demonstrated: caffeinated eyes with arctic eyebrows, and a smile pasted from *Hello* magazine. He exchanged uplifting words with one or two of the students, selecting the more olive-skinned, I noted. It was like a minor royal working a parade of ball boys at Wimbledon.

"What a spectacle, my lad, what a spectacle," he said finally, approaching me on the lawn beside the fountain. We watched a while as the boys cheerfully sailed the ocean blue, crying *Ahoy, Ahoy* as the buckets passed along the rows.

Dennis continued: "Man and bucket in perfect harmony. Is Mr Greatsholme here to see his doings?"

I shook my head. "He is in deep hiding, by order of the

Archivist. An inadvertent sighting today would be, as it were, maximally unhelpful."

"Shame, shame. It is rare that one is emotionally moved by buckets. And yet…"

"It is the scale, Dennis." I swept my hand across the court. "A king inspires an army and the army, in turn, inspires the king."

"Is that me, is it? King of all the buckets?" he said, with a wired chuckle.

"*Acting* king of all the buckets."

He knew I meant it kindly and applauded me lightly on the shoulder. "Or perhaps, more fitting, Acting Ruler of the Queen's Navy. Regardless, this temporary monarch has an appointment on his temporary throne, so I shall leave you and the army and navy to your duties."

He left me and picked his way through a writhing snake of buckets. "Keep it up, lads, keep it up," he called out. Then he spun back to me and wagged a finger. "And Dr Flowers: don't forget your speech."

I had forgotten my speech.

Race day at last, the day of reckoning.

The final few hours before the event passed in a smear. I danced on a lit hob from place to place, verifying and validating and vomiting.

Amanda remained caged. Seb remained hidden. Conor and his colleague Manish lay low somewhere thereabouts. Dennis rested, after yesterday's exertions, until he was ceremonially required. The counting machines and tellers were primed. The Archivist watched.

All other available hands pitched in with Helen to register arriving competitors and assign numbers and buckets, via a scenic queue through college ("Keep off the Grass. We accept donations via PayPal"). My attempts to enlist Claire in Helen's

The Speech

team had produced the perfect excuse: she was a competitor herself. Her husband Ken's spirit was willing but his flesh was Greek, attending a mop symposium in Athens.

Also taking part, I was rather moved to learn, was Seb's sister Pamela: another of the family here to seek closure for the terrible deeds enacted in the name of fish paper and in the hunt for profit. I hoped to meet her. The events of her youth, her dice with death, were still undoubtedly raw despite the passing of the years.

Another turn of the screw of pressure, then. A fresh injection of laxative.

A long wooden dais had been raised beside the closed road by the college front gate, at the race's start line, and draped in college colours. Barriers had been erected in strategic positions along the course to ensure passage. High-visibility jobsworths were posted where required.

The race would begin at noon, by the *Yankee Doodle* chime of the college clock. It was a fine day for autumn: bursts of sunshine under hasty clouds, with a danger of light showers much later. An overnight drizzle had brought a fresh, earthy smell to the fore.

Multi-coloured competitors swarmed along St Andrew's Street toward Emmanuel College, teasing muscles into warmth. It was not, of course, a timed race, though the generally accepted belief was that you must avoid wallet fatigue and keep at least in distant view of the leading positions. Others felt a slower pace and an elaborate costume might better tempt the givers. The race might ultimately be won by tortoise or hare.

As the ceremonies approached, an elastic barrier decorated in — of course — short stripes of pink and grey was drawn across the road. The limbering runners made final preparations, practising bucket-rattling and affixing numbers and home-made charity identifiers. It was a column of babble, of shared tactics and jokes, of groans and shrieks and wishes of good luck from families waving and chivvying from the sidelines. The excitement rose. Various deodorants and aftershaves and perfumes mingled in my nostrils like an evacuated chemistry lab.

The projector in the management office high opposite once again shone the *Band on the Run* image onto the college façade, visible only dimly in the sunlight. It was almost a subconscious reminder, as with the Archivist's cameras above the gate and elsewhere, and the knowledge that Amanda was secreted behind glass somewhere above us.

I climbed the dais with Dennis and representatives from the three other participating colleges, and of course the city council, always on the sniff for a snatch of publicity. To my left, the writhing mass of participants. Ahead by the Grand Arcade gateway a phalanx of cameras and press, with the scandal bringing the national TV news scurrying to our doorstep. To my right, an empty road toward Christ's and beyond, lined along both sides two or three deep with locals and tourists and cash.

Five minutes until the race, and I discovered myself standing before an open microphone, all faces toward me, gripping tightly onto my hastily written speech and onto my bowels. I wore a smile like a choppy sea.

Before I had uttered a word, the cry "Where's the spy, Spencer?" came from the press box and I very nearly Shatnered myself. I recognised the caller: it was Wantage from the *Bugle*, there alongside his editor. Another cry came, a similar retort, then a third. I raised my hand, and there was a tense silence. I cleared my throat, thankfully not into the microphone.

"Acting Master, distinguished guests, fellow Paulines," I began and was momentarily disoriented by my own echo, a foreign voice mocking my words. "My Lords, as we have one or two, Ladies, fewer, and gentlemen. I stand here upon this dais, beside this fine college, before you all, beneath some fashion of a cloud. I hazard to identify it meteorologically as a *Bugulonimbus*." There was scattered laughter.

The Speech

"It has precipitated somewhat, and moistened us with its onion tears of outrage. We stand dampened and dripping with disreputable allegations, denied mendaciously the opportunity and chance to inflate the umbrella of truth, or to don the wax jacket of justice.

"And yet, ladies and gentlemen, today brings sunshine." As if on cue a cloud drew back, and I heard a single cheer. "Sunshine dries the ground, and with the furnace of our internal fire dries the skin. Sunshine brings light to the dark and gloomy niches, where lies do plot and huddle and conspire. Sunshine, ladies and gentlemen, brings the glory of truth.

"I admit freely to you, at this time, at this place, that none of us, neither student nor staff, within the Holy and Glorious College of St Paul, pretends perfection. I have glanced at the low-slung trouser of temptation. I have taken succour from the intimate company of gin. Who here can claim otherwise? Vodka drinkers, perhaps, but let us speak no more of them.

"Let us not forget that this college, too, is sainted but not saintly. Our founder James Drybutter: vilified, ostracised. And yet we persist. We have seen bad times before, and yet we persist. We have nothing if not stamina, ladies and gentlemen.

"History shall favour our words, my friends. You shall see. Enough of that for now.

"To the race. St Paul's, St John's, St George's in the guise of Corpus Christi, St Ringo in the guise of Downing, and back to this line. Let me here now thank those three other colleges, in fact all four, for their assistance and encouragement." Generous applause.

"Ladies and gentlemen, remember that the race is how *much*, not how *fast*. Stamina, you see? But please also remember that you must return here with your buckets by three o'clock or the police will be banging upon our door with truncheons raised. We have seen this before, too.

"I should also like to extend gracious thanks to our sponsor, who I know stands anonymously somewhere amongst us. He gave generously so that *you* might give generously, and so that goodness in all its pleasant and many forms shall ultimately vanquish a suitably large subset of ills.

"And finally I thank you, our competitors, for your efforts this afternoon. I wish you all great luck. Please do your best to fill both your buckets and your boots. Do not forget there is an award and great honour for the one amongst you who collects the greatest amount, which shall be presented here upon this dais once the counting is concluded.

"And now may I introduce our dear Acting Master, Professor Dennis Sauvage, to, as it were, get you off."

I receded from the microphone with vigour and to kind and loud applause. The press box remained silent, knowing it had a further opportunity to ask questions after the race, where I was unlikely to be allowed to exercise my rhetoric in quite so unrestrained a fashion.

Dennis shook my hand warmly before he took his amplified turn. The minute hand teetered on the cusp. "Thank you, Spencer. Fine words, fine words, from a fine fellow, a fine fellow. I apologise for my internal echo, do not adjust your sets, your sets."

I heard a rattle behind and above, as a window began to be opened.

Dennis continued: "The chimes begin any moment. The old *Yank*, as we call it. I once knew an old yank. Frightful fellow, frightful fellow. All rather — what's the expression — *in your face*. Anyhow. On the first bong, I think, the first bong, we shall set you free."

There were more rattles. Dennis peered back and up and moistened a lip nervously. I looked too. It seemed to be a window in Amanda's apartments. A growing inch or two of space through which she could perhaps bellow.

The Speech

I nodded at Dennis and encouraged him to speak on.

"Though, I think we might be a fraction, a fraction early. Longer speech next time, I propose. What, uh, what lovely weather."

The clock hand remained stubbornly unmoved, the chimes absent without *exeat*. Each second languished.

A panic stabbed me: Amanda did, after all, have her supporters within college. Might they have smuggled in a screwdriver to unlock the window? And sabotaged the clock? She could under no circumstances, by crook or hook, be allowed to interfere. My own watch claimed high noon: time to act.

"Dennis: begin the race," I hissed urgently.

"I might say—" came Amanda's warble through the gap.

Dennis jumped at the microphone, which shrieked along the street. "Bugger this for a soldier," he cried. "On your marks, get set, get set, go!"

The retaining elastic sprang back violently and the runners surged to cheers and laughter from the crowd that drowned out any contribution Amanda might have wished to make. I hoped the TV news reporters were now too occupied apologising for Dennis's choice of words to inquire as to the who, what and why regarding our window heckler.

I also hoped the Archivist was now dispatching elves *en grande masse* to reseal the gap. Although legs and brain wished it I could not leave the dais to rage into the Hub. My duties until the competitors passed were to smile and wave and point at strangers as if I knew them. I hogged the microphone and bleated encouragement whenever I could make out faint words of the opposite behind me. I did in a risky moment venture one glance up to the window only to see two purple eyes glare and spit down at me through this devil's letterbox. I spun back forward, swallowing down the bile and redoubling my concentration upon the race.

I was glad to do so. Despite my early misgivings about the

task and despite the grief and upheaval I had inflicted upon my beloved St Paul's, we were unequivocally doing good these three bucketing hours. The batty old woman attempting to wrench her way back into the limelight had somehow injected verdant new life into me while simultaneously heaving at the rug upon which I stood. A curious and unrecommended form of leadership, I concluded, waving and pointing at a pantomime horse.

I began almost to relax. It was at this inopportune moment that I was tapped on the shoulder by the Archivist.

twenty-two
The Race

I watched the blood drain from Spencer's face as if the little short guy who'd tapped him on the shoulder had pulled out a plug in his neck. His jaw clanged to the floor. The guy quickly dragged him stumbling off the dais and through the gate into the sanctuary of the college.

Seb and I had been watching discreetly from the corner, where the college turned down Emmanuel Street — Seb was wearing a dark blue branded hoody and sunglasses, turning him from a Chinese spy into a twat-faced rapper. We decided that whatever was happening now meant it was time for us to join the party. Arthur on the gate took one look at us and waved us through. He must've been fed up with the sight of us by then.

We found the two men arguing behind the porters' lodge, well out of sight of the street. I caught the word "missing" and barged into the conversation like a proper journalist.

"What's going on?" I said. "Who's missing?"

Spencer spat back: "Amanda. Amanda!" Arms flapping about in full-on fart dispersal. "All this surveillance, all this monitoring, and she vanishes from beneath the Archivist's nose."

He pointed angrily at the short guy: grey, owl-eyes, Einstein hair. So that was the Archivist, I thought. I was relieved to discover it wasn't Quiff after all — that would've been a bit of a cheese grater to the head. To be honest though I'd expected the Archivist to be someone with greater presence, a bit more oomph. A Christopher Lee type with a hatful of sparks. Instead he was more of a pale old gonk. The great-grandfather of all the gonks, maybe, his hair without its synthetic sheen after all those years in dark rooms underground being blasted by TV screens.

"Some kind of malfunction, I suspect," he said to Spencer, barely acknowledging us. "Not entirely uncommon — we do have a number of interrelated systems and every system has its teething troubles and ongoing issues. Occasionally the connections break down, or there are incompatible protocols, or rats."

"Bit convenient, though, isn't it?" I said. "For her, right now."

"Where has she gone?" said Seb.

The Archivist finally turned to us. "Mr Geraghty, Mr Greatsholme. Please. With respect, this is college business."

I cocked my head and found myself bristling. "College business? Hey, like it or not, buddy, we're tied up in all this," I said. "I've just lost my crappy little job as part of this game of Risk for Toffs youse all seem to be playing. I think you'll find college business *is* my business. Well, it's not, but it sounded a hell of a good line in my head. Listen, I apologise for using the word buddy. It was either that or Albert. It's the hair."

Seb touched my arm to silence me, about a minute too late. "How can we help?" he said.

The Archivist looked at us both, probably weighing us up from our TV highlights, our *best bits*. "The last confirmed sighting was at the back gate, a few minutes ago."

"Escaping? Where to?" said Seb.

I knew. "She's gonna go straight for Geoff and Simon."

"My conclusion also," said the Archivist.

"And so how do we counter?" said Spencer.

"Spencer," I said. "You stay here and deal with the race. Seb and I will track her down. *All is in hand*, as your man there once said. What's she wearing?"

Purple, the pair said simultaneously.

"Purple what?"

Purple everything.

Right, I thought. Easy enough. She might have had a head start but she'd be taking the long way round, and even with the streets full of fancy dress I was sure we could spot a purple dragon lady.

Seb and I went back onto St Andrew's Street. There were still racers passing slowly by, with the little old Acting Master guy shouting at them over the mike. Peeking through the dais and around his legs I could see Simon over in the press box but I couldn't make out Geoff.

"Do you see Geoff anywhere?" I said to Seb. "He's probably standing behind a cake."

"You never stop joking, do you?" he replied evenly. "Even now."

"I'm not giving you my *knock knock* collection, if that's what you want. He might've trundled off for a different camera angle, I suppose." I kept hunting for the editor in the crowds opposite while also scanning left and right for the Master.

Seb said nothing.

"It's what I do, OK? Think of it as a coping mechanism for life. It was either this or holy orders, and I couldn't have handled all that sex. Is it a problem? Are you looking? Keep looking. I know you can't take your eyes off me, but keep looking."

"I have an idea. If you track Burnett, I will lure Wantage out. Attract his fire." Seb pulled his hood down and took off his sunglasses, fully exposing the face that was on the front of the *Bugle* the previous morning. "You know, I think I could do with a jog."

He vaulted the spectators' barrier onto the tarmac of St Andrew's Street and quickly stretched his calf muscles. Then he jinked through the fag-end competitors over to the press box and acted suspiciously for a few seconds, untying and tying his shoelaces.

It didn't take long for Simon to spot him, and to draw Geoff out. Seb did a decent impression of a startled sheep when he realised he'd been rumbled and darted into the crowd of competitors ahead. Simon barged through a squealing mass of spectators and a gap in the barrier to haul himself onto the road in pursuit, camera flapping around his neck. Unless he had some marathon-running skills I hadn't heard of, I knew I wouldn't see him for a while.

That left Geoff, who in the excitement I almost lost again: he was waddling along the pavement past the bus stops, perhaps thinking he could cut across town and roll into King's Parade to form a kind of dam to stop Seb getting any further.

I figured my best bet, since I couldn't see Amanda, was to keep Geoff in my sights. If I could keep him in view then I could spot if the purple woman was anywhere nearby and I could do something that I hadn't quite figured out yet, and which wouldn't involve my own personal injury, to avoid the two meeting and the universe exploding or whatever was going to happen when her anti-matter met his enormous great sphere of matter.

Excusing my way through some undergrads holding up a dirty banner I found a policed gap in the barriers and sweet-talked the steward into letting me across the road by showing him my press card and my dimples. I didn't do vaulting. Vaulting is like sport, and sport is something masochists do — like dieting and budgeting. I didn't need to hurry that much: Geoff was not one of life's sprinters. The only danger of me losing my breath was if he saw a BOGOF on jammy doughnuts.

My guess about his tactics was right: he followed the line of the crowds for a while then turned up Petty Cury towards the market, planning to bypass a great chunk of the race route. And that's when I spotted the flaw in my own plan. If I followed him that way and the Master hadn't yet seen him, we might never find

The Race

her. And if I didn't follow him and she *had* seen him, then she'd find him, and he might intercept Seb. Stupid plan, who thought this one up? We should've just got the new Master to broadcast a bounty on her head, or something, make it part of the event. *Hunt the purple monster and win an undergraduate.*

I was trying to figure out whether to follow Geoff or not when I felt a tap on my shoulder. It was one of the St Paul's students I'd met before, one of the elves as Spencer called them — the *all is in hand* elf who wouldn't let us visit the Archivist when I wanted him to hack out the suspicious log entries for Manish and me, not that he did, the git.

"Jeez, what do *you* want," I said. "Are you gonna tell me it's *all in hand* again? You must have, like, forty-nine hands or something."

"Sir, the Archivist did send me, it's true," he said, "but only to say we've had a sighting. Heading for Bar Humbug, sir. I suggest we—"

With the elf in tow I changed direction and sped towards Humbug. "Doesn't he have a phone?" I said. "He's hardly a technophobe. I bet he has a *Mission Impossible* ring tone, doesn't he?"

"He believed you might need some assistance with the Master."

"Did he now. Are you like the horse-whisperer? Are you a Master-whisperer? Do you, like blow up her nose?"

We'd gone about ten seconds through the shoppers and the race-watchers towards Humbug when my phone rang. I nearly didn't notice — there was far too much noise and vibration going on to notice the noise and vibration. I slowed to answer it. It was Spencer.

"Conor," he said urgently. "There is a fox in the hen house. *All is in hand*. He never uttered those words. The Archivist never uttered those words."

"What do you mean? What does that matter?"

"He never uttered those words and he never despatched Beardsley to intercept us. It seems the malfunctions in the Archivist's systems extended from the technical and on to the personal. You must be on your guard."

"Right. Shit." I slowed further at some Peruvian buskers having a bad day for a large number of reasons. "So if I were to say I were on my way to Humbug..."

"Why are you going to that place? Not her milk of magnesia by a long stretch."

Dead stop.

Spencer twigged. "Am I to understand that you are currently, as it were, with company?"

"That's a bit personal now. Yeah, I am, but I wouldn't go out and buy a hat just yet, you know?" The blond elf looked on, confused. I turned away from him and the buskers. "Well, that explains a lot."

The elf grabbed my arm and tried to twist me around. "We must get to Humbug," he said.

"You go on ahead," I said to him and shook free. "I have a thing with a thing about a—"

I started running back to Petty Cury, as fast as I could through the crowds, to catch up with Geoff.

On the phone to Spencer: "Always the cute ones, dammit. Can you send reinforcements? Does that Archivist fella have an army of elves or gonks or something he can dispatch? A squadron would do. Elf ninjas? Petty Cury, heading up to King's Parade."

I hung up. I had no idea whether the elf was following me. I just had to get back onto Geoff's slimy little trail before Amanda grabbed him.

The crowds were harder to force through in this direction, against the flow of the competitors. I was briefly in the slipstream of a strident young mum with a snow-plough buggy that sliced

The Race

a path through anything or anyone that didn't jump out of the way quickly enough, until she peeled off elsewhere. And then I was nearly bowled over by a git on a bike trying to cycle his way along the pavement with music coming from a plastic bag hanging from his handlebars like the shittiest ice cream van you can think of.

Progress got easier when I turned back on to Petty Cury and it wasn't long before I picked out Geoff again: his fastest speed was amble and he was being distracted by a chocolate shop.

And there, head to toe in purple, sights set and course laid in, was Amanda. With her long, flowing dress hiding what I assumed were purple legs, it was like she was hovering in his direction like a Geoff-seeking missile.

I scrabbled through the middle of a flock of French schoolchildren with bright yellow backpacks perfecting their moody misery and dancing around a fresh pack of Gauloise.

"Excusez-moi, je suis homosexuel," I said, and they scattered.

She was about a dozen metres or so behind Geoff and gaining fast.

I'd reached sniffing distance, Ralgex with undertones of TCP, when the elf finally caught up and dragged me to a stop, pinning my arm in both of his.

"You must not interfere," he said, out of breath. "It is the Master's right."

"I'm doing this for your college, you arsehole," I said, struggling.

"She will tell only the truth."

I looked him in the eye. "Sometimes, kid, the truth isn't good for you. Watch out for the elves at your six."

"I'm not an idiot—"

A six-pack of elves pounced and grabbed him and muffled his cries and quickly carried him away, aloft, like ants wrangling a twig. Nobody paid them any attention: student town, occ. These things happen.

I settled in behind Amanda just a few paces this side of Geoff and — my turn — tapped her on the shoulder.

She swung round, the long skirt following at its leisure. "What of it?"

"That's some outfit you've got on there, Professor."

"Of which concern is it of yours?"

I waited a second as Geoff receded. Then, best reporter's bollocks. "Geoff has asked me to interview you for the *Bugle*. We've heard you've got an amazing story for us. We're thinking like a double-page spread, maybe with a fashion special. *Amanda Chatteris Reveals All* kind of a thing. *The St Paul's Diet*, which from what I've heard would be two square meals a day in the canteen. I wonder if you could just come with me?"

"This Geoff walks there." She pointed towards him, ambling into the distance. "Am I not to speak directly upon him?"

I put a hand on her elbow and started walking her slowly back towards college. "You see, about that. He's a bit undercover at the moment. I know, you wouldn't know it to look at him. That's the beauty of it. He's actually a great fan of purple. Doesn't wear it often, it makes him look like a bowling ball. So how's your day been?"

After the second elf death squad, or whatever the collective noun is, had found me and taken charge of Amanda, I went off in search of Geoff again. He was still the loose cannonball. I could maybe still throw myself in front of him to stop him throwing himself in front of Seb. But he was nowhere to be seen, which to say the least was unusual for him. He'd managed to fade into the crowds like a chubby ghost, or maybe he'd found a fellow cockney somewhere and was reminiscing over a plate of apples and pears. In pie form, probably.

I know, enough with the fat jokes. In truth it's a defence

The Race

mechanism. At school it was kill or be killed and by the time I'd hit puberty I had the holy trinity: fat, ginger and queer. I fought the flab mostly by fighting the kids who were ripping the shit. The other two weren't so easy. I could've dyed my hair black and gone all freckle-me-emo but I could never pull off all the tears and the cutting. And going out with girls? Jeez, I had to draw a line somewhere.

That was all long gone, much like my job at the *Bugle*. And I'd begun to realise that one thing schools and newspapers had in common was bullying. The difference was, at the newspaper the bullies were the ones paying the wages.

So my grand idea to launch a new paper once the *Bugle* had lost its horn wasn't feeling quite so attractive right then. I didn't want to turn into a bully. The world had enough of those.

I made my way back to St Paul's. It was about half way through the three hours of the race, and the first buckets were crossing the finish line carried by scarlet and steaming bodies with double-length arms. Every finisher was awarded a medal in college colours — a lot cheaper than it looked, Seb had told me — and the bucket was labelled and sealed and carted off to be counted and audited.

I'd watched the competitors streaming in for a few minutes when I saw Seb himself jog easily over the finish line, barely puffing, and with no sign of Simon. He refused a medal with a shake of the head and a smile.

"You forgot to take a bucket," I called out to him in the queue of finishers.

He turned out his pockets to show a decent few coins and notes. "I did OK, I think. Not everyone reads the *Bugle*."

He distributed the cash between the buckets of a few people before and after him, with a wink, and skipped out of the queue to join me. I gave him a hug. He was hot and clammy and smelled of *man*.

"I'm sorry, I lost Geoff," I said. "Shit happened. Did he give you any trouble?"

"I waved at him as he was attempting to force his way onto the course. He seemed a little distraught that a policeman would not let him do whatever he wanted. Oh: did you get her?"

"All is in hand," I said.

twenty-three
The End

The buckets of donations began their tireless march through Helen's magnificent system in the dining hall, watched by many student faces pressed against the windows. The tellers recruited by our dear Bursar, all of whom were of the lady persuasion, processed and counted the monies via the machines wherever possible. They double-checked and triple-checked under the protective but lightly manic gaze of Helen herself and two rather stern-looking gentlemen *sans* hair and *avec* clipboard, independently auditing. Two pearl accountants rolling within a cash and teller oyster.

Dennis and I were inside the hall officially assessing progress, but mentally as excited as the window-pressers. One of the clipboards instructed us at the tip of his pencil not to pass beyond a crude line of benches — a rudimentary infection control barrier of sorts.

I said that such a barrier might be of considerable assistance during those worrying times in which the college kitchen was in full operation, and the acting Master revealed to me in delight that improving college cuisine was high upon his list, his list.

Amanda's escape and subsequent recapture, as it were, had revealed a small cell of undesirables within the Archivist's circle: a Romulan cabal on Vulcan, perhaps. The Archivist was at that moment undertaking a purge, an elf pogrom: young Beardsley, who had so nearly misdirected Conor, had swiftly capitulated and blabbed without significant prodding, aware how his college and career prospects were rebalancing unfavourably before his traitorous eyes.

The purple lady herself was returned to her quarters with a fresh detail on guard. She would, I was told, be *dealt with* presently in an unspecified manner. I confess the thought rather unnerved me.

"The snow falls heavily upon Amanda," said Dennis as we watched the tellers at work. "I fear she is lost in a blizzard, a blizzard."

I remembered the explanation Dennis and the Archivist had given me before: an obsession with the screens, an overpowering need to know, an overwhelmingness of raw data, an inability to comprehend.

"Do you not feel... responsible? At least in some measure?" I said, kindly. "You and the Archivist might have assisted her. Given her some fashion of umbrella against the weather, or at least a warm fire and a mug of your finest peppermint tea."

He removed his spectacles and wiped them upon his gown. I doubted this did more than redistribute the dirt and grease. "My boy, you are right, of course."

"I mean no deep criticism."

"No, no." He waved his hand and smiled. "Wood and trees, my lad, wood and trees. When the ground is hard and dry the rain slips off, yet the fault is neither the ground's nor the rain's, but the sun's."

"I am not entirely convinced I follow."

"Let me put it another way, another way. There is no black, there is no white—"

"—All is grey, above, below and beyond," I finished with him. I suspected that was the closest to an explanation I would receive.

"It has been snowing on Amanda for many years, many years.

The End

Be careful which clouds you stand beneath, my boy."

I nodded. This was either sage advice requiring great consideration or Dennis's hearing aid was rebroadcasting the weather forecast on Radio 4.

I had begun to formulate a reply when an exclamation came from a teller, a noise like the truculent squeak of a forty-a-day supermarket trolley. She held up a piece of paper extracted from a bucket: not a banknote, plainly. It had the size and proportions of a cheque. As her neighbouring tellers caught sight the squeak rippled through the ranks. Faces at the windows shuffled and bounced. Helen rushed across and inspected the cheque, and her eyes and mouth snapped into O shapes that mirrored, I quickly gathered, the trailing and non-decimal zeroes written thereupon.

"Dennis, Spencer," the Bursar said, not altogether calmly, a distinct vibrato in her voice. "I believe we have our winner."

Dennis tapped a finger upon the dais microphone to verify its function. "If I might have your attention, your attention," he said to the expectant crowd.

I stood beside him. The many hundreds of competitors, reunited with their audited and resealed buckets, were arrayed before us in their costumes and with their friends and family. College staff and many students and the tellers and auditors and others such as Conor and Seb gathered to one side and behind in anticipation. The press crowded opposite in their raised box of lenses, the walled camera garden.

Silence fell.

"We should now like to award the prize to the winner."

A buzz of anticipation and cheers, hijacked by Wantage. "Bring out the spy first! He was here earlier, I saw him. Where's the spy?" he called out.

"Goodness, such noise, such noise. I must say the—"

Another journalist joined in. "Where's Wang Ming? Why are you hiding a spy?"

The crowd became jittery and restless, some swivelling to the source of the interruption. One person, competitor or not I couldn't say, called for silence from the press box. Others agreed, and still more disagreed.

Dennis looked ill at ease. This was transparently unfair on him: he was not responsible for any of what had happened. I touched him lightly on the arm and offered myself as a substitute. He gladly stepped aside and I gulped out a smile.

"Please, gentlemen, ladies," I said, holding up my hands in peace. "I shall remove all doubts that might even now be simmering."

"Bring him out!" cried Wantage.

"Mr Wantage, please, I fear the ambulance might not reach you through the crowds should you suffer an emergency illness with your present language."

There was laughter, not all of it at his expense. He continued with his heckling. I turned from the microphone, cleared my throat and shook away the cobwebs.

"Do shut up, dear," I said. Stronger laughter. Wantage quietened.

"You are all aware of the press coverage. Of the allegations against us. That we harbour a spy. Preposterous. I tell you now and here, preposterous. Why, I was discussing over afternoon tea with Professors Hitler and Stalin only the other day—" I paused for further generous laughter, which nearly came.

"We do accommodate, this much is true. Our undergraduates pride themselves on their abilities to bunk up to make room for one more. And occasionally these visitors will play under a different flag. We teach them our ways. We guide them through the intricacies of our common etiquette, whether they drive right or left, whether they bat under the North Star or the Southern

The End

Cross or, indeed, equatorially.

"But a spy, ladies and gentlemen? No. St Paul's hides no spy. The *Bugle* is mistaken. The article is wrong. Its writer, Mr Simon Wantage, has, I fear, a most vivid imagination. And I shall now not only rebut his and his paper's allegation, I shall refute it. There is indeed a person, a guest, within college, but he is not this hypothetical Wang Ming of whom Mr Wantage wrote. This guest is responsible for making today happen. This guest is our sponsor. Without him none of you would be here. Without him none of your charities would benefit. He is no spy."

I turned and located the familiar face of Seb beside Conor amongst the college staff. I beckoned him to the dais. "Ladies and gentlemen, our sponsor."

There was applause: polite and slightly confused. Seb squeezed past people to the rear of the dais then jumped, red-faced, into the limelight and forced a small embarrassed wave.

Wantage called out: "We have proof! Documentary evidence in black and white!"

There is no black, there is no white, I thought.

I returned to the microphone. "*Quid est veritas*, Mr Wantage. *Caveat navigatrum*. Might I respectfully suggest that you shouldn't believe everything you read on the internet." This brought scattered laughter and applause. "Let me say that had I believed everything I had read or seen on the internet regarding certain Hollywood actors I might at this moment be languishing under several rather merciless restraining orders. I suggest and recommend you take an equally cynical view.

"And now I want to return to our scheduled programme, unless Mr Wantage would care to make a further fool of himself? Good."

I paused for a second, not wishing to rush straight into happier announcements while a foul mood still hung about the street.

"Tell us about the Archivist!" The moment roused Geoff at last from his long silence, and yet even this was half-hearted: the final syllable withered away in a sudden regret, strangled at birth.

A smile crept slowly across my face as various figures on and off the dais tensed. "Oh, Mr Burnett," I said calmly. "The Archivist is the college record keeper. He has many stories to tell. I look forward to his autobiography: don't you?"

Answer came there none.

I reintroduced Dennis to the microphone for the remaining announcements and shuffled alongside Seb.

"Why did you invite me up here?" he whispered to me.

I shushed him, nodding towards Dennis.

"Goodness, we must make some progress now, some progress, or it shall be Christmas. So, to our winner. The person who collected the greatest sum for his, or indeed her, designated charity. All of you have been rather magnificent, of course. But I must say we have a clear winner, a clear winner, courtesy of a large individual donation submitted quite fairly, I must assure you, within the bucket.

"The winner, to be celebrated for the upcoming year as our honorary Fifth Beatle, joining St Paul, St John, St Ringo, St Ringo and St George, is…"

He paused.

"You know, I don't watch those dreadful talent shows, but we must have a delay, a delay, mustn't we. The winner is: Pamela Pedrosa. A lady, I surmise. Pamela Pedrosa."

I heard a shriek and a small cheer from the crowd, and the winner swam through the faces to claim her crown.

Seb leaned to me and whispered: "Ah, that's why."

My grin was unconfined. It was an unusual feeling.

Pamela found her way to a gap in the barrier and onto the dais, passing Seb and I with a quick smile. The crowd applauded unselfishly as Dennis presented her with a trophy — a gold-plated halo on a stick, embedded into an engraved base — and

The End

invited her, if she would like, to say a few words perhaps about her selected charity.

"Thank you, thank you," she said. "Such an honour, thank you Master. My name is Pamela Pedrosa. I would like to tell you a short story, a story about why I chose to support this particular charity. The story begins long before I was married, when I was a girl, and my name was Pamela Greatsholme…"

Seb watched proudly as his sister spoke.

The unused buckets dotting New Court had been pushed to the sides and open marquees erected around the fountain, under which college dignitaries and undergraduates and special guests swooned over tables laden with food neither concocted nor dredged up by our kitchen, and thus edible.

I saw Jonathan clinking glasses with his friends from *Cream*, and a few admirers. Hints of Cody leaked into his body language: he had a certain confidence about him, a poise, absent before.

The skies above the north range, although cast orange by the bus terminal beyond, sparkled blue and green and red and not purple with the crack and fizz of fireworks supplied, of course, by Seb.

His sister Pamela had spoken movingly to the crowd of what had happened to her in her youth, and to her family, and who had perpetrated it. Burnett and Wantage had attempted to slink silently away unnoticed, but had already been sufficiently clamorous to make such a getaway impossible. Various fit and healthy members of the crowd, and their smartphones, assured that. The TV coverage they had themselves triggered proved their final undoing, and it was apparent to all that the *Bugle* had tootled its last Last Post.

Pamela and Seb were chatting together, catching up away from tedious drunken interruptions by well-meaning sycophants such as myself — although I was still not daring to admit alcohol into my bloodstream, lest I dive clothed or unclothed into the fountain *again*. Alas, I had no company with which to dive, in any case. I stood by myself, possibly exuding a beatific glow, holding a plate of identifiable food and a glass of an exotic formulation apparently called an *orange juice*. I felt sure it would be unlikely to catch on.

Helen approached with Conor's former colleague, Manish, at her elbow. I reconfigured the contents of my hands so we could shake, and I thanked him for his noble sacrifice and promised assistance to find him new employment.

"On a related topic," said Helen, "I have some rather good news. The college is already attracting an increased level of interest from potential students. Our supply of college prospecti is dropping to dangerous levels. Even our page on the Wikipedia has seen some activity. And I was thinking…"

"I'm retiring from SPAIN with immediate effect, you should know that," I said.

"Good! Excellent! I mean, we'll need someone new focused upon these matters, which fits entirely with my plan. And my plan is standing here with us."

I looked at Manish brightly.

"I'd like to join the college, be a press and publicity guy," he said. "I know I'm not exactly your usual type. But, you owe me big time. And you can't turn me down because I'm straight — it's the law."

"Very true," I said. "There will need to be formalities, of course. All by the book. Helen has mastery of the book. I doubt my opinion is relevant but I have no objection. Perhaps you should speak to Dennis — he is about here somewhere."

They agreed and set off in search.

I returned to savouring the delights of unreconstructed chicken. Who knew it had a texture? Such wonders.

I heard Conor's voice across the court. He had earlier dashed

The End

off mysteriously, claiming an unspecified *scoop* which seemed rather unlikely under the circumstances. I had suspected this was his way of telling us he had some form of a date, as yet unidentified, and we might or might not see him that evening. I turned to greet him.

"Hey Spencer," he said. "You know that scoop I was telling you about?"

He had brought a guest. It was Eddie, from Bar Humbug.

"Hello darling," he said, twinkling rather. "I've given myself the night off. I was told you needed a plus one, and you know how I feel about looking after the old and vulnerable in society, don't you? Now then, free food, is it? I'm positively waif-like."

I laughed and turned to Conor: "How did you know?"

Conor tapped his nose. "Eyes everywhere, me."

Eddie put his arm in mine and began to inch me towards the buffet. Then I heard my name called from behind. I stopped and spun around.

Manish stood with Helen and Dennis, holding one thumb victoriously aloft. Dennis, his impish grin restored, saw and copied him. I raised my soft glass in congratulation.

I turned back again to Eddie to resume, not exactly where we left off however many months ago it was, but in the immediate vicinity thereof. I was in time to see Pamela introduced to Conor, and for Seb's arm to snake around Conor's waist and come to rest peacefully and happily.

There was no sign of the Archivist or Amanda.

Also by Anthony Camber

Disunited

anthonycamber.com/disunited/

A life, a team, a sport — changed forever

When footballer Danny Prince transfers to a top club across town, he has everything he ever wanted: a lucrative career with a promising future, and a boyfriend who reads the Guardian. But it probably wasn't a good idea to celebrate the move in a gay nightclub. Accidentally snapped in a compromising photo that goes viral, he steps off the dance floor into a life flipped upside-down.

Football's last taboo: an out gay player.

Still, surely his new teammates will stick by him? And his manager, carved from granite, with lava for blood. And the club's owner, a Kazakh oil magnate with a limp and a past. And the media. And not forgetting the club's supporters…

Darkly funny yet pulling no punches, *Disunited* mixes the sweet, sour and spice of Danny's new life on and off the pitch.

Loyalty versus honesty, risk versus reward, defence versus attack. Danny versus the world.

Disunited: it's a book of two halves.

"Plenty of dark humour." – *FourFourTwo Magazine,* April 2013

"A feat of writing genius … this book must be read. ★ ★ ★ ★ ★"
– *So So Gay Magazine*

Till Undeath Do Us Part

anthonycamber.com/till-undeath-do-us-part/

Josh and Olly: students, rowers, lovers.
A research experiment that goes wrong.
The end, and the beginning.
Till undeath do us part.

Set in and around King's College, Cambridge, this poignant and darkly comic story, a gothic horror for the modern age, follows undergraduate Olly Coll as he struggles to survive after his boyfriend, graduate student Josh Greenwood, inadvertently starts a zombie outbreak that threatens the city and beyond.

Top-ten bestseller in Amazon UK's gay literature category

Nominated for Best Book in the 2012 So So Gay Awards

"Will keep you on the edge of your seat ... an amazing conclusion ... a skilled storyteller" – *Kyle West, author "Apocalypse (The Wasteland Chronicles)"*

"Stands proud in the genre ... Perfect blend of gothic horror, romance, comedy and zombies. Like Shaun of the Dead, but gayer. ★ ★ ★ ★ ★ "— *So So Gay Magazine*

Contact the author

You can get in touch with Anthony Camber at:

anthonycamber.com
twitter.com/anthonycamber
facebook.com/AnthonyCamber
plus.google.com/102396025019089047369
goodreads.com/author/show/5781825.Anthony_Camber
librarything.com/author/camberanthony